BARTER ISLAND

BARTER ISLAND

7/26/07

PETER SCOTT

For Lisa w/ many fond
Memories.

Peter Scott

Down East Books
Camden, Maine

Cover photograph by Greg Currier

ISBN-10: 0-89272-739-X
ISBN-13: 978-0-89272-739-1

Printed at Versa Press, Inc., East Peoria, Illinois

5   4   3   2   1

Down East Books
Camden, Maine
A division of Down East Enterprise, Inc.
Book orders: 800-685-7962
www.downeastbooks.com
Distributed to the trade by National Book Network, Inc.

Library of Congress Cataloging-in-Publication Data

Scott, Peter, 1945-
   Barter Island / Peter Scott.
       p. cm.
   ISBN-13: 978-0-89272-739-1 (trade pbk. : alk. paper)
   ISBN-10: 0-89272-739-X (trade pbk. : alk. paper)
      1. Islands--Maine--Fiction. 2. Vietnam War, 1961-1975--Veterans--
Fiction. 3. Hippies--Fiction. 4. Social conflict--Fiction. 5. Maine--Social life
and customs--Fiction. I. Title.
      PS3569.C675B37 2007
      813'.54--dc22
                                          2007003355

This book is dedicated to my friends, infantrymen all,
who await me on the high ground

ONE

*They say they come down here to find themselves. To look inside
themselves and see what's in there. The thing that surprises me is how
long it takes them to realize that there's nothing there to find
out. Whatever in hell made them think there was, do you suppose?*
-Junior Chafin

On the island's town landing, Gus Barter sits atop an upturned lobster crate watching the afternoon mail boat approach. His legs are
double crossed, the toe of his right foot tucked behind his left
ankle to prevent the foot from jigging. He is bent forward slightly, and his
hands, denied a lap by his stomach, rest on his thighs, nestled palms up and
fingers limp, like a master's pencil-sketch study of hardworking hands asleep.
When a high, white cloud slips past the westering sun, Gus takes his sunshades out of his shirt pocket, clips them onto his glasses, and blinks to
adjust his eyes.

After a long day bent over his boat's engine, he has come over to town
to meet the late boat and offer David Harper a ride to his parents' house in
the cove. Gus has not seen David since he visited the island on leave from the
army three years ago, or perhaps it was four. He has known David since he
was a little boy; David and Gus's own son, John, played and fished together

every summer until they both grew up and went away. And now David, the one who survived, is coming back, perhaps for good, or so Gus hears, and he is suffering serious crosscurrents of emotion as he watches the boat approach.

At Gus's side stands Junior Chafin, who has come to meet the boat for his weekly delivery of Fleischmann's gin and has too many scruples to be sitting on a trap or crate owned by a west-side fisherman. Ever in motion of some sort, Junior stands in his rolled-down rubber boots, packing a Pall Mall on his thumbnail, then scratching a match on the railing and muttering to Gus, who he knows is not listening, that there won't be any lobsters at all anymore if they keep letting new Stonington guys set out their gear in Barter Island waters.

As the mail boat slips in to the float, both men—Gus is on his feet now—strain forward (without appearing to, they believe) to get a better look at the three creatures sitting in the bow. In the center is a male wearing a full, brown beard and a long ponytail that appears to have been rinsed in used motor oil. His fringed, sleeveless buckskin vest is decorated with sewn flowers, buttons with messages, and a rainbow; his sunken, sunburned chest is bedecked with strings of beads. On either side of him—he is laughing—sits a girl. One wears the kind of shapeless dress that Gus saw a Hawaiian queen wearing in *National Geographic*; she is pale, full-bodied but pretty, with a tiny mouth and rosy cheeks, and her hair is held by a beaded headband. The other is a beautiful olive-skinned girl, who wears her long, black hair in braided pigtails, the same style of headband as the Hawaiian queen, a garland of cow vetch, and a sleeveless T-shirt that is a cosmos of mixed colors. Her shorts are cut from a pair of jeans, her beads fall between her full and quite pert breasts that sway ever so slightly when she moves, and her long and lovely legs are hairy from her knees to her sandals. At the threesome's feet, a filthy, tailless mongrel dog with pointed ears sits ready to pounce on anything small enough to massacre.

As the mail boat ties up to the float, Gus and Junior step back from the edge of the wharf full of wonder.

"What the hell?" Gus asks. "Those are Indians!"

"Those aren't Indians, you goddamn fool. Indians can't grow beards. Those are hippies." Junior picks a bit of tobacco from the tip of his tongue and flicks it away.

"They're not going to come ashore here, are they?"

"How the hell should I know, dear?"

"They're getting up!" Gus takes two more baby steps backward. "He's picking up his knapsack! You're the goddamn constable, Junior—do something! Tell the captain not to let them off. Tell him to take them back where they came from, to the goddamn mainland."

As Bernadine and Kimberly Bowen ascend the gangplank carrying between them a large, loaded basket of folded laundry, the tailless mongrel dog runs between Bernadine's legs, nearly upending her and sending summer people's towels and sheets overboard. The dog strikes the wharf on the run and streaks up the hill, heading, Gus is certain, directly for the chicken coop behind the parsonage.

"Jesus Christ Almighty, there."

His brimming knapsack on his back, the red sash that serves as his belt fluttering in the breeze, following his companion in the shapeless muumuu, the leader of the pack pulls an American Flyer wagon laden with cloth and burlap sacks up the gangplank. Behind the little red wagon, the braless nymph in pigtails is bent over to steady the load and push. Following her, his eyes level with and attached to her flawless thighs and straining buttocks, a thin young man in a white T-shirt and blue jeans carries an olive-drab duffel bag over his shoulder and a box of groceries under his arm.

On the wharf, the bearded creature asks Bernadine how to get to the park campground, and she points the way. As they pass the staring fishermen, the male says "Peace," and the nymph with the buoyant breasts flashes them a V sign.

"Peace, my ass," says Junior under his breath.

Gus grunts, then tells Junior, "I've got a mind to go up to your house and strap on that .38 and come back down here and order that human garbage off the island."

"This isn't a war, you know. Those aren't communist spies come here to do us damage."

"Maybe not to you it isn't. I feel like I've been through this before. Invaded. The island threatened."

"Oh Gus." Bernadine hefts her end of the laundry basket. "Don't be silly. They're harmless. They're . . . they're exciting, and they're *different*. They're a breath of fresh air."

"I wouldn't call their air fresh, exactly." The young man in the white T-shirt sets down his groceries and duffel bag. "I followed them up the gangplank. Not fresh."

"Well, look who's here," Junior says. "I wouldn't of recognized you with that head full of curls. Welcome home, David; or welcome back, anyway."

"Home, I hope, for a while at least."

David shakes hands with Junior, and then with Gus, who takes his hand in two of his own and holds it with deep affection and a measure of trepidation. *You won't mention it, David, will you?* Gus pleads silently. *It, or him; especially him. I know you won't. I have to believe it.*

"You wouldn't be headed over to the east side, would you?" asks David.

"Well of course I am," Gus laughs. "I came over to give you a ride, for Christ's sake, you and your gear. Is there more than this?"

"Another box of groceries and a case of beer." David takes a second to look around him appreciatively: at the dozen houses built on the road in "town"; at the post office and store, and on the hill beneath the mountain, the high white steeple of the island church. "How the hell did you know I'd be on this boat?"

"Maggie told me. She stopped me on the road."

"How did *she* know?"

"I don't know. You get your other boxes, and I'll bring the jeep down. There comes Junior with your case of beer and his jug. I'd get that beer away from him right now if I was you."

***

Gus's ancient green-and-white Willys is as familiar to David, who has ridden in it almost every summer since he can remember, as practically anything he knows. The plywood covering the hole in the floor at his feet still lets dust in around its edges; the seat cushions are still decomposing and are still covered with blankets; the driver's side windshield wiper is still missing–where the hell would you find a windshield wiper for a '50 Willys?–and the interior still smells of used oil, sweat, rubber, bait, and a fresh whiff of spruce from the two wheel chocks stored behind the seat.

Driving through town, they wave at Skeet in his porch rocker. He lifts a hand in response. They pass a young woman in the doorway of the post office who catches David's eye; she is wearing shorts, a flannel shirt open at the throat, and a white ball cap that can't contain the reddish hair spilling onto her back. When he turns his head to see her better–so many freckles!–he finds that she is watching him too. She smiles slightly.

Gus says, "Humph."

"Do you have telephones down here yet?"

"Telephones?" Gus asks. "Hell no." As the Willys gains the top of the steep town hill, clouds cover the sun again and Gus takes off his sunshades. "You watch," he says. "When we get around to the east side there'll be a thick of fog offshore. The wind's backing to the east, and that'll bring it in."

David nods. "Then how did Maggie know I was going to be on the late boat?"

"I don't know," Gus says. "The Pringle girl, Meredith, saw you in the grocery in Stonington, and when she came home on the noon boat she told Leah in the post office, then Leah told Maggie when she came for her mail, I suppose. I don't know."

"I should stop and see Maggie," says David.

"She won't expect you until tomorrow. She'll let you get settled in first. Your mother wrote that you were coming sometime in early June, so Maggie and mother opened the house and cleaned for you."

"They didn't have to do that, I could have . . ."

"They did it for your mother, then." *Those two and others down here, Gus thinks, would of liked to do something more to celebrate your safe return, after two years, from that ungodly goddamn dog-shit war, but they didn't do any such thing because they knew I couldn't of stood it: they think it would of sent me back into that dark corner. And it would of.*

Gus turns down the steep gravel road into the cove and shifts into first gear to save wear on the brakes. The thick, tangled oaks in the cove are showing early green. The dark creek they cross twice is up and running, the sky is still, and, as Gus predicted, a thick fog bank looms in the east. They pass Maggie's little gray house, the cove and Gus's boat, the *Betty B.*, asleep on her slack mooring line, and turn uphill to cross the meadow to the Harper house, whose pale yellow seems even duller in contrast with the bright explosion of the huge forsythia in the dooryard. Gus turns the Willys around in the drive and gets out to help David unload.

"Just set them here," says David. "I'll carry them in. Can I buy you a beer? It was cold an hour ago."

"No thanks, maybe next time," says Gus, who suddenly seems physically uncertain, as though he is going to bump into something or stumble while standing still. He looks away, then turns back to David and proffers a hand, which David takes, smiling.

"Welcome home, David," Gus says softly, then does an abrupt about-face, fumbles into the Willys, and drives away.

✳✳✳

In her west window, from which the sun has just withdrawn its light and warmth, Maggie Bowen sits wrapped in a plaid blanket in her wicker chair. A weighty poetry anthology lies open in her lap, and her reading glasses–the pair with archaic little round lenses that she bought before the war and has kept in a felt case, scratchless, since–rest on the end of her nose. Her eyes are closed, the better to see, and she sits upright in her chair. The Willys has just passed, returning from dropping off David up the cove road. Maggie's eyes are shut to see him, David, again, for a closer look.

She did not expect the curls, nor that the breeze in the car window would set them in such soft motion. Now, on second sight, she decides she likes them and smiles to think how surprised she was at first sight.

What must Gus think, she wonders. What did he say when he saw that hair? Probably nothing, but he will certainly tease David mercilessly when he feels comfortable enough with him again; tease him as he always has, play-fully, but with a purpose.

Though he has not said so, Maggie knows that Gus has awaited David's arrival with both dread and hope. He dreads the prospect of seeing David daily, alive and well and growing into a man while his son, John, is dead and in the earth. He fears that David will ask about John, how he was killed, and rip open the wound that nearly killed the father along with the son.

They say that soldiers don't like to talk about their experiences; if that is so for David, having him around, perhaps even taking him on his boat as a stern man, which Gus badly needs, will be a blessing for him. Remorse is memory awake, though, as Emily Dickinson says, and the best grief is tongueless, but it might soothe Gus some to talk a little about his loss; per-haps a cautious whispered memory at first, a sweet silly little incident recalled to open the valve of grief and guilt just a tad. Killed in Hue, the Imperial City, for God's sake; it sounds like a cruel fairy tale.

David's poor mother, such a fragile thing, sounds in her letters so over-wrought with worry about him that she might leave the professor to his own sabbatical and come back from France to hover closer to David, or she will ruin the sabbatical with her worrying. She has been afraid for him since he chose to stay in Vietnam with his natives, as she calls them, for a second year, and lost his pretty fiancée as a consequence. She was afraid for him when he came home—so confused, so angry, she said, so hermetic. She was afraid when he dropped out of college without finishing the semester, acting like a resentful outcast, or so she said. Now that he has come down here to the island, to live alone in the house, she is afraid that he will never be able to recover and cope with the world at large. Perhaps he won't. Maggie wonders why David or anyone would want to, but she will try to coax him back to college as his mother asked, and she will enlist Gus to help, as she promised. But not yet. Let him rest, she thinks; let him settle in; let him find his own way.

Her guess is that he wants to rediscover a perfect island world that no longer exists. It did once, in a way, and Gus will assure him of that, but now it is all gone, the good with the bad. It certainly never existed in the way that David must remember or dream that it did: a place he remembers as a carefree child playing among the rocks in the cove, paddling in the skiffs at the town float, catching mackerel in a world of perfectly protected innocence; a place that he would like to recapture as a refuge, a sanctuary from the war and bitter disappointment and betrayal upon coming home. Now, Maggie believes, he is hoping to reconstruct his two years in an unclean jungle fortress living and fighting with savages into something gentle and sublime, transforming the *Heart of Darkness* into *The Swiss Family Robinson* to protect himself from tormenting memories. God help him.

And here comes the fog again. She should have known when the trees were still for so long. Another chill night and morning; another delay of the lilac's bloom. But it will be nice having someone else in the cove; someone new but familiar; someone nearby in the night. He'll have eaten some of the ginger snaps by now, found the cold milk in the icebox as well. Settling in, sniffing about, getting a little fire going in the stove as she should do. Sanctuary. Maggie wonders how he will get on with the other newcomers, especially with the schoolteacher's husband, who tells such horrifying, bloodthirsty stories about his experiences in Vietnam that even the men in their cups cringe and slip away. Perhaps David will avoid him as Gus does.

***

The house that David's parents bought from Maggie Bowen in the early 1950s is still called Ava's house by the natives of Barter Island, especially those on the east side of the island, who sincerely mean that they still consider it to be Ava's house, though the Harpers have owned it for nearly twenty years and Ava, the last of the Coombs family to live there, has been dead for thirty. When David's father, the distant professor, insisted that they add a family room with a fireplace and a master bedroom above it, his wife was equally insistent that they restore the original house exactly the way it was in its heyday. She maintains Ava's wicker chair, draped with her afghan, as a sort of shrine in the front parlor window.

The house sits on a slope above the cove and is fronted by a long, wide meadow wrapped around by stone walls. Behind it, the ground—granite outcroppings and a thick spruce forest—continues to rise to the cliffs on the northern end of the island's east side. On the edge of the granite precipice sits the little cabin that Ava's brother, Walter, built for a retreat the year before they both died.

Relishing the cool evening silence, David decides not to run the generator but lights the kerosene lamps in the kitchen and parlor instead. When he lights the wall lamp over the sink, he notices that the calendar is blank but for today, June 6, which is filled with his name and a question mark. The fog has brought in the rich salt smell of the sea and a stillness that comforts David, calms him. He moves slowly, unpacking the boxes of groceries and arranging the kitchen. When he is done, he pries open a beer with the Pepsi-Cola bottle opener on the wall by the door and eats a couple of ginger snaps. He leans Maggie's short welcome note up against the little vase of forget-me-nots, thinking that he has been welcomed more here on the island than any place he has been in the six months that he has been back.

He lugs his duffel bag up the narrow staircase and plumps it onto the bed in the little room that he and his brother shared in summers. He remembers how he loved lying in this bed under the eaves listening to the steady night rain on the roof or the murmur of his parents' voices downstairs. He remembers how he liked to linger on cold and damp mornings reading under the covers while his brother slept curled up beneath the slanting eaves. But now the room seems confining, close. The view from the only window is of the rise of boulders, stumps, and trees beneath the shoulder of the hill behind the house, and it makes him feel uneasy, leaves him with a strange but somehow familiar sense of discomfort, even dread. He shakes it off with a dramatic little shiver, smiles at his foolishness, then descends the stairs to explore the rest of the house.

The old parlor and new family room have been swept and dusted and—he sniffs—undoubtedly aired out by Maggie and Leah. They have laid a fire in the fireplace, which he will light later against the fog and chill, and the woodbox has been filled. He remembers interminable Monopoly games with his brother—and parents, too, sometimes—on the lobster-trap coffee table between the couch and the fire; hot chocolate with marshmallows; whispered stories about old grandfather Amos's ghost risen from his grave under the oaks to visit the cabin and the cliff where German spies murdered him. David lifts a framed photograph from the shelf and wonders at it. It is of him in his army greens on the parade field at Smoke Bomb Hill, and it is the day he was awarded his Green Beret. *How young he was; how fucking gung ho and naive.* He places the photo facedown on the shelf.

He opens another bottle of beer, takes a handful of kitchen matches from the dispenser above the stove, then goes out the front door to sit on the stoop, smoke, and watch Gus's boat and skiff sway on their moorings. But the fog, which has only begun to come in, is just thick enough to hide the boats and the water beyond the meadow, so he starts down the path to the wharf and cove, cigarette and beer in hand. He thinks of the girl in the post office doorway, that she is tall, that she must be in her mid-twenties, and that she is probably not summer people as it is so early in the season.

Every evening at this time for almost two years, he walked Neang from the compound to the shrine at the canal on the outskirts of the hamlet. At first he walked with her as a courtesy, a bodyguard against local communist guerrillas who might want to punish her for working for the Americans, or "enlist" her to serve as a porter, a messenger, or even a soldier. She wore the same cotton shirt and pants every day, her hair bobbed to just below her ears, and her feet slapping in plastic sandals. She did not tease and tickle him like she did Byrnes and Ski in the team house kitchen, but she sang American pop tunes with him, quietly, as they walked. *You know the gypsy with the gold-capped tooth.* In his second year, she sometimes held his hand and swung their arms softly.

He was armed with his .45 and was usually shirtless. She carried leftovers from the evening meal in a red plastic basket, and she smelled of detergent, spices, and sweet-scented hair oil. On evenings when she knew that her mother was visiting her aunt in Ap Moi and might see them when she came walking home, they waited for Chau Sinh to bathe at the well, then he accompanied them, chaperoned them, in his sarong with a carbine over his shoulder. When Chau Sinh and Neang spoke in Khmer, Neang translated for David; when he and Neang were alone, they spoke a patois of Khmer, Vietnamese, and English that the Americans and Khmer in the outpost used. In his last months, David carried a cold beer with him, and they often stopped to sit on the stone steps of the little shrine to watch the sun go down over the distant Cambodian mountains that were getting more crowded every day with North Vietnamese regulars massing to come across the border. Neang sat close to him, her shoulder against his, once in a while her head resting there. They talked in simple sentences built from three languages about her dreams to go to school in Saigon, her fears for her family and village, her love of dancing. He tried to explain why the American Special Forces were leaving, why he could not stay. He said that he wanted her to go to America with him. Although she said that she would like to but must stay with her family, he knew that she would not like to, and wondered if she would like America at all if she did. He wondered if he would.

On the wharf, he flicks the lighted end of his cigarette into the water and pockets the filter. Off to his right, on the top of the high granite outcropping in the mouth of the cove in front of Maggie's house, he thinks he sees movement, something dark and thick, bear-like in silhouette. He remembers that Maggie sometimes sits out there in the evening under a blanket to watch the flash of Mount Desert Light, but tonight it is too foggy to see the light, and the shape he sees is larger than Maggie. If it is Maggie, there is someone under the blanket with her. But when he moves uphill toward the house and looks back, he sees the shape move again, and he sees that it is Maggie, alone, who is standing and turning to go back inside out of the foggy cold.

TWO

A year or two out in the open, on the water, nothing closing in on him, ought to cure him of that.
—Gus Barter

Gus pours half of the boiling water in the kettle over his breakfast dishes in the sink, then the other half into his thermos, where two fresh tea bags wait to be steeped. He visits the outhouse—no need for a lamp as the sun has nearly risen—and moving quietly to not wake Betty, he returns to the kitchen to wash, shave, and make up his lunch. Today Gus finds his favorite, pimento loaf, in the fridge and peels two slices from the plastic package. He slathers a slice of bread with mayonnaise, lays down a slice of pimento loaf, slathers that with mustard, lays down another slice, and slathers that with mayonnaise before he wraps the sandwich in waxed paper. He cuts a wedge of Boston cream pie and wraps it, then adds a bruised banana from the bowl on the table to his dinner pail before he closes it. In the mudroom, Gus remembers to change the newspaper padding in the soles of his fishing boots and to sprinkle mustard powder into each to absorb the pain in his arches. When he has donned his jacket and flannel cap, he thinks to go back in and give Betty a kiss for remembering to buy the pimento loaf, but he decides not to disturb her and lets himself out of the house without a sound.

He parks the Willys at the top of the hill above the cove, walks downhill, crosses the creek, passes Maggie's well as he crosses her lawn, then cuts
through the tall meadow grass on the path that he re-creates every spring
with repeated use. This morning the dew is heavy, and Gus's black rubber
boots are glistening wet to his calves from the drooping timothy on the sides
of his skinny path. The sun is just peeping above the horizon beyond the cove;
the tide is coming and will be for two more hours. The sea is very nearly flat
calm, and what little breeze there is is southwesterly: the finest kind of morning for setting out traps.

Aboard the *Betty B.*, Gus blinks at a pair of shags on the ledge who have
opened their wings for drying in the slanting morning sunlight, then starts
up the Chrysler V-8 to let her idle and see how she sounds. He watches the
swaying eelgrass in the clear cove water and remembers the story of his great-
great-uncle Henry Coombs who was said to have walked ashore from out here
in the middle of the cove, his head bobbing just underwater, pushing aside
eelgrass, in fulfillment of some witch's prediction. Gus shakes his head smiling, thinking that his grandfather, who told him that story, believed in ghosts
and was said to converse with them regularly. He thinks that he misses his
grandfather as he misses his son, John, and he quickly shuts them both out of
his waking mind.

As he brings the *Betty B.* in alongside the wharf and ties off the bowline,
he notices a pair of leather boots and jeans and looks up to see David standing behind the stacked traps. David is smiling; his hands are tucked in the
front pouch of a hooded sweatshirt, his curls flattened by a blue wool watch
cap.

"You could of said something," Gus scolds. "You nearly scared me to
death. Here, take this stern line, would you, if you can remember how to tie
a hitch."

"I guess so." David handles the line gingerly but ties it right.

"What's the matter with your hands?" Gus asks.

"I blistered them the day before yesterday turning over my garden,
breaking up that goddamn sod. It's been a while since I worked with my
hands."

"College will do that to you. Since you're standing there you might start
handing me over those ballast stones," Gus says. "I want to ask you why you
quit college, but I won't. There, those flat ones first."

David hands two flat brick-sized stones at a time, feeling his blisters stretch and split as he spreads his hands to hold the stones. He thinks that the remark about college and not asking means that he, David, should refrain from asking about a certain other tender subject, though he might want to.

"I finished putting in the garden yesterday. I wonder if I could go along with you today and help out. I'd really like to get out on the water."

"Didn't I see you clearing brush up around the cabin the other day? You've been busy."

"Sure, that was me. I've cleared most of the spruce behind the cabin too. I've been sleeping up there these last few nights. I really like it; it's open, up on the high ground, clear to the sea on all sides but one. I noticed that you don't fish the shore along the cliffs in front of the cabin; those are your waters, aren't they? Did you ever fish along there?"

"You can start handing me traps," Gus says, gesturing at the stack. "Those ones first. No, I haven't ever fished along there; no one has in a long time. A Stonington guy tried putting a string in there a few years ago, but I tied him off; he took the warning. They're light, aren't they?"

"Jesus, I guess so." David hefts a trap over his head with ease. "I've never handled traps that weren't already soaked. Is it because of what happened to your grandfather on the cabin cliff that you don't fish there? Out of respect for him?"

"Not out of respect, I don't think. It's just that I don't like being there, that's all."

"I can't count how many times I've told that story in the last few years: him murdered by German spies, about you and Maggie and the depth charges. People say it's bullshit."

"It is, but it isn't either. He was up there one night—the Coastal Picket—keeping a lookout for U-boats, and he slipped and fell. Hand me those traps from that row there. We only have room for five more. You're talkative today, aren't you? You ought to go make yourself a lunch if you're coming out with me. You must of lost twenty pounds since I saw you last."

"I don't want to hold you up," David says.

"You'll want a lunch."

"If I get hungry I'll have some of yours."

"Like hell you will. Come on aboard."

✳✳✳

Two miles wide and six miles long, Barter Island lies north to south off the mid-Maine coast. With the exception of a few islands–York, that was once inhabited but is now populated by sheep–and other high, bare outcroppings that are nesting islands and rookeries for seabirds, Barter Island is the last piece of land before open ocean. The waters off the east side of Barter Island are prime lobstering grounds and are fished primarily by Gus Barter and Junior Chafin, who are the last male scions of their respective families and inherited their fishing grounds from their ancestors, Cornish fishermen who claimed them in the early 1800s. Their claim to these waters, where they set out their traps in strings of ten, is not legal but is sanctified by tradition and protected by violence if need be. In midsummer, when the lobsters come clambering in from deep water to the rocky coastline to find a crevice or cave to hide in while they shed their shells and grow others, and then crawl out, famished, the first baited traps to welcome them more often than not belong to Gus and Junior.

"Maybe you should throw a line over the traps." Gus has been watching the pyramid of traps on the stern as he steers with one hand and opens his thermos with the other. "They're dry and it's going to breeze up some with this coming tide."

David starts to the stern, glad to have something to do.

"Take this line." Gus tosses him a short coil. "Snug but not too tight would be best. If it's tied too tight, one might squirt out of the middle and take the whole stack overboard with it."

As they pass the southern point of York Island, out of protected waters and into the tidal rip toward open sea, David stands in the middle of the deck in the chill morning sunlight, relishing the vastness of the open sea beyond, the lifting breeze and chop, and the isolation. There is no one in sight on the water, there is little chance of encountering strangers, and best of all, there is no chance of being surprised by anyone.

As they set the southern string at ten fathoms, David puts two or three ballast stones in each trap, baits it, ties it shut, and waits for Gus to raise his forefinger before he tips the trap over the washboard and watches it slowly sink. Gus curses the third trap: it does not have enough weight and drifts farther north than he wants it to before it sinks. David is lulled by the rocking of the boat, the rhythm of the work, the sun in his face.

On the way back to the cove to pick up another string of traps, David would like to sit out on the transom, but he does not want to look like a tourist, so he stands under the house with Gus.

Steering with a raised knee, Gus pours a cup of tea. "If you want some, there's plenty. There's a porcelain cup down below; it's white."

"No thanks."

They ride in silence. David remembers days with Gus on the water when he was a boy. He remembers the summer when Gus's son, John, left to join the army and he, David, filled in as Gus's stern man. He remembers how puffed up he was when his parents or other summer people saw him coming into the cove on the *Betty B.* and cleaning up the boat after a day of hauling traps. He remembers how large he felt in his high rubber boots, how important.

Gus pours another cup of tea and dumps the tea bags overboard. He remembers that when he and his brother Melvin were kids they read somewhere that Iroquois boys practiced for war by shooting arrows at one another and slapping them aside before they struck flesh. He remembers how he and Melvin practiced doing the same in the meadow with blunt arrows and how he, Gus, got quite good at it. Today he thinks that he is doing the same thing: slapping aside arrows of memory launched by the presence of David, who was not only a friend of his son's but was also in Vietnam. The arrows that come straight at him–John baiting a trap and pushing it overboard–are easy to deflect; those that come unexpected, from an angle–that David might talk about what violent death looks like and sounds like–are harder to slap aside, but Gus remains alert, determined not to be pierced.

"There's Junior." Gus nods toward the starboard bow and steps out behind the house to raise a hand in greeting to Junior at the wheel of *Myrmaid* several hundred yards to the east. Junior does the same.

"He's alone. I wonder where his stern man is, what's his name?"

"Simon Cooper." David says.

"You know him?"

"I've met him. We've talked a little a couple of times at the store. He's wound pretty tight. It feels like he's liable to start throwing punches any second."

Neither man mentions that it is commonly believed by islanders that Simon Cooper bristles and spins and sputters like a Tasmanian devil because of his horrible experiences in the war. Neither man aboard the *Betty B.* this morning wants to be reminded of terror and fury. They are silent as they dodge those arrows.

"He's been here two years, and you still don't know his name," David says. "Jesus."

"You've been here two weeks and you already know everybody, it seems– all the new ones."

"I haven't met the McGregors. I've seen her a couple of times, but I haven't seen or met him."

"You could of seen him five minutes ago if you would of looked. In Eaton Cove, in his garden, digging."

When they return from the cove with a second pyramid of traps on the transom, the wind has stiffened. David stands on the starboard side watching the shoreline slip by, waiting to pass Eaton Cove and see the McGregor house and perhaps Eliot as well. Gus sticks a broom handle in the wheel to hold it and steps back to tug at the pyramid lashing to be sure that it's secured well enough for the increasing sea.

The warps for the second string of traps are set at fifteen fathoms. Gus throws the boat out of gear and steps back for a look around. His last buoy in the first string is one hundred yards closer to shore, and Junior's string of blue and white buoys is well off to the port side. Gus nods to David who pulls the top trap down to the washboard.

"What was that flash? Did you see that?" David points astern of the *Betty B.*, where nothing is visible. "Oh, of course–sun on a windshield. I'd forgotten."

"That's probably Roger Weed from Stonington, setting out traps past the York Ledges. He'd be setting out down here if he dared to. Junior thinks him and his uncle are going to try it again this year. There are too many Stonington boats, and they've bought too many traps. They're desperate and they'll fish our waters if they can. They know me and Junior don't have sons or even nephews to inherit our waters. They're like turkey buzzards dancing around a half-dead dog in the road, pecking at him when they can, just waiting, and not too damn patiently either."

It is late morning when they finish setting the second string parallel to the shore. The tide is at flood, the breeze is southwest at ten knots, and the sun is high over the mountainous ridge of the island's spine. Gus steers into the lee of The Battery, a rugged, slanting wall of brownish granite that stretches for one hundred yards just off the island shore. Out of the wind, David sheds his cap and sweatshirt and basks in the sun and breeze, thinking how far sweeter this is than the steaming heat of the airless rice paddies. It was here at The Battery, he remembers, where he caught his first mackerel, in this boat, when he was something like twelve years old.

Gus, who sheds neither his cap nor his flannel shirt, taps the *Betty B.* out of gear, cuts back to a low idle, and goes below, saying that he does not want to shut her off so early in the season for fear that she might not start again. He returns with a bottle of Jim Beam and two cans of Coca-Cola hugged against his chest. He gives David a porcelain cup and a hand line.

"You might bait that and throw it over. There aren't many flounder anymore, but you might get a fair-sized mackerel in here. I'm going to make myself a little something to drink. How about you?"

David would like that very much. He baits the large hook and lowers it overboard, jigging it, while Gus pours them a half-cup of bourbon and an equal amount of soda, then stirs the drinks with a wooden claw peg. He returns from a second trip below with a short stool on which he perches, legs crossed and recrossed, toe tucked behind ankle, within reach of the gear shift and throttle lest they drift too close to The Battery while he drinks. David sits on the washboard, with the line in one hand, and his cup in the other. The sweetened bourbon goes down nicely, and in empty stomachs the first cup warms and spreads and softly glows when it finds its way to their faces. David smiles seraphically at all he sees around him. Gus pulls out part of his undershirt and cleans his glasses, looking vague-eyed and vulnerable without them.

"I got something!" David sets his cup down and stands to haul in his line. It is a flounder, brown and two-eyed on one side, pale and eyeless on the other. The fish is weighty and well over a foot and a half long. He unhooks it and hands it to Gus, who drops it into a bucket.

"He's a nice one. You almost never see a good-sized flounder like that anymore. There's no better-tasting fish," Gus says, pleased. "We caught that one on one drink; let's see how many we can catch on a second drink."

David lets the weighted hook strike bottom, then draws it up a foot or so, jigging it with his index finger. Well into their second cup, Gus begins to tell the story of how old Dennis Eaton nearly bled to death when he fell with a gallon jug of rum and sliced his wrist open. David, who remembers the story well, listens with pleasure, as Gus punctuates each sentence with a chuckle, anticipating the punch line.

"He said when they finally got him to the hospital they pumped two pints into him, a Christly quart of blood, and didn't he feel invigorated with all that young blood in him? He recommended it to old Virgil Gross as a kind of elixir."

They laugh and shake their heads appreciatively.

"Not getting anything here? I'll move us over closer to the rocks, and we can try it there while we finish this drink." The tiny spider-webs of capillaries on Gus's cheeks and nose are flushed crimson.

David drops his line back over and knocks back half his cupful. He sits in the sun jigging his line and thinking that he would like to drop a hint that would launch Gus into one of his stories about the Coastal Picket and the lighthouse crew and the battle against the U-boats long ago, familiar stories intoned by Gus as fond memories on which David could sail, not back to the old days, but to the careless days when he and young John listened to the same stories on this deck, in the fish shack, riding in the Willys. But he senses that Gus does not want to break the companionable silence in which they sit now, that he has fallen silent because of one memory, and that he cannot or will not brook another of any kind. David scratches a kitchen match to flame on the washboard and lights a cigarette. *Light it up!* He shakes his head abruptly, as if trying to wake himself and begins to pull in the line.

Passing Eaton Cove this time, riding in a strained silence that he does not understand but will not question, David sees the McGregors. Eliot is at the edge of a large, fenced-in symmetrical garden beneath a huge rock maple, apparently digging, but upon closer inspection David sees that he is turning over a mound of loose soil. His wife is carrying two buckets that pull her shoulders earthward. As they pass close to the open shore of the cove, Eliot looks over his shoulder at the sound of their engine, and Gus waves. Christine McGregor sets down one of her buckets and waves back. Her husband, whose expression reminds David of Ebenezer Scrooge, does not.

"I guess it's true that he's not too friendly," David says. "She seems nice enough."

"She dresses like a man, dungarees, short hair, that feed cap," Gus observes. "Still, she has nice teeth." Gus is not watching the cove recede as David is.

"That's not all that's nice-looking about her," he says. "She must be twenty years younger than him."

"They eat nuts and berries and plain oats in a bowl," Gus tells the windshield. "He preaches against eating meat or fish or eggs or lobsters. They don't use money except to buy fuel for his truck. They eat carrots and spinach, roots and leaves, and probably bugs too. Christ," he scoffs. "what's this world coming to? They pay their taxes with rhubarb? What's happening to our island?"

"Hippies that work. Brown ricers," David says.

"What?"

"If they don't use money, how did they buy that house and land?"

"Hah." Gus is sarcastic. "That's another story. They both went to high-toned colleges. You don't go out of your way to live poor if you aren't rich, do you?"

David has no answer. He feels that he is somehow responsible for Gus's shift from a laughing delight in the day to a smoldering anger that he has never before seen and cannot comprehend.

As they turn into the cove, Gus says, still to the windshield, "I'm going to have my lunch here at the wharf before I head back out. You don't have to go with me if you don't want to. I've handled these traps alone for years. You've got other things to do."

"No. I'd like to go with you, unless you don't want me to."

"Well, why don't you go up the hill to the house and make yourself a sandwich. We'll load back up after we eat. How's that?"

"Good," says David. "You were right. I am hungry. I'll be quick about it."

✳✳✳

Fat Albert, the 1946 Chevrolet truck, has been without doors for longer than anyone, including its owner, Fuddy McFarland, can remember. Tonight Fuddy and his lifelong companion, Skippy Groth, are riding in Fat Albert to the party in Bill's workshop on the west side of the island. There is a sweating six-pack of Ballantine Ale in tall cans on the seat between them. Fat Albert is coughing and rattling its way up Bridge Hill in first gear.

Fuddy and Skippy live together in their father's house—they are cousins with the same father—in Squeaker Cove on the southern end of the island. Though they have not washed or changed their clothes or shaved for the party, they have dribbled a little of their late father's scented hair oil onto their chests beneath their undershirts. They are both of late middle age, but Skippy, whose cleft palate and lip are made hideous by four remaining teeth, two on top and

two below, still has the heart and mind of a boy. Skippy's speech is so gar-
bled, so bubbling, that he would sound the same if he were trying to speak
under-water, and only Fuddy and a couple of others can understand him
fairly well. He and Fuddy may be related, but they do not look alike: Fuddy
is tall, thin, and clumsy; Skippy is stocky and surprisingly agile. Fuddy has
tiny eyes and a sharp nose and chin that seem to be tending toward one
another; Skippy is round-faced and bug-eyed. Fuddy still has his teeth, but
they are so begrimed and encrusted with mold that he appears toothless from
a distance; his breath reminds his friends of rancid clam broth. They make
good money digging clams primarily because of Skippy's ability to hear clams
that are hidden in the mud; for this people like to call him gifted, a term the
men use for Fuddy as well, but for a different reason.

At the top of Bridge Hill, Fuddy lets Fat Albert coast a bit to catch its
breath, and Skippy pokes him and points ahead at David who is walking
along the side of the road carrying a six-pack. Fuddy pumps, then applies the
brakes, and Fat Albert squeals to a stop next to David, who has turned. It is
the summer solstice, and at nearly 9:00 P.M. it is still light enough to see that
David is smiling.

Fuddy waves David into the cab, and Skippy moves to the middle of
the seat with the six-pack in his lap. David has seen Fuddy several times
since he has come back, but this is the first time he has seen Skippy. With
one foot on the running board, David, who smells of Old Spice and sham-
poo, reaches for Skippy's reluctant hand and shakes it as he climbs onto the
seat.

"I haven't seen you in years, Skippy," David declares. "You look just the
same as you did in '66. No, better."

Skippy, delighted and frightened, averts his big blue eyes and covers his
mangled mouth with his hand.

"I told him you was here," Fuddy says. "You wouldn't have a cigarette,
would you? I been out all day." Fuddy has his eye on the pack of Marlboros
in David's shirt pocket.

David knocks out four cigarettes for Fuddy and offers one to Skippy,
who shakes his head.

"Thanks," Fuddy says. "They make him dizzy and being dizzy scares
him."

David scratches a kitchen match on the dash, cups it, lights Fuddy's cigarette and his own, then asks Skippy, "You going to the shop party or to the library?"

Skippy is confused, but Fuddy laughs. "The liberry? Ha ha. Skippy don't dance, but he likes to watch and he likes the music. Hey Skippy?"

David thinks that he has hardly seen the cousins in almost five years, and he had forgotten how ripe they are close-up. Theirs is a unique fragrance, a potpourri of intestinal gases, decaying vegetable matter, used motor oil, body odor, and rotting bait. David is reminded of the open sewage ditch behind Ba Xoai village.

Past the gravel pit, they round the bend in time to see the rays of the disappearing sun on the pink underbellies of the clouds and to see two more pedestrians walking westward. They are two of the three hippies that David saw the day that he arrived, who he thought, and heard, had left the island weeks ago.

Fuddy stops beside them. "Hullo. You want a ride?"

"Right on," says the bearded one. He laughs happily. His hair is loose and hangs to his shoulders but does not stir in the breeze.

His companion is the girl whose adorable buttocks David followed up the gangplank his first day on the island. She too has loosened her hair, and she too smiles brightly. She is wearing a loosely fitting cotton peasant dress of many colors that is gathered about her ample breasts and puffed full in the sleeves.

"I'm Willow," says the bearded one. He takes David's hand in the thumb-wrapping, soul brother handshake popular among black soldiers. "And this is Autumn."

"Hi!" Autumn says.

David introduces himself and the cousins and invites the couple to climb aboard. Willow is carrying a woven, purse-like bag over his shoulder. He places it in the bed of the truck and climbs up behind it.

"Far out!" says Autumn, as she too climbs on.

***

There are typically three kinds of parties on Barter Island. The smallest and most frequently attended is the card party. From late September, when the bugs and summer people have finally gone, to the beginning of fishing season in late spring, card parties are held every other week or so at various houses. The host or hostess–card parties are for men at one house, women at another on different nights–provides the house and tables and tea and lemonade for the ladies, coffee and Postum for the men. One or two guest volunteers provide sweet snacks. The men's parties are thick with pipe and cigarette smoke and laced with jokes and off-color comments; at the ladies' parties no one smokes or swears and everyone talks; at neither is alcohol of any kind served or consumed. The game at both parties is "83," a locally grown hybrid of hearts and bridge.

In the summer months, two or three dances are held at the town hall, a prodigious stone building erected by summer people at the turn of the century on the edge of the little town. They are contra dances, and they are attended by islanders and summer residents alike, as many as one hundred people of all ages. Reverend Hotchkiss calls the dances: "The Lady of the Lake," "The March and Circle," "Boston Fancy," and Skippy's favorite, "Duck for the Oyster, Dive for the Clam." The music on stage is provided by Bernadine Bowen, in white, sequined cowboy boots, on the accordion, Alice Hotchkiss on the piano, and Teddy Hatch on the fiddle and squeezebox. The hall is hung with streamers, bunting, and sometimes balloons. The islanders wear their Sunday clothes; no hats for the women or ties for the men, but pretty dresses, dancing shoes, and shirts ironed and starched. The summer people wear polo shirts and shorts and Top-Siders, madras summer dresses or skirts and villager blouses. Chairs line the walls for those too shy to dance and those who prefer to watch and comment. There is fruit punch and sweets on the decorative table in the entry. Alcohol and tobacco are taboo inside, but outside across the road at the edge of the dark alder grove, the island men sit on tailgates and bumpers to smoke and quietly drink rum or rye mixed with anything that may be found in the trunks and truck beds. For most married couples, churchgoers, families, and old folks, the dance ends at midnight with the playing of "Good Night, Irene." For the teens and young singles it continues elsewhere: in backseats of cars, in moonlit meadows, in boathouses, and at the pond, where the sand beach and picnic tables are littered with beer cans and piles of recently shed clothing.

The shop party toward which Fat Albert labors is the third kind. It was not advertised days before on posters in the store as are the dances at the town hall but was proclaimed by Bernadine at noon that day and advertised by selective word of mouth to about forty people, most of them islanders from teens to forties, and new year-rounders like David, of which there are about a dozen. When Fat Albert shudders to a halt off the side of the road behind a dilapidated old Ford, another truck pulls in behind it. Willow and Autumn jump down waving and calling out thank-you's on their way to join a group of young drinkers in front of Bill's shop. Watching Autumn glide past, David notices that she is barefoot and wonders what, if anything, she is wearing beneath her soft dress.

As daylight wanes, the party shows signs of beginning: Simon Cooper has cleared a breach in the tumble of retired lobster traps on the north side of Bill's wide workshop and inched his Ford Galaxie over the boulders up to the window to attach the wires of the record player inside to the car's battery; the older partygoers—Gus and Betty, Junior and Myrtle, Fuddy and Skippy among them—have settled into chairs along the south wall beneath ranks of green and white buoys hanging in the rafters above, with plastic cups and cans of beer in their laps; a gaggle of girls and young women are arguing and laughing, some nervously, by the record player on the workbench-turned-bar. Chief among them is the lithe and lovely Dianne "Boo" Barnes, in shorts and flannel shirt, who argues that the Mamas and the Papas are way too lame and insists on early Beatles, posing with the album cover as if offering it in a television ad, bringing fits of laughter from the girls and appreciative leers from the young men who lounge in the wide doorway, their eyes fixed on her flawless thighs.

Outside, in the increasing shadow of a spruce wood, well away from the workshop and the new arrivals in the road, and purposely down wind, a group of young men gathers to get their personalities going. On the hood of a colorless old car, Willow sits cross-legged rolling joints for his new brothers. An eager deerfly circles his shaggy head, providing him with a vibrant halo that is seen but not appreciated by the others. Willow is wearing a tie-dyed T-shirt, sandals, and striped bell-bottoms; the others, to a man, are dressed in flannel shirts, jeans, and leather boots; a few of the younger ones have begun to grow their hair. Simon Cooper is passing a half-gallon jug of coffee brandy to follow the fifth of Black Velvet that is making the rounds. Several have settled in, sitting on the ground, on the tailgate of a pickup, or on the hood with Willow; others, David and Simon among them, remain standing, and depart singly or in pairs to join the dance, and yet others, who have seen the smoky circle and flickering matches from a distance, join the group to replace them.

The floor of Bill's shop is of heavy-duty plywood affixed to sturdy stringers, but even so it is in motion beneath the feet of the dancers when David and Simon return from Willow's uplifting council fire. The music is Rolling Stones, heavy on the bass, and the dancers are mostly girls and young women, who are twisting, waving their arms, and leaping around playfully in pairs, in groups, sometimes alone. Boo shouts something in Nancy Cooper's ear, and they laugh as Nancy drags her husband Simon onto the dance floor. Boo does the same to David, and he and Simon, awkward and self-conscious under the eyes of the older men, strive to appear relaxed and at ease. A few more young men are pulled from the bar and shadows, and when the crowd on the dance floor morphs into a circle, Betty takes Gus's drink out of his hand, sets it on the floor, and leads him to join the dancing, much to the grim disapproval of Myrtle Chafin, who shakes her chin in tiny rapid motions at Junior. When "Ruby Tuesday" begins, the dancers, sweaty and winded, take the person next to them as a partner and dance a kind of clumsy gitdown waltz. David is next to Nancy Cooper; he puts his arm around her waist and takes her outstretched hand and they laugh as they bump into others on the floor. David steals a look at Nancy's neck, the damp auburn ringlets that fall around her ear; when he looks at her lips and her eyes, which meet his, he realizes that she has been watching him and he reddens to his neck. Nancy smiles and rolls her green eyes.

As the records are being changed, people drift to the bar and disparate corners to address their drinks and pour new ones. Gus waves David over to where he and Betty are sitting by the cold woodstove. Gus hands David a plastic kitchen glass, a gas station giveaway, and from an insulated bag with fading hunting scenes on its sides, he pours David three fingers of Jim Beam, adds a handful of ice, and tops it off with soda. Betty is mixing her new drink with a spoon. Gus is perspiring and grinning at David.

"You best behave yourself," Gus says. "This is a small island."

"Look at who's talking." Betty laughs.

"Look at who's laughing."

David says that he is going to sit out the next one and go outside for some air and to cool off. The music starts again, even louder; it is Fleetwood Mac, who has been down one time, been down two times, but is never going back again.

Betty shouts good luck to David and smiles knowingly as she sees him pulled back onto the dance floor before he can make it to the door.

"They love those curls and how shy he is," Betty says to Gus, who cannot hear her.

This time two circles are formed, and David's is the closer to the door. In the other, in the pale light, a boy points an index finger to the top of his head and tries a wild spin, loses control, and sprays those nearest to him with beer before he falls in a laughing heap. Perspiring, his head pounding, David remembers the *romvong*, the gentle Khmer circle dance that Neang tried to teach him in the golden light on those humid evenings at Ba Xoai. When his circle, in slow motion, brings him around to the door, he slips out of the workshop, picking up his drink from the paint shelf on the way.

He stands in the road with his back to the shop and closes his eyes for twenty seconds to see better in the dark. He feels as though he is alone, passing in the dark between two distant but somehow similar worlds, and this new one seems to be his destination, unlike the hostile college campus. When he opens his eyes, he can see the smoky circle of young men and their twinkling matches, and looking up he sees that the sky is crowded with stars, so many, so clear, that he can barely identify familiar constellations. The air is cool and smells of balsam and salt water. He thinks that he would like to sit alone for a while and looks around for Fat Albert.

"Christ, I almost bumped into you."

Simon Cooper pulls to a halt on David's right. He laughs, and David closes his eyes while Simon lights his cigarette with a Zippo, then lights his own.

"What do you think?" Simon exhales.

"About this place? I think it's incredibly beautiful; I had almost forgotten. And friendly, too."

"Friendly! Yeah, at first," Simon says. "But in the winter it's a different story. You'll find out if you stay that long. They can smile and smile at you the whole time, and get you in the ass when you bend over. You were a Green Beret."

"Yes. And you were with the First Cav? What was your MOS?"

"Eleven bravo. Yours?"

"Same. Infantry."

"I was with the Seventh Cavalry to be exact." Simon flatfoots half of his drink, his interest gradually shifting to the jug of coffee brandy in the group beyond.

"Garryowen," David says, naming the martial tune of the Seventh Cavalry.

"What? What's that?"

David pauses, puzzled that Simon doesn't seem to recognize the song, Custer's tune.

The music stops and someone replaces Fleetwood Mac with "Love Me Tender." A group of laughing girls and young women, drinks in their hands, passes David and Simon in the dark and assembles at a nearby truck bed, smoking and talking in excited whispers. David can just barely make out the figure of Autumn, who is sitting cross-legged on the tailgate, busily preparing a treat in her lap for her new sisters.

"A Green Beret, eh?" Simon leans against the side of a car. "We called you Green Weenies. That stupid song: 'Fighting soldiers from the sky, Fearless men who jump and die.' That's pretty dumb, isn't it?"

"How so?"

"Who the hell would want to do that? Jump and die? Why not jump and live? You must not have jumped." Simon laughs at his own cleverness. David manages a smile that Simon does not see.

"Or else I did, and I'm dead, and I just don't know it."

"That's possible, I guess. You wouldn't know you were dead if you were."

"No, I guess not."

Simon seems thoughtful, his eye on the group of men in the distance. A sudden brisk breeze runs in off the water and along the road, soughing through the spruce.

"I was at the Ia Drang," Simon says.

"Jesus Christ." David is astonished. Simon knew that he would be and is quiet while it sinks in.

"But I thought . . ." David begins, then stops in midquestion.

Simon sniffs the air. "Smell that? That's wicked good dope that hippie brought. Let's get over there before they smoke the joint down." He knocks back the rest of his drink and starts off into the dark.

Gus and Betty are slow dancing by the window, enjoying the old Elvis favorites and the breeze. Junior and Myrtle are dancing nearby; Myrtle is glaring over her husband's shoulder at Betty's backside and hips, which are moving slowly against Gus.

"What's that smell?" Junior wants to know. It is sweeter than tobacco and has a pleasant after-sniff.

"I smell it, too," says Betty over Gus's shoulder. "I think it's dope."

"Those hippies are back, as if you didn't notice." Myrtle holds Junior at arm's length and gives him a look.

"Camping at the park again, I guess."

"No, I hear they're camping on McGregor's land, up across the road toward the mountain, just below the Black Dinah."

"Christ," Gus says.

Soon the shop is full to capacity, throbbing with dancers and an insistent bass from the record player. People have to cup their hands over another's ear and shout into it to be heard. The shuddering shop floor causes the record player's needle to skip its way through songs. Autumn sits on the far end of the workbench/bar, her bare legs dangling and dancing over the edge, her puffy sleeves pushed up to her shoulders. She is examining a newly sewn bait bag, her mouth half open in wonderment at the stitching. High on beer, marijuana, rum, and life, she feels an almost overwhelming wave of joy to be among such *real* people; people so generous, so accepting; people who are embracing her, welcoming her and Willow and Meadow Dawn. Now they are all virtual brothers and sisters. Her joy melts into compassion for the humble and the plain—no phony-ass suburban businessmen here. The homely and the unlovely people before her grow lovely in her eyes, and she knows that she is seeing beyond physical corruption and into the pure beauty of their souls: Skippy's bright eyes and childlike wonder; the earthen and uncorrupted color and appearance of Fuddy, who with such delight and innocence slaps his knee in time to the music. Both men seem so lonely, so bereft of a woman's touch. How long must it have been since someone held their heads against a soft breast?

The needle slides on the record, and the crowd stops, turns to see Bernadine standing before the record player with a replacement in hand. Someone whistles for quiet, and Bernadine, beaming, her high a natural one, announces a Sadie Hawkins dance.

Autumn is astonished. How fucking cosmic can a coincidence be? It's as though Bernadine could hear her thoughts. As though they have already made a spiritual connection.

Autumn pushes her way through the murmuring, laughing crowd on the dance floor and approaches Skippy, who looks up to see her coming, then ducks his head as low as it will go.

Autumn stands over him, a sunburst of sisterly love, and asks him if he will dance with her. "I mean, you gave me a ride and all."

Skippy neither raises his head nor replies. Autumn looks at Fuddy for direction; he shakes his head no, and waves a hand as if trying to erase the idea from her mind.

"Then will *you*?" Autumn is determined. She takes the can of Ballantine from Fuddy's hand and pulls him to his feet. He stands beside her, glances once at her, then faces Bernadine, his hand still in Autumn's, waiting, as are the others in the room who have already paired, until all the males have a partner or have escaped the shop. Bernadine puts on her favorite Beatles tune, "The Fool on the Hill," and someone shuts out one of the three lights in the room.

When the song begins, Fuddy, expressionless, his eyes on the near distance, lets Autumn lead him, holding her apart, but, in spite of himself, relishing the warmth of her body and the feel of the soft flesh of her back beneath the thin dress. To the other island men on the dance floor who wink at him and make lascivious faces, he returns a tiny grin with squinched lips.

To Autumn, whose bare feet move slowly with Fuddy's, her partner is not only a lonely man, a man of the sea and forest, but he is the whole island community, her bodhisattva, and she wants more than anything, ever, to engulf him with love. She pulls him closer, caressing his chest with soft strokes of her breasts and tightened nipples, then she presses her whole body against his, her head lying tenderly on his mephitic shoulder, her eyes closed to the dance floor, but wide open on Nirvana.

When she moves her hips against his, softly, side to side, she feels something that reminds her of an animated film in which a brontosaurus, feeding in a swamp, slowly raises his long, mammoth, outstretched neck from the mire, and straightens it to test the air, alert to danger or opportunity or both. As the song ends and the couples glide to their rest, several of the island men exchange knowing looks as Autumn leads Fuddy out the door into the night. One says to another in a whisper that it looks like yet another girl has discovered Fuddy's gift.

Now Bernadine, with her shy, smiling husband, Bill, at her side and a broom in her hand, announces to the crowd that is far too subdued for her liking, that it's time for the limbo. She is answered with whoops and cheers and a general rush to refurbish drinks. Bernadine has misplaced the limbo record, so she tells those assembling around her that she is substituting Jimmie Cliff's song for the "real one."

The Barter Island shop-party version of limbo holds that the contestants must go under the broom with their drinks in hand, and they cannot spill a drop. Nancy Cooper goes first, with the broom waist high, and slides under with ease to the applause of the crowd. Simon follows her, and halfway through, his chin under the broom, he plumps onto the floor seated, but is satisfied that he has not spilled any rum. The crowd boos him. Another young man goes under successfully, to further applause.

Outside, under a ceiling of stars, Autumn leads Fuddy through the puckerbrush and into an overgrown apple orchard behind the workshop. Beneath a young apple tree, whose last blossoms are visible in the starlight, Autumn kisses Fuddy, in whose mouth her tongue tastes Mother Earth, Gaia herself, and all the sweet detritus of the natural world. Cautiously, reverently, she unzips him and releases his prodigious gift. Neither speaks as Fuddy sinks to the ground, seated with his back against the little tree trunk. Autumn, as speechless as her lover, lifts her dress over her head, revealing that she is naked beneath, and lowers herself carefully athwart his hips, her hands on his shoulders to receive the pleasure and pain of his first entrance as slowly and appreciably as she can. Fuddy holds a soft, firm melonous buttock in each hand and buries his furry face between her breasts. As she lifts herself for the first time, not kneeling, but squatting flat-footed, ready to launch a series of divine deep-knee bends—celestial calisthenics—she makes a soft sound in her throat that sounds like a groan but is her mantra. "Om. Mani padme. Om." Fuddy, who is at this moment the happiest man on Barter Island, hums, "She'll be coming around the mountain when she comes" ever so slowly and softly to himself.

Inside, the broom is just above Bernadine and Bill's knees, and the competition has dwindled to Nancy Cooper and Boo. The crowd is raucous. Bets are laid. Drinks are poured. Beers are chugged. When the music begins, Bernadine checks Nancy's cup to be sure that it is at least half full, and Nancy, slowly, with great care, leans back as far as she can and starts under the broom. The crowd claps in rhythm, while some cheer, and others hoot. When Nancy falls onto her back, there is a universal groan from the crowd, then applause for a noble try and not a drop spilled. Now it is Boo's turn, and there is a hush while her drink is inspected. The music begins suddenly and she leans back, her feet spread wide, her shoulders nearly touching the floor, and begins to move beneath the broom, an inch at a time. As she does, the crowd claps in unison and chants "Go! Go!" and "Do it! Do it!" and "Yes. Yes. Yes." The eyes of the young men caress her spreading thighs.

Outside, Autumn is moving quicker now, perspiring and chanting her mantra with a beatific smile on her face. She hears the voices of the crowd within and is filled with wonder at how in touch the people of this magical island are with her and Fuddy. In another coincidence of cosmic proportions, Boo rises from the broom, Autumn and Fuddy reach the mountaintop at the same time, and the crowd shouts "Hurray! Wow! Way to go!" Fuddy shudders, and Autumn collapses in his lap, her wet lips parted for the final escaping holy syllable: "Om."

✳✳✳

At six in the morning, Maggie stands on her front porch in the soft sunlight. She is wearing her robe open at the neck to gather the warmth from the sun, which is slowly rising over the water and even more slowly trying to burn its way through the morning haze. The cove is silent, as is the sea. It is Sunday and no early boats are roaring and growling past to fish off of Head Harbor; Gus is not banging about in the cove. The only sounds are the thin, liquid song of a hermit thrush deep in the woods beyond the graveyard and the throaty bark of a high-soaring gull overhead. Scattered on the lawn are dozens of little dew-laden spider-webs that Leah used to call tiny trampolines for elves and fairies when she was little. This Sunday morning, Maggie decides, she will go to church. And this morning she will walk.

At the top of Bridge Hill, warmed by the climb, she stops to remove her sweater and tie it around her shoulders, as they liked to do in the 1940s and '50s. She remembers her mother's claim that there was once a path that led from the east side over the mountain through the notch, then down into town by the blacksmith's and the sweet shop, following, no doubt, the creek that ran between them. Maggie wonders, as she has a thousand times, where the path met the road, where she might find it again. Past the bog where the skunk cabbage is unfurling, she walks under a Cooper's hawk, waiting in the tall birch tree for a hapless mouse or green snake to brave the open road. At the top of town hill, looking southwest past the white church steeple out to

Saddleback Rock and Brimstone Island miles distant on the copper sea, she thinks that she will never, ever, tire of this sight, of this island, of these beauteous forms.

With the midmorning sun on her back, Maggie walks in one of the deep ruts of the wagon road that runs across the high meadow toward the island church. The meadow, a plateau of sorts above the town, has begun to show green, and the two shadbush trees at its edge by one of the Barter family plots are abloom in dark pink blossoms. Ahead she can see west-siders and summer people who have climbed the boardwalk up from town to mingle in the churchyard. Any minute now, she thinks, the cars from the east side will begin to pull into the old meadow road behind her. Maggie smiles imperceptibly. Her first memory of crossing this meadow toward the thin white steeple is of her riding in her mother's lap on the wagon seat on a morning such as this. In another memory she is sitting between her father and mother on a blowy autumn morning, their legs covered by wool blankets. She remembers driving the wagon herself, with little Leah on the open seat beside her. Then she is in a Model T, and finally in a procession of cars, all Ford sedans, she the solitary schoolteacher on a rainy Sunday morning. An agnostic all her life (with occasional spells of atheism), Maggie does not attend church out of belief, but out of a habit of being and a love of music and that certain slant of light from the windows.

Today when she turns to see Gus and Betty in the Willys, she has to shield her eyes from the sun. Behind the Willys come Junior and Myrtle in the green truck, and both vehicles creep past her, with waves from the occupants, and pull over into the shade to join her on the lawn beneath the church steps. Myrtle is wearing a blue dress with tiny white dots and a flowered hat of white, woven plastic. Betty, like Maggie, wears a plain skirt and white blouse. The men, both deacons who must pass the basket, are in their Sunday suits; Gus's red hair is still wet and slicked back. When they have exchanged nods and smiles and inane comments with others, the five from the east side turn inward to one another.

"So tell me, Gus, if you would, how David is doing," Maggie says.

"Good, I guess. He's doing good. He's a good stern man. I ought to pay him better."

"I'm sure you should."

"I don't know how good he feels this morning though."

"No." Maggie agrees. "I heard him come down the cove road last night, his footsteps on the gravel in a pattern I've heard many times over the years. Like this."

She takes three unsteady steps forward, saying "Step. Step. Step," then, leaning precariously, she adds three shaky steps to the left, saying "Shuffle. Shuffle. Shuffle." Betty laughs, and the little groups of people still outside watch with amusement.

"Maggie, don't! Stop it, for pity's sake," hisses Myrtle.

Maggie smiles at Gus and repeats the little pantomime, saying, "Shamble. Shamble. Shamble," this time veering to the right.

"Maggie. Stop it. This is church!"

"Maggie laughs and desists. "Oh, Myrtle. You needn't worry. I am seventy-five years old and beyond reproach."

"Whatever that means."

"It's not important that you know. Though it might matter that you know to be merry near a church is hardly un-Christian."

The last of the other churchgoers are mounting the stairs to enter through the front door, and the five from the east side, Myrtle and Betty in the lead, follow.

"David's a good boy, I think," Gus tells Maggie.

"Not a boy anymore." Maggie is suddenly thoughtful. "There's a strain of elderly in him now."

"I suppose there is."

Inside, Maggie parts with the two couples and climbs the back stairs to the tiny balcony where she likes to sit to view the congregation as well as the service. Today, as always, the families from the west side of the island sit by the tall windows on the east side of the aisle with the more prestigious of the summer people, those whose families have spent generations summering on the island and who own the largest cottages on Point Lookout, the summer colony. On the west side of the aisle sit the families from the east side of the island; the arrangement is an inversion that Maggie enjoys. In the summer, the west-siders must mop their brows in the heat of the morning sun that streams through the windows, much to the satisfaction of the east-siders. In the winter, the west-siders enjoy the warmth of the sun, while the east-siders shiver on the shaded side.

In his story for the children, before the formal service, Reverend Hotchkiss explains that Jonah was gobbled up by the whale because he refused to take the word of God to the people of Nineveh, whom he despised because they were different from the Israelites and had different customs and ways of behaving and praising the Lord. When the reverend is done and dismisses the children, Maggie wonders if their parents, who are poisoning their children with suspicion and fear of the ungodly clan camped in the forest, heard his message. She doubts it, but she sings "Beulah Land" with them nevertheless.

THREE

Fear tastes like a rusty knife and do not let her into your house.
Courage tastes like blood. Stand up straight. Admire the world. Relish
the love of a gentle woman. Trust in the Lord.
—John Cheever, *The Wapshot Chronicle*

Simon Cooper takes the church key from its hook on the boat's bulkhead, pops open a longneck, and scales the cap out into the harbor by snapping it smartly between his thumb and middle finger. The *Myrmaid* is tied up at the public landing in Stonington and Simon is waiting for Junior to park his truck up in the schoolyard and walk back down to the landing. They have been off-island all day shopping in Ellsworth for groceries, hardware supplies, a new tire for Simon's Galaxie on the island, feed for Junior's chickens, and, of course, rum, which is not sold on Barter Island. Simon flatfoots half the bottle of beer and sits on the transom. It is six o'clock, and the Stonington fishing fleet is in; the wind is picking up in the bay, which makes Simon wish Junior would hurry. When Tim Shepard told them an hour ago that it was breezing up pretty seriously out in the bay, Simon suggested that they spend the night in Stonington, but Junior just laughed. Junior, like many older Barter Island men, would rather face midnight in the midst of a winter gale in a leaky dinghy without oars than spend the night in Stonington, a disposition that Simon and the other newcomers do not understand.

This is Simon's fifth beer, or perhaps his sixth; he is not counting. Fortunately the tide is at its lowest, and this affords him the opportunity to take a leak overboard without being seen. He zips up, then decides that he is not going to wait for Junior to pass down the feed sack and the tire but will bring them down himself. The sack is sixty pounds, and the tire, including the rim, weighs as much, but Simon has always been known for his physical strength and is proud of it; he has the shoulders and back and neck and arms of a professional wrestler, and he is fond of flexing when he yawns and stretches. He climbs the rickety wharf ladder, and disappointed not to have an audience, carries the tire down to the deck in one hand, teetering momentarily with each step, snatching each rung with the other hand as he descends. He finishes his beer and opens another, then goes back up for the feed sack. High-riding clouds have hidden the sun, and the entire fleet in the harbor is straining on its moorings, bows into the wind. The *Myrmaid* is bumping and grinding against the float.

As Simon shoulders the feed sack, he looks again for an audience and sees Junior come around the corner of the Atlantic Avenue hardware store with David Harper, who is carrying a box of groceries. Simon shoulders the sack with exaggerated ease and shouts "About time!" as he steps onto the top rung of the ladder.

"Look who I found," says Junior, as he approaches the ladder.

"I thought I was going to have to spend the night in my car." David hands his box to Junior, who passes it to Simon. "I got behind a truck coming down from Bucksport and couldn't pass him until I got to Blue Hill; by then I knew I had missed the damn mail boat."

Junior starts up the engine and Simon throws off the lines. As they turn out into the harbor, Simon opens a beer and hands it to David, who accepts it gratefully.

"You ought to drink a beer once in a while, Junior." Simon opens another for himself. "It's got vitamins and good healthy stuff like malt in it."

"Beer gives me the shits." Junior loosens the arm that holds the windshield open, then tightens it down to close it against the wind.

Crossing under the lee of Crotch Island and the granite quarry, the water is fairly calm, but the few spruce on the height above the quarry are tipped toward them, bent by the wind pushing against the far side of the island. Junior takes care to weave through the lobster buoys, watching for toggle lines that stretch near the surface on the low tide.

When they are past the lee of Crotch Island, the wind coming across the bay gives them a sudden shove on the starboard side, and Junior has to heave on the wheel to bring the bow back around. The chop that slaps against the hull is spraying cold and wet and douses Simon and David. Simon swears mightily and negotiates the dancing deck to get a hold on the house support. David makes his way forward to the port side of the house, saying to Junior that it's going to be a pretty good ride.

"Pain in the ass," Junior growls. He pulls his cap down and steers with his elbows as he buttons the top of his flannel shirt. Beside him, Simon is wide-eyed: his legs are spread for balance and the hand that grips the upright is as white as the painted surface it grasps. David, who loves a wild ride, whoops; Junior rolls his eyes at him and shakes his grim head.

Simon swallows the remainder of his beer and tosses the bottle overboard, watching it tumble in the wind and disappear beneath the waves and spray.

"That's a returnable," Junior says, not taking his eyes off the bow. "You just threw away a nickel."

Simon holds on to the bait barrel for balance and takes another bottle from the case. He opens it, offers it to David, who shakes his head and shows him that his bottle is still half full. Simon grabs the upright and presses his back against the bulkhead to avoid the spray; he shivers and wishes he had had the sense to claim the lee side of the boat's house as David has done. While David drinks his beer and watches the small, rocky, uninhabited islands slide by on their port side, Simon has to turn up his collar to keep the cold spray from running down inside his shirt.

A sonorous groan beneath the deck turns all three toward the stern. It is followed by a vicious, rhythmic slapping against the stern hull.

Junior swears and throws the boat out of gear.

"What the hell?" Simon wants to know.

"We've got a line in the damn wheel; that slapping was the buoy. We've wrapped up a hell of a length of somebody's line in the propeller."

"Oh my God! Oh shit!" Simon cries out in a voice that Junior does not recognize. Junior looks at his stern man, who is standing wide-eyed and gap-mouthed at his side, as if he did not know that Simon was aboard his boat, or that he has been drinking, or both.

"We're going to draw onto those rocks. We'll be smashed to bits. If we try to jump for it, we'll drown. We'll be crushed by the boat."

"We're dragging a trap, for Christ's sake. With any luck there's a pair. David, take the gaff and go up forward and see if you can gaff another trap or two and cleat them off; they'll slow us down some. Where did I put that mirror?" Junior pulls the throttle back to idle, wipes his face with his sleeve, nudges Simon aside, and goes below.

Simon, his usual voice returned, asks what he should do. "I'm good for it, Captain," he claims.

Junior emerges holding a pole with a car's rearview mirror attached to the end and tilted at a forty-five-degree angle.

"Bring the knife." Junior nods toward the large filet knife that is strapped to the bulkhead for emergency cutting of a running line wrapped around someone's leg. "And put that goddamn beer bottle down."

As Junior and Simon lean out over the transom, stretching to see what the mirror reflects beneath the surface, David shouts over the wind that he has cleated one line and will cleat one more in a second. When he gaffs the second buoy and cleats it on the bow, the *Myrmaid* swings slightly, her bow into the wind now, and slows her slide toward the barnacled granite ledges to their lee, dragging at least two, but more likely four, sunken lobster traps. Crouching and grasping the coaming with his free hand, David makes his way back to the deck and watches Junior and Simon struggle with gaff and mirror to untangle the rope and buoy and toggle from the propeller. The mirror is nearly useless in the chop and the angled evening light, and Junior can manage to unravel only enough of the line to free the buoy.

Junior gives it up with a groan and sits up on the transom, cleaning the brine from his glasses with his handkerchief. Simon, desperate, continues to claw at the huge knot around the propeller with the gaff.

David sits on the case of beer, facing Junior who appears to be without hope. David's curls are soaked and sticky with salt on the left side and raised by the wind in silly-looking spires on top.

"You ought to get a haircut," Junior says.

David laughs, relieved for a moment. "You think we can raise somebody on the CB? I don't suppose there's anyone out on the water at this time of day, it being Saturday, but maybe someone could come out from the island or from Stonington."

"Oh Jesus Christ! We're fucked." Simon cries.

"Even if somebody is up on the radio, which I doubt," Junior says, looking toward the two nearest islands, which are growing larger ever so slowly on their lee, "we'll strike the rocks before anybody can get out here. Maybe we can gaff some more buoys, but unless this wind lets off, no amount of dragging traps is going to keep us off those rocks, unless one or two seize up on a boulder on the bottom. But this bottom is sand. Can you swim? I can't."

"Oh Jesus Christ." Simon is on his knees on the transom, tugging on the buoy as frantically as a little boy trying to pull a horse out of a barn fire.

"All you're doing is making it tighter, for God's sake."

Simon lets up and throws the buoy over the stern. "I'm going to dive down there and cut us loose."

"Like hell. You can't swim, and you're Christly drunk."

"So the fuck what. I can swim good enough anyway. I'm not going to let go of the boat, and the beer will keep me warm. I'll have some of that Jim Beam, too, so's I don't freeze."

"The alcohol will make you colder; it thins your blood. I'll go," David says. "I can swim."

"The hell it does," says Simon. "If it does then why do Saint Bernard dogs carry little kegs of brandy to save people from freezing in the snow?"

"I don't know," David says. He begins to unlace his boots, hoping that Junior does not notice that his hands are shaking.

"That cold water will suck the breath right out of you."

"It'll shrink your peter."

David stands up and takes off his pants and shirt, shivering in the cold wind in his jockey shorts and T-shirt. "Let me get in before you give me the knife."

David sits on the leeward washboard, then turns to kneel with his back to the water so he does not have to let go of the boat. A sudden slapping wave throws Simon against the bait barrel and dumps David overboard. David tumbles into the water, then shoots to the surface gasping for air and taking Junior's outstretched hand.

"I had no idea," David is sucking for air, his mouth wide open. A thousand-pound block of ice sits on his chest.

"Come back aboard," Junior says.

"Let me try." David kicks violently as he treads water, trying to warm his blood. Junior hands him the knife, and with an insuck of breath, he ducks under the hull.

It is darker than he imagined it would be, and he thinks that the cold will crush him in a second. Terrified, he kicks toward the stern, far more buoyant than he would have believed, but held under with his back scraping against the rough keel above. David cannot hear the boat's idling engine, though he can feel it on his back. As if in a silent nightmare, suspended in terror, he cuts with a sawing motion at the line knotted around the propeller, sees through the haze that he has cut through at least three strands, then with a mighty kick, he surfaces for air. He hears voices but does not heed them.

Certain that he is going to die this time, and somehow not alarmed by the certainty, he dives again and saws at the wrapped line with all of his strength, his spine against the keel and his legs spread for balance. He sees a dark brown ribbon slipping away from the bundled line, cuts with his soul into it, and with a tug, pulls the last of the line free of the wheel.

At the surface, his mouth wide open for air, he takes in a mouthful of water, coughs it out and gasps, making a noise that he has heard before in another place of terror and knows is not his own.

Clambering at the hull of the boat, reaching for the four outstretched arms above him, David lets the knife drop below him and feels himself being pulled aboard, as cold and lifeless, as blue-lipped and rigid, as any dead Viet Cong in the concertina wire on the camp perimeter the morning after a ground attack. The top of his head is being squeezed unbearably, and his left index finger is screaming in pain.

Sitting on the deck, shaking, his teeth clattering, he listens detached to Simon screaming in horror, asking him what he did to his finger. When he looks, he sees that he has cut through his finger at the tip, and that the piece with the nail is hanging by a bloody thread. Junior gently puts the severed end back in place and ties it tightly with his handkerchief before he strips David of his wet T-shirt and wraps him in dry clothes.

When Junior has calmed Simon, the two of them, with little help from David, move him to a lobster crate beside the exhaust pipe for warmth, and drape him with Junior's slicker. Junior tells Simon to race the engine while he uncleats the buoys at the bow, then they steam for the island, making a run for the protection of the cove and dry clothes on shore.

✳✳✳

Gus's mother, Leah Barter keeps fit by walking a brisk two miles every day, in rain or shine or sleet or snow, but never on ice. Today the sun is bright in a cobalt sky, and a stiff breeze is keeping the late-summer bugs under cover, except, of course, the occasional, circling deer-fly. Leah wears a denim jumper recently sewn from a borrowed pattern, walking shoes from a catalog, and a wide-brimmed straw hat to protect her fair-skinned face from the sun. Around her neck, strung on a piece of cod line, hangs a tin can for raspberries, and in her hand is a small, galvanized pail for blueberries.

She is walking and picking along the road, humming a Perry Como tune, when she spies her Aunt Maggie, who is equipped in the same manner, passing beneath the tall birch, which leans over the road, in her approach from the east side on her morning outing. Neither is surprised to see the other; both smile and raise a hand in greeting. Maggie's copious hair, whose auburn sheen has grown dim of late, is bound up on her head and pushed under a soft, colorless beret-like cap. She is wearing baggy khaki trousers held up by a thin, blue belt that make her appear even thinner than she is.

When Leah's mother died fifty-three years ago, Maggie held Leah in her lap and from that moment in her dead sister's kitchen, under a cloud of sorrow and remorse, Maggie devoted herself to raising her niece, foreswearing love and marriage and approval of the elderly island women to do so. They lived alone together—Maggie, the island schoolteacher, and Leah, her seemingly perpetual student—until Leah married soon after she finished school and moved to the west side to live in her husband Cecil's house, where she raised her son, Gus, and was widowed nearly twenty years ago. Now Maggie and Leah see each other nearly every day at the post office, at the store, over tea, for a walk, sometimes for a shared supper. In a small town on a small island at sea, miles from the teeming world, the two women's lives, both conscious and unconscious, spoken and assumed, have become so entwined that they often need not speak to converse and often choose not to speak at all. Content in their mutual affection and understanding of one another, they share forgiveness and a mutual love for Gus and for Leah's long-departed father, Amos Coombs.

This morning they meet at a tangle of raspberry bushes between the road and the town gravel pit. Maggie says what a beautiful day it is and sets her little pail of blueberries down to pick into her tin can; Leah knows that the two inches of blueberries in Maggie's bucket are from the patch at the edge of the bog down the road. She tells Maggie that she wishes she wouldn't wear that old hat. Maggie dismisses the comment with a wave of her hand and before she edges sideways into the prickly bushes, says that Leah's new jumper is some cunning.

As they pick, Leah working the edges of the patch while Maggie pushes into the center, Leah resumes her soft humming, and Maggie rolls each berry with her thumb over a curved forefinger into her cupped palm. A flight of cedar waxwings, early in their trip south, settles into the neighboring raspberry patch twenty yards away and, with a flurry of wings but little noise, begins to eat. Maggie removes the can from her neck, steps to the edge of the patch, and picks up several stones, each the size of a robin's egg, then unleashes a barrage at the birds. She startles them with the first stones, adjusts her range, and fires for effect to send them flying for their lives with the second barrage.

"That's my cobbler you're eating, " she tells them. "Winged beggars."

The unmistakable chugging sound of an aged truck running on six of its eight cylinders precedes the vehicle up the road from the west side of the island. Without looking up, Leah and Maggie know by its sound that it is the McGregor truck, undoubtedly—at this time of day—come from meeting the noon boat. When the dull green truck with its rounded cab top approaches, downshifting to take the turn, the pickers look up to see Christine McGregor behind the wheel, a bare forearm hanging out of the window, a red bandana around her head holding her short, unruly hair in place. She smiles and waves, and the pickers respond in kind. The truck, with an unusually heavy load, is listing badly to starboard on a flattened spring.

As it passes, Leah and Maggie see Willow and Autumn sitting cross-legged on a mound of sailcloth that is piled higher than the sides of the truck bed. They sit with their backs against the cab; Willow is grinning and calls out a merry greeting to the pickers. He laughs and accepts a miniature pipe from Autumn, who says something lost in the wind as they sail by and waves, her palm swaying back and forth high over her head like the arm of a metronome. A coal black puppy of uncertain breed sits between them, its eyes wide with fear on its first truck ride, its soft fur rippling in the wind. When it sees Maggie and Leah, it rises clumsily and starts toward the rear of the truck, yipping. Willow slaps it upside the head, knocking it off its feet, then grabs it by the neck to slam it back against the cab.

Leah returns the waves, but her thin lips are pressed in a tight line, and her tiny brown eyes are alight with contempt.

"Slut," she says.

"Leah!" Maggie turns aside so that Leah will not see her little smile.

"Well, she is. Half the town saw her take Fuddy outside. For pity's sake. It's an abomination." Leah picks furiously, gets pricked, and sucks her finger.

"She isn't the first to–how should I say it–discover Fuddy," Maggie says. She is crouched out of sight behind a large bush; her voice filters through the prickers and leaves.

"I still think it's disgusting. She's so young, so public, such a brazen little . . ."

"Nymph," Maggie finishes for Leah.

"She's a slut, a brazen hussy. The way she dresses, if you call that dressing. It's one thing to couple in the woods with that smelly man of hers, but with Fuddy it's grotesque, filthy."

"Odoriferous," Maggie says, then laughs, delighted by the word. "Perhaps she's just altruistic."

"Oh, Maggie." Leah finds her anger cooling; she tries to stoke it again but cannot.

"I'm surprised to hear such vitriol from you, dear. From the woman who once years ago so vehemently defended Betty after her indiscretion with the Coast Guardsman, the woman who single-handedly faced down the Rebekahs and half the indignant island."

"That was different," Leah says. "You did too. That was war time and private, and besides, she paid the price with an unwanted child and seventeen years of exile from this island, banished by the biddies."

"And now she's your daughter-in-law. A happy ending."

"Yes, and I am grateful for that every day, for Gus's sake and for my own."

Maggie picks up her blueberry pail, empties the brimming can of raspberries into it, wipes her brow, and starts slowly for the patch that she saved from the waxwings. Leah walks behind, fanning herself with her wide hat.

"I just wish those hippies had never come down here, and I'm afraid they're here for more than a visit; everyone is. Myrtle thinks we should run them off the island."

"Myrtle," Maggie says. "Who does Myrtle mean by 'we'? None of us has the right to force them off the island. They're camped on private land with permission; they're free to live as they please, with or without our approval."

"They take drugs. They copulate like rabbits. They're filthy and lazy."

"I don't say that I like the way they behave. I admit to an odor of corruption which I find foul, but they have as much right as any of us to live as they please."

"Gus heard their dog running deer up by Old Cove the other day. It wasn't either of Junior's dogs—Gus knows their barks—it was that nasty-looking mangy thing they came ashore with and let run up there. And now they have another one."

"If it is running deer, someone should talk to them and put a stop to it," Maggie says. "Just as we would with anyone else. We don't want anyone's dog running the poor deer into the water, drowning them."

"I know it. Then they get carried away in the currents, and they're wasted." Leah is thinking of the sweet aroma of venison stew.

"Myrtle's downwind from the hippie camp up in the woods. She can smell their fires. She's terrified lest they catch the forest on fire and burn the island over, her house first."

Maggie, who thinks Leah sees far too much of Myrtle Chafin, changes the subject to the new radio station called National Public Radio and tries to imitate the pompous modulation of an announcer's voice, but she fails.

"His name is Robert something, and he is an intellectual boor, but he's also brilliant and plays wonderful music. You really should listen, Leah, in the morning; *Morning Pro Musica,* it's called. Should we ever get electricity down here, I'm going to get a radio with speakers."

"Oh Maggie, you would not."

"Would not what, dear?"

"Would not want electricity and certainly would not want big booming speakers in your house," Leah says.

"No, I don't suppose I would." With thumb and forefinger, Maggie gingerly lifts a lower branch of the bush that is heavy with fruit and rests it atop another branch. "Look at all these berries beneath, where the waxwings couldn't get to them; I'll have that cobbler, at least."

✳✳✳

With Gus's old McCullough chain saw, which rattles more than it roars and drifts off line when it cuts, David is taking down another oak on the wooded cliff just north of the cabin. It is a gray afternoon, the tail end of a long windy day. The wind is southerly, gusting at times south by west; it is not cold, but it is raw and persistent and has a tinge of autumn to it. Even though he is out on the exposed cliffs—now far more exposed than before because of the clearing that he has been doing around the cabin's perimeter—and though he is in the lee of the island's high, forested ridge, David fears that the wind is strong enough to push the falling oak into the limbs of other trees and hang it up there, rather than let it fall into the clearing. He has learned from Gus and from practice to judge the direction a tree will want to fall, how and where to cut a decent wedge, and how to use a back cut. This time he is lucky: the oak, perhaps forty feet tall, teeters a moment, balancing by waving its boughs like a boy flaps his arms when crossing a narrow log bridge, then chooses to fall into the clearing in a slow, soft ride to the ground.

Pleased, David shuts off the saw and sits on the stump for a cigarette break. He sniffs a sweet handful of fresh sawdust and thinks that he can tell that this is an oak by the smell of it, without even looking at the tree, and the thought pleases him. He feels the wind flatten his curls against the back of his head, watches his smoke disappear quickly in a thin trail, and thinks that Chau Sinh would not like all this cutting of trees; none of the Khmers would.

Shit, Trung-si, *you don't need to clear a field of fire up here; those trees, they liked protecting that house from the wind and rain.* When the team was on recon patrols, sneaking around in the mountains across the border, Chau Sinh and the others would collect things that they liked on the way through the forest—a certain stone from a stream, a tiny monkey skull, a round green-and-yellow bud, a sloughed snake skin—and save them wrapped in a banana leaf in the pockets of their black shorts. When they made camp, and a little fire when they dared to, Chau Sinh broke dead limbs from the nearby trees; when he did so, he left one of the trinkets he had collected at the foot of the tree in recompense.

David wipes his face on his sleeve and stands to stretch. He will limb this tree, drag the limbs into the woods, then cut it up into fireplace lengths for splitting. The trees he has cut and split this summer, he has used to replace the cured firewood that he lugged up to the cabin from the house and stacked and covered behind the cabin. He has put up two cords—a lot of wood for a fireplace—and dreams of having a fire every night during the winter, less for heat than for pleasure.

In the old wooden wheelbarrow, said to have been made by Uncle Walter himself, David has pushed two man-sized propane tanks for the stove and little heater up the steep path, over humped boulders, the iron-rimmed wheel sinking into the soft moss and decaying spruce needles. He has caulked all the windows, applying two layers to those on the north and east sides. He has borrowed a stiff chimney brush from Junior and cleaned the cabin's chimney with care. He has brought the heavy, brightly patterned quilt, apparently sewn by Ava herself, up from the house and spread it over the wide bed. He has closed off the screen porch with plastic sheeting buttressed by strips of trap laths. Because the cabin sits on boulders a few inches off the ground, David has wrapped a skirt of tar paper around her and banked that with sawdust to insulate the cabin knee high.

In the floor of the tiny kitchen, he has fashioned a small trapdoor with brass fittings; beneath it sits an insulated milk box he found at the flea market in Searsport, in which he will keep his beer and cheese cool with ice in fair weather and protected from freezing in foul. He has covered the mouse holes in the cupboards with flattened tin cans. He has filled two shelves with books shipped from home, books from his boyhood: adventures illustrated by Howard Pyle and N. C. Wyeth, all of Kenneth Robert's novels, and Allan Eckert's narrative histories of wars in the frontier forests. He has wheeled up the path two loads of *National Geographic* magazines he found in the attic of the main house.

He has cleared all the oak and spruce from the front of the cabin, for the view, he tells visitors; on the north and south sides of the cabin, he has cut away all the trees and brush down to blueberry level; and behind the cabin he has trimmed the woods back fifty feet or more. The clearings of the sides and back are to preclude rot in the cabin floor and walls, or so he tells visitors.

David pushes his cigarette end deep into the soft soil and stands to survey the cabin, the clearing, the cliffs, the sea below, and the darkening horizon afar. He opens and closes his rough, calloused hands and smiles with great satisfaction at all he sees around him. A gull scales by at eye level, flying eighty feet over the water, and tips its wing in greeting.

He stands on the front stoop, his arms akimbo. The tide is going, drawing south into the incoming blow; the meeting of wave and wind raises hackles of white spray over all the ocean that David can see, even to Mount Desert, the farthest island visible. After five years of living in close quarters with strangers, even closer quarters with foreigners in a foreign land, he is more than ready for some privacy, some solitude. Perhaps it is unrealistic, this island and cabin living. Perhaps it is, as others have suggested, a form of denial, a vain attempt to escape the indifference and outright hate in the real world, as others have suggested. He doesn't care. Fuck the real world. Fuck them all. Fuck all the fucking realists. Wipe them out. Wipe out all of them except for the six you save for pallbearers.

He will close off the kitchen down in the main house and eat his meals there, keeping the kerosene stove burning low and using the refrigerator for storage. He will keep cheese and crackers and beer in the cabin and have a morning cup of coffee there, but he will take his other meals at the kitchen table where he has eaten since he was eleven years old. He will bathe in the kitchen, too, hauling water from the well and washing in the big tub by the stove, as his mother once bathed him on cold nights. He will take his time to move up to the cabin entirely, on his own and in his own place. He will get to know the yard and its surroundings and the path to the cabin as well as Gus knows the cove, well enough to negotiate any path without a light in a dense, black night of fog. On the radio news he will not listen to politicians or protesters or pundits, nor will he read about any of them. He will put in a garden in the spring and learn to put up rhubarb jam and to pickle green beans. In the winter, when fishing is done, he will cut trees for the sawmill and go to bed tired and sore to sleep the whole night through. He will teach himself to pull down the blinds and shut the curtains against the cold, even though it will mean blocking his view of the perimeter he has cut around the cabin. He will listen to the Red Sox games and to college football and *Reading Aloud*, and he will enjoy picture magazines by the fire—*Scottish Fields* and *Newsweek* from Maggie, *Playboy*, purchased in Searsport and smuggled onto the island beneath his groceries. He will not challenge Simon. He will spend stormy evenings safe by the fire above the edge of the sea, the front-porch door creaking in the wind like the swinging sign over the door of the Admiral Benbow Inn in *Treasure Island*.

It is dusk when he sets his plate of fried mackerel and rice by a tall, brown bottle of beer on the table in Ava's kitchen. He has left the windows and kitchen door open to smell the sea and hear the windy rivers in the tree-tops. The tabletop is scratched, and its edges are worn smooth by a hundred years of daily use. David keeps the table waxed, as did those before him, and the wax reflects the glow of the kerosene lamp in a burnished aura of light. He spoils the kerosene's soft light with the metallic blue flare of the gas lamps so that he can see to eat and read in the approaching dark. He sits facing the open screen door and windows overlooking the wide shadowed meadow and the cove beyond. Behind him, and behind the curtains that cover the back windows, the hillside looms; it crouches behind his back.

Their camp was named Ba Xaoi for the village it sat beside beneath Nui Cam, "Cam Mountain." Ba Xaoi, "under the shoulder," described the Special

Forces fighting camp even better than it did the village; the camp's eastern wall and concertina wire ran along the boulders at the base of the mountain. Anyone on the mountain's slope could look and fire directly into the rickety wooden watchtower in the camp's center; they could fire down into the mortar pit, the team house, and the barracks and houses for the Khmer and American defenders. On any night, indeed, on any day, a sizable communist force could overcome the listening post on the summit of the mountain, and attack downhill into the camp behind a mortar barrage and hail of small-arms fire. This happened three times while David was at the camp, or more accurately, twice; the first time the communists launched a ground attack, they struck from the hillside in a feint to cover for a larger ground attack on the southern flank. They lighted the fire arrow that night to direct the fire of the helicopter gunships called in, and it worked.

When David has washed the dishes and shut the kitchen down for the evening, he pushes a bottle of beer into each of the back pockets of his jeans. He carries a flashlight but, though there is no moonlight, is determined not to use it, to find his way up the path to the cabin by memory and feel. He passes the well, its cover a vague shape at the edge of the meadow, and climbs over the tumbled stone wall without faltering. The twin paper birch trunks are a vague, ghosty white; he touches them as he steps along the path between them. But as he climbs toward the high ground, he walks into a massive juniper shrub, then into a sharp trap of broken branches of a fallen spruce, and blunders face-first into a witches'-broom the size of a bushel basket, saving his face from laceration only with an upraised hand. Defeated, he switches on the flashlight and finds the path ten feet to his left.

The sudden light reminds him of shielding his eyes from the red beam of someone's flashlight and then the sickening shift of weight in the back of the open jeep as he hit the brakes. He remembers the stinging smell of burning palm fronds, the scattered crackling of small-arms fire in the village behind him, the red light playing over the backseat, the thin alto voice of the lieutenant from Maryland, amazed at first, then outraged.

"Jesus Christ, Sergeant! Jesus fucking Christ!"

David steps over the fallen spruce and onto the path. He strikes a kitchen match on a boulder to light a cigarette and looks directly into the flame, assuring himself that he doesn't care that it will ruin his night vision. He will try the path without a light again tomorrow night, and the next night, and the next, until he can walk it in the dark. He feels certain that he will do it, that he will get to the high ground unscathed.

FOUR

We do not eat milk products. We eat honey, but we struggle with the morality of it, as taking honey exploits bees.
—Christine McGregor

Gus does not stand at his workbench, nor does he sit on the stool; rather he stands leaning his rump against it as his Uncle Walter used to do when he was building traps down in the fish house. In the late afternoon sunlight that filters through his shop's milky window-panes, he is fine-sanding the stern of the model Novi boat that he is making for his Aunt Maggie, one last, soft sanding before he glues the rudder in place. He has been working on the model for two years now; it is perfect in scale—thirty-two inches in length over all—and it will be perfect in detail. He hopes to have it finished for Christmas this year, but he has only a little over two months to get it done and he does not dare hurry it. It will be paint-ed white with a blue boot stripe just as the real boat was when his grandfa-ther fished in it, and the model will bear the name *Amos Coombs* in tiny brass letters he got from a mail-order catalog last spring—the name that he and Maggie put on the stern years ago when the boat was passed on to them. The little buoy that he will affix to the roof of the boat's house will be painted with Amos's colors: red with a yellow spindle.

Though the barrel woodstove has been shut down for a couple of hours and the door of the shop is thrown open, it is still quite warm. Gus has stripped down to his long-john shirt, pushed up the sleeves, and unbuttoned the top, but he is still too warm and wants a breath of air. He sits on the doorstep and cleans his glasses on his shirt. The purple martins skitter through the air above the dooryard and go whipping in and out of their house; this year there are eight or nine pairs in their house by the clothesline, more than most years. Betty claims that it is the new pink paint job she gave the house that attracts them; Gus thinks it's the mosquitoes and flies, the reason for having a martin house in your dooryard in the first place.

That maple. It is the only tree in the half-acre grass and gravel dooryard; it always has been, which is why it is so full and stately in shape. The lowering sun on the far side makes the reddening leaves blush even deeper than they did in the direct morning light. Two of the three lower limbs are as big around as Jake Gardinier's flexed bicep; the third is thinner and tends around toward the sun. From the thickest limb hangs the old slant-six engine that John took out of Junior's Falcon; it is still suspended over the hoodless maw of the Ford truck that John bought to put it in. A scrap of dried and shredded plastic, a remnant of the larger piece that once covered the engine, still flaps in the breeze. Gus knows that he should take down the engine and haul it and the truck frame off into the woods, but he has yet to do it, Betty's monthly reminders notwithstanding. From the other strong limb hangs the old tire swing, a U.S. baldy worn so thin that it shows threads in two places. The swing has been there since they moved back to the island, the year both his father and his first wife died and John was just eight. The ground beneath the tire, which was once worn bare by dragging soles, is now grown up in bayberry shrubs.

Gus remembers a sharp morning in the fall of that difficult year. The maple was not nearly so big then but had the same husky shape, promising to grow as it has done. The tire swing had been up for only a month or so. The night before, they had a hard frost that left a thin, etched pane of ice on the puddle by the well, and his morning chores left melted boot prints in the hoary grass. He was standing right here in the door of the shop, dressed to go haul his traps, and Betty was on the kitchen stoop seeing John off to school with his Mighty Mouse lunch box. As if one of them had spoken, all three had looked up at the top of the maple at the same time. The sun had just risen above the spruce surrounding the yard and was shining full on the tree; within seconds it melted the light film of frost on the leaves. They sparkled briefly, then began to fall in a slow rain of crimson orange onto the tire and the ground around like yellow butterflies.

"What do you think of that?" Gus remembers asking John, who was wearing a coonskin cap with dangling tail. "Some pretty, isn't it?"

"I guess it is," John said, turning toward the road. "It's kinda sad too."

That night at supper, Betty had called it a little miracle. John reached for the sliced bread.

The sound of a car on the crushed shells in the drive turns Gus's head back to the present. It is Junior and Myrtle come to supper in their dull blue Rambler. It must be exactly five o'clock, he thinks; you can set your watch by Myrtle Chafin's visits. Gus rises from the ship's doorstep to greet them as they let themselves out of the car.

"You didn't need to get dressed up just for us," says Myrtle. She is opening the back door on the far side of the car and she is not smiling.

"I've got my shirt in the shop. You don't think Betty would let me in the house without one, do you?"

Myrtle lifts a pie tin from the floor of the backseat and marches toward the kitchen door. Junior stands next to Gus. He is wearing one of his good flannel shirts, which is parted between buttons showing slashes of white undershirt over his taut distended belly; his suspenders, russet with black stripes, are also parted over his belly, stretched to hold up his green Dickies workpants.

"I hope it's rhubarb," says Gus of the pie.

"If this goddamn wind don't shift, I'm going to go crazy. I'm going to kill myself or kill her," says Junior, who spits.

"Did you bring us a sup of something?"

"No, Christ."

"You wait just a minute. Go on inside the shop," says Gus. With a cautious glance toward the kitchen window, he goes to the woodpile and returns to the shop with a green bottle.

While Gus wipes out two cups with a soft rag, Junior lifts the model boat from its cradle and admires its lines for the hundredth time. Gus pours them both a few fingers of Bacardi, which he tops off with Coke. They touch cups and drink appreciatively.

"What the hell does the wind direction have to do with killing your wife?" Gus asks.

"As if you didn't know, dear." Junior wipes a screwdriver on his pant leg and stirs his drink with it. "Fire is the thing she harps on most. If it isn't raining, and she smells the hippies' campfire, the whole goddamn island might as well be a raging forest fire headed for our bedroom."

"If it was that much drier, I could see her point. Betty, she . . ."

"Then it's the goddamn dogs. Just when you think everything is okay because they're off the island, it's their dogs. They keep them tied up since McGregor talked to them about the dogs running deer; at least when they're gone they tie them up. It isn't long before the damn things get hungry and start their yapping and whining. The wind carries their voices right in through our windows. You can hear them over the generator and the TV both some nights."

"We can hear them sometimes," Gus says. "Poor things."

"And then when there's no fire smell, you get a whiff that smells like an outhouse." This time, Junior pours.

"Maybe they got a hole to shit in."

They turn to the open door toward the sound of a car passing on the road: it is a big V-8, and the driver slaps the gas pedal twice to make it roar up in greeting as he passes. The men in the shop know that it is Simon Cooper in his Galaxie.

"That's his first time today," Gus observes, as he picks a bit of something from his drink. "Usually by this time on Sunday he's driven past at least twice. He says he doesn't speed."

"I know it," says Junior. "I once asked him how come the last time I heard him go by, he got from our house to the end of the pavement and back—six miles—in five minutes. He laughed and said he turned around at the farm."

"He been drinking today?"

"I don't doubt it, dear. He says he gets bored when he's not out to haul, that he can tinker with his engine only for so long. So he goes driving, back and forth, back and forth. His wife hates it."

"So does mine. Bored? What the hell?"

"He says that when you've been in combat, everything afterwards is boring. He says unless you been there, like he has, you can't understand."

"I guess he's right," Gus says. "It's going to be another long winter for that poor bastard."

"You want to talk to somebody else who would like to see those hippies off the island, talk to him. He told me he'd burn them out if he thought he could get away with it. He says he'd hate to have to do it—the smell of burning human flesh would bring back so many bad memories—but he would if need be."

"I believe it. I don't know about that guy. We ought to go in, I guess."

Gus finishes his drink, and Junior does the same.

***

Maggie puts out her right leg for balance and opens the bulkhead doors, first one, then the other. As she descends the cellar stairs, she sweeps the dark doorframe with her arm to clear it of spiders and their webs before she passes through. She steps onto the floorboards and stands still to let her eyes adjust to the dark. The light from the stairway behind her falls first on the glistening tiers of Mason jars, so recently washed and filled that there is not a jot or tittle of dust on any one of them. She ties back her hair, so thin, rolls up her sleeves, takes hold of the smooth, cold handles on the sidecar pump, and begins to push and pull in a rocking rhythm that she has known for so long. She listens to the well water gushing with each stroke through the pipes over her head to fill the fifty-gallon drum up on the landing by her bedroom door. Though the pumping is rigorous and daily (she attributes her longevity to this pump), she would rather use gravity feed than pump by hand at the kitchen sink and have to lug buckets to the bathtub.

She rides on the rhythm of her motion over to the shelves of jars. They are a great satisfaction to her: pickled pole beans, tomatoes, cuke slices, and oh, that rhubarb. She is glad to have had Leah's migraine, poor girl, as an excuse not to accept Betty's invitation to supper. She would far rather take muffins and vegetable soup over to Leah and bide with her in the dark bedroom than sit before Betty's sublime pot roast and listen to Myrtle bitch and moan about the hippies' campfire, their pornographic antics, and their mistreatment of their dogs. All of this from someone who has hated dogs since she was three and has never once in her years on the east side with Junior worried a fig about campfires down in the park or hunters' campfires in the fall. Now the perceived cruelty to dogs and the whiff of campfires are calamities, harbingers of Armageddon. And the whole damn problem can be traced to the communists, Junior will be sure to add.

She pauses, brushes a few loose hairs from her forehead with the spotted back of her hand, and faces the eastern cellar wall for the last fifty strokes, each harder than the one before as the barrel fills.

She stops at eighty-five strokes, which she knows has filled the barrel to two inches below the rim, and turns toward the waning light from the stairs. Leah's soup will have to come from a can on such short notice, but the bran muffins are fresh, and while the soup warms there will be time for a glass of sherry and the evening news here at home before she goes.

September 7, 1970

Dear Ruth,

While I was pumping this afternoon, it occurred to me that the new people on the island and the new ideas they have brought with them have quite literally shaken some of us older ones to our foundations. What brought that on? Down in the cellar, pumping and staring at the walls, I wondered if Amos's great-grandparents had any idea of the kind of traffic that we would get on our tiny road these days. They could not have imagined, could they? If they had, they would not have built the house a foot from the road bed, such a narrow way between the house and the ledges. The stones are so wide and heavy, settled securely far deeper than any frost heave might go, that they must have had help to set them in this square cellar: oxen and block and tackle, neighbors; so heavy and settled so deep under such weight that no cement was needed.

But now when a truck comes by or that Simon Cooper's grumbling hot rod on its way to visit David at night, I lie there in the dark and believe that I can feel those great granite blocks shivering from his engine, the wide weight of his oversized auto. Last night he came by again, late, nine-ish, the second time in a week. But this time he drove up to Ava's and turned around (if you can imagine turning a car that size around in the dark on the edge of the drop-off in Ava's dooryard), and after a few minutes started honking his damn horn over and over, it resounding on the surface of the cove until my head ached. David must have been up at the cabin, and his visitor must not have wanted to dare the path in the dark, or perhaps he was too drunk. They say that he shows up at David's already drunk, uninvited, unexpected, unwanted, and brings along a half gallon of whiskey and a large bottle of ginger ale and stays until he can barely walk to his car. He can't be insulted: David said he once asked him to leave, begging fatigue, and he was answered with invective, that Simon almost blew his top like a volcano. Perhaps this time David was up at the cabin and feigning sleep, though it is hard to imagine that he could pretend not to have been awakened by that raffish horn.

Simon's poor wife seems such a pleasant girl—articulate and even pretty. She must be powerless to keep him at home, or she doesn't care to. Betty says she is terribly embarrassed, and for good reason.

There, now I've rambled on like a nervous, old gossip, like poor Myrtle about whom I complain. I hope you didn't read the above, or if you did, took it with a grain of salt. I love you for listening, dear one.

It's late. You're undoubtedly asleep by now, as I will soon be. Sleep well.

Maggie

PS: I imagined for an instant, or I dreamt, half asleep in my afternoon chair, that Simon wandered off on one of his drunken coastal rambles, as is his wont, and did not return. Gone. Leaving David and Nancy to find one another and live together (I am so bad!) here in the cove, a quiet, loving couple.

* * *

Junior parks at the side of the road on the little hill one hundred feet from the entrance to the narrow rutted road into Eaton Cove and the McGregors'. When Gus gets out to chock the wheels and slams his door shut, the hippie dogs up in the woods on the mountainside across the road bark feebly, quit, then bark again when Junior climbs out and slams his door shut.

"If you'd get a new battery you wouldn't have to worry about jump-starting her; we could of driven in there." Gus pronounces it *bat-tray*; he pushes a piece of stove wood under the front tire and gives it a kick to secure it. "I don't suppose you brought along a flashlight," he says.

"I did, dear, but it doesn't work," Junior confesses.

"Jesus flippin' Christ," says Gus, pleased to be deeply disgusted. "I don't know why we didn't come in daylight then."

"I know why we didn't come in daylight; we didn't come in daylight because you had to have your goddamn supper first."

"No need to get salty," Gus says.

The road into Eaton Cove is deeply rutted from two centuries of passing wagon wheels and tires; it leads through a thick forest of spruce and birch and poplar before it opens onto a wide field, then shore and sea beyond. Tonight, in the last of the evening light, the ruts and grassy hump between are covered with a blanket of wet yellow leaves that show the way into the forest. Gus and Junior, who have not approached Eaton Cove from land since they were boys, and only then on a dare, take a rut each and walk slowly, side by side, feeling their way into the darkness. The moon, nearly full, is on the rise, but its light does not penetrate the tunnel of trees. Junior will never say so, but he is grateful that Gus agreed to come with him; and Gus, who wishes now that he had not agreed to come, will not say that he is scared shitless.

Years ago, when the WPA men were building Barter Island's only road, first old Martha Eaton died, then her husband, Minot, followed her shortly afterwards. They were prayed over and buried together in the little family plot north of the house on a rise in the field by the shore. One Friday, young Winslow Dixon and a few other Deer Isle boys who were working on the road got into some rum. Winslow fell asleep under a tree. When he woke up it was dark, and he had missed the late boat going home. Too embarrassed to knock on anyone's door, he walked to Eaton Cove and spent the night in the empty house. He said he heard growling and scratching all night long. In the morning, sleepless, hungover, and skittish, he started out to walk to the town landing. As he crossed the field, he saw out of the corner of his eye what he thought must be a sleeping doe; when he looked again he saw that it was a dog, a huge dog, lying asleep or dead in the open gate of the Eaton graveyard. He whistled, but the dog did not budge. Fearfully, he approached the animal, and as he did he saw another dog, then a third and a fourth—four huge, black dogs, dead, their eyes wide open, their tongues caked with dirt and hanging loose. When Winslow saw that holes had been dug into both of the fresh Eaton graves and saw bloodied bits of a white linen dress near one of the dogs, he began to run. He arrived on Gus's grandfather's doorstep frothing at the mouth and bleeding from the nose, his eyes rolling around in their sockets. Amos said that he had to slap him to bring him around, slap him so hard that he left a pink handprint on his cheek. When he finally got the boy to talk, Amos laughed, dismissing it as a nightmare and blaming the jug of rum. But the boy insisted, so Amos drove him over to Eaton Cove where Winslow waited in the truck and Amos walked in to view the carnage.

No dead dogs. No bloody linen. No holes in the graves. Amos drove the boy to the town landing and promised him that he would not tell a soul about what the boy thought he had seen. Winslow never came back to Barter Island, not to work on the road crew, nor to visit ever again in his lifetime. Not long after the boy's run-in with the hounds of hell, Amos amused a rum-soaked group of fishermen with Winslow's story outside the town hall during a dance, adding that actually the graves had been disturbed, only recently filled in, packed flat not by shovels but by human hands, and that he would swear on the Bible that this was true. His audience grinned into their cups, knowing Amos was lying but happy with his story.

"You believed he saw the Crawling Ones, didn't you?" Junior whispered to Gus in the dark, feeling his way in the rut with his feet, wishing he had his flashlight.

"I told Amos I didn't, but I tell you I never looked over at Eaton Cove when we passed by it in the dark on the way out to haul. Winslow said he saw them, her in a white linen dress, Minot in a brown suit, crawling across the field, all tattered, their skin hanging loose in shreds, raising their heads to sniff the darkness like deer do. What the hell did you bring it up now for?"

"Because we're both thinking about it, is why."

"Did you ever tell anybody that Amos told us he really did find the grave disturbed; he wasn't lying."

"Hell no, dear. We cut our palms and shook hands to mix our blood when we swore to stay secret. I still have the scar."

"So do I," Gus says.

As one, they slow their pace to peer at their palms, but neither can see his scar in the dark.

Close to the end of the Eaton Cove road, the trees thin and moonlight sifts through the branches to better light their way. They can hear waves splashing on the near ledges and smell the water, as well as a dampish hint of a hardwood stove-fire tamped down for the night. When the road ends and the field stands open in the silvery light before them, Gus and Junior instinctively reach out to hold a restraining hand across the other's chest, as if they are about to collide with something . . . or see something crawling beneath the moon. With their hands still crossing one another's chest, Gus scans the open field to their left, and Junior reconnoiters to their right.

The small rectangular house that Minot Eaton's grandfather built has been recently shingled from peak to sill with good cedar shakes and stained to last for years. The two front windows and a row of small panes over the front door that face the land are alight with the yellow orange glow of candle or lamp flame; they do not cast a shaft of light onto the meadow grass as bulb light would but burn warmly in the first-floor rooms and the attached kitchen. The house and outbuildings throw dark shadows on the pearly meadow and bald, gray granite outcroppings nearby that protrude like the heads of buried giants, worn smooth by the glacier that moved a boulder the size of a hay mound onto the shore of the little cove. Where the open ground lies flat, on Junior's side, a wide, fenced garden spreads southward. Beyond the thin stream of chimney smoke that trails off to the northeast, the rippled sea sparkles, then goes dark, as does the meadow when a passing cloud covers the moon.

And in the dark the two men scurry across the meadow from the road's opening, as edgy and circumspect as two mice running in the open, certain that a screech owl is watching from the near trees, praying that he has already eaten his fill for the evening.

Junior hitches up his trousers and catches his breath before he knocks on the sturdy oak door. Neither looks behind as they listen to approaching footsteps inside. In a bulky, colorless wool sweater and baggy slacks, Christine McGregor opens the door and invites them in, obviously delighted to have company. With her hair gathered tight behind her head and her freckled cheeks pink from the kitchen stove, she looks much younger than her late twenties. As they follow her through the entryway, Junior thinks he would rather be back out in the moonlight. Gus thinks that he has never before been anxious entering a neighbor's house on Barter Island—no neighbors had ever seemed so foreign, so baffling in their behavior as the McGregors. The wainscoting that Gus remembers from years ago is painted a bluish gray, the walls, once a faded floral design, are white and clean, the linoleum floors have been peeled off and the wide pine floorboards have been sanded down to the shiny square heads of the original nails. The color from wood and lamplight is of polished brass; the smell inside is of fresh-cut spruce and spices.

As they enter the old parlor, Eliot McGregor stands to greet them, setting his pencil down on the wide, polished worktable that sits squarely between two windows and is lighted by a wall lamp and two table lamps. Centered on the bare, white wall between the windows is a sampler framed in walnut; the lettering is gold gothic on a forest green background and says,

FIDELITY TO TRUTH BUTTERS NO PARSNIPS, the meaning of which floats past the heads of the two visitors as they remove their caps and shake hands with Eliot. He seems taller contained in this room, looking even more like young Abe Lincoln than Gus had imagined before now. His cropped beard is white beneath the lower lip and on both sides of his chin, and when he speaks he shows two huge, white, gapped front teeth. His shirt and trousers are rough work clothes, stiff and clean, stone-washed by hand, patched on the elbows and knees. Gus thinks he must be at least a decade older than Christine.

While Eliot and Christine go into the kitchen—he for two chairs, she to put the kettle on—Gus and Junior stand silently and steal a secret look around the room. There are no carpets on the floor or decoration of any kind on the walls. A wooden rocker and end table sit beneath the beams hung with drying herbs. On the rocker seat is a knitted cushion; on the little table are a porcelain washbowl and pitcher, from which rises a bright purple spray of New England aster and joe-pye weed. With an eye on the kitchen door, Gus looks over the worktable where the McGregors were sitting when Junior knocked. On each end is a loose-leaf notebook filled with figures and several pencils of half-length, sharpened to a pinpoint. In the middle of the table, between two lamps, is a meticulous sketch of a small dam and pond done to scale on graph paper, with heights and depths and widths noted.

When they are settled in straight-back wooden chairs in an awkward semicircle around the big table, cups of chamomile tea sweetened with honey balanced on their knees, Gus and Junior find themselves speechless: locked shut like scared clams.

Christine talks about the weather and asks after their families; they reply in half syllables and loud sniffs of agreement. Eliot asks about lobstering, and both fishermen agree in clipped phrases that it's been a particularly bad year; there are fewer lobsters than ever, and Stonington men are putting out so much gear that there won't be any lobsters left in a couple of years. When their host and hostess have exhausted their attempts at conversation, there is a long painful silence as the guests avoid the eyes of their hosts and concentrate on their tea.

Eliot uncrosses his legs and crosses them again. Afraid that he might offend, Eliot asks carefully whether their visit is a social one or an official one. Christine blushes slightly; the visitors are relieved and open their shells slightly. All three look at Junior, the constable.

"I guess it's both," Junior begins, picking his words. "I mean, I haven't been to visit since right after you moved in; you'd just finished putting in the windows. It's not really official because it's not town business proper. I mean, it's east-side business."

"I see," says Eliot, who knows what's coming.

Junior wipes the perspiration from his forehead. "You mind if we smoke?" he asks.

Eliot and Christine exchange looks. "Actually we do," Eliot says. "If you want to step outside, we can go with you."

"No, it's not necessary," says Junior, who would like to know why Gus isn't helping out here, goddamn him. "I mean, what we came about is the people camped on your land up on our side of the road. Their fires are to our windward, and the women worry. I mean, we all do, when it's dry. And the dogs."

"They've tied the dogs since we asked them to," Christine says. "They didn't realize that they were running deer and how harmful that can be."

"They tied them up, but when they're not here the dogs bark all night long. They'll freeze to death in a month or so, if they don't starve first."

"When they go off-island, I feed the dogs," Christine says. "They are doing pick-up work on the mainland to get cash for their winter supplies, digging clams and worms, too. When the cold comes, they'll move down here to the island. They want to start from scratch, independent of the cash economy. They already have a fair shelter, and this winter they are going to clear ten acres for a subsistence garden like ours."

Eliot, who is taking his tea by the teaspoon, listens intently and with pride as Christine explains; then he interrupts.

"You see, we support young people who want to live as far from the marketplace as possible; who want to live strenuous, simple, productive lives; who eschew an acquisitive culture that worships wealth and luxury; and who want to go back to the land. How can we *not* support them?"

Junior and Gus are not sure how to respond; they wait for Eliot to say more.

"You've come to ask us to ask them to move elsewhere, I assume," Eliot offers.

Junior and Gus nod several times each.

"There are two problems: one is ethical, which you've just heard a little about; the other is practical."

"Practical?" Gus asks.

"Yes," Christine begins.

"Yes," says Eliot. "You see, we sold them the ten acres on the mountainside that they have settled on. That is their land."

"But how could you? I mean, how could they . . . ?"

"I guess that the particulars of the sale are our business—not to be rude, Junior," Eliot sips his spoon.

"You needn't worry about an open fire much longer," Christine offers. "They're looking for a small woodstove, even now, for inside their shelter."

Junior finishes his tea, which he likes better cold. In his mind, he can hear Myrtle—not shrill, but hissing, her angriest noise: *Sold it to them? They'll be here permanently? Sold it to them? They'll drive us out. And you say you can't do anything?*

Gus sees Junior finish off his tea and does the same, relieved that nothing further can be said, eager to get out the door and up the road.

When they take their leave, Eliot and Christine walk them to the door. Christine says that she is glad that they came. "I hope you understand us a little. No, I am sure that you do," she says.

Junior and Gus say good-night and start nonchalantly in the moonlight across the meadow toward the road. When Gus hears the door shut behind him, he looks toward the graveyard and picks up speed. Junior does not look back or around, but keeps pace with Gus.

Eliot watches them out the window. "Understand us, perhaps, but agree with us? I doubt it."

Christine does not reply. The teacups ring together as she gathers them.

Eliot chuckles. "I had no idea that Junior could move so quickly. I wonder what his all-fired hurry is."

When they reach the shelter of the dark, rutted road, Gus is breathing hard, and Junior is bent over, supporting himself with his hands on his knees, and gasping for air. Gus does not look back at the moonlit meadow. When he catches his breath, he asks Junior what the hell that was all about. Junior does not answer; he is afraid he is going to faint from want of air. When he finally stops gasping, he straightens, heaves his belt back up under his belly, and reaches for a cigarette.

"What was what all about?" he asks.

"That running back there just now," Gus says in return. "What the hell got into you? You think you saw something back there?"

"No–Christ." Junior lights his cigarette and takes a long satisfying drag. "You started scurrying, and I did too. I thought you saw something. I didn't want to get left behind. When I caught up, you started going faster. It like to killed me."

Gus starts up the road in the same rut he followed coming in, and Junior puffs to keep up.

"How the hell can they buy land? They're digging clams and doing pick-up work, and they bought ten acres of land? I guess maybe they could have worked something out, paying on time or with labor. But Jesus."

"Maybe Eliot's lying," wheezes Junior. He is straining to enjoy his smoke and keep up with Gus in the dark. "Myrtle's going to drive me out of the house when she hears this. She already drove me out of the kitchen. Can't smoke in his house. What the hell."

"You're going to have to go up there and talk to them. Maybe Willow will let you rub up against one of his women."

"The hell," says Junior.

FIVE

That boy is obscene; he is an outrage; he's a loose cannonball that could get people killed, yet Junior loves him. God knows why, but he does.
—*Myrtle Chafin*

It is a cold, dark, drizzling November day. Since late morning the wind has been light and easterly, pushing a salty, soaking dampness in off the sea and across the island. Gus's long johns, which had been nearly dried on the clothesline at midmorning, are now dripping from the frayed cuffs and sleeves; Betty's bras, nightgown, and undies were wafting in the breeze earlier but are sodden now and dripping. Smoke from the burning brush on the reverend's lot across the road from the Barters' disappears in the haze among the spruce trees. David and Simon have been at work since early morning clearing the lot in front of the reverend's cabin, and Betty Barter, who has just finished cleaning up after a noon dinner of SpaghettiOs, Wonder Bread, and boiled carrots, is watching them from the kitchen window.

A few feet from Betty, Gus sits at the table just inside the living room; he is framed by the kitchen doorway, over which are mounted his Krag rifle and 12-gauge pump shotgun. Gus is bent over the *Bangor Daily News* (which he likes to call the Bangor Barely News) that is spread on the table before him. At his right hand is an empty cup of tea; in the saucer and on his trousers are the remnants of a store-bought, powdered-sugar donut. He skips an article about antiwar demonstrations in Orono, and another about a civic club luncheon. On his way to the back pages for the comics, weather, and puzzles, he glimpses an article that says that U.S. Special Forces have officially turned their border camps over to the Vietnamese. Gus thinks what a coincidence it is that David is right across the road and that the fucking war is everywhere and will not leave him alone. He encircles the word *gulf* (vertical and upside down) in the newspaper's Wonderword puzzle and begins a drizzly afternoon search for more hidden words.

As Betty suspected when she saw them steamed open earlier, the quahogs that Gus dug that morning are especially tough. She scoops the clams out of their shells, which she drops into the bucket at her feet, loud to remind Gus to empty it later, and begins to chop up the meaty necks for tonight's chowder. Betty at forty-two, is, as Maggie often says, "still quite handsome." Though a little heavier than she was in her youth, she is in excellent health. When she's at work on something outside, her thick hair wrapped in a kerchief, her sleeves rolled, her cheeks pink, she reminds Gus of Rosie the Riveter in the old WWII posters, a comparison that Betty likes. She will not mention to Gus that the quahogs are unusually tough; it would result in a sermon about how the Deer Isle men are digging up all the clams everywhere to sell, and soon there won't be any left for the people who count on them for eating. She opens her window a tad and wipes a wide circular hole in the steamy glass.

Beyond her pink martin house and across the road she can see David and Simon at work cutting brush and limbing trees. They are feeding a fire that smolders, then leaps up and erupts in flame. They are both in T-shirts, warmed by the fire and the work: David's T-shirt is olive drab; Simon's is white with a black smear over his belly that is discernible from a hundred yards away. This is their second day at work in this spot. When they are done and have cleared and burned all the crowded spruce shrubs and trees, Betty will be able to see the reverend's cabin from her kitchen window, and as a consequence, she will have a view of the sea and Mount Desert Island as well, something she hasn't seen from her house since they first moved in fifteen years ago. As David drags a bundle of spruce limbs toward the fire, he passes Simon who is standing at the open trunk of his car gesticulating and obviously talking passionately about something. David seems to pay him no mind, in the same posture that Gus assumes when Junior gets on a rant.

Betty clears the circle on the glass again.

"Well," she says. "Guess who's come back."

Gus, who can damn well guess who has come back, does not reply.

"All three of them, and a goat to boot," says Betty.

"A goat? Jesus Christ, what next? A goddamn goat."

Willow, pulling an overburdened wagon, and Autumn, tugging along a scruffy goat, stop in the road next to Simon's two-tone Galaxie to chat with the brush burners and wait for Meadow Dawn to catch up. After a brief minute, Autumn ties the goat to the bumper of the car, while Simon opens the trunk and hands around what appear to be bottles of beer. Autumn is wearing a sheepskin jacket and a many-colored knit stocking cap; Willow is wrapped in scarves and sweaters and wearing what look like Eskimo boots to Betty, though she could be wrong.

"It looks like they've stopped to socialize and to have a bottle of beer," Betty says. "Come see the goat." She drops the clam stomachs into the pail and washes her hands thoroughly.

"No thanks," says Gus, encircling *tidbit* in his puzzle. He doesn't have to look to see what's going on. He knows that when they start to get cold they'll move to the fire and smoke cigarettes and drink beer. Laughing, no doubt. John would of kept working, said hello, but kept working, beer or no beer. That is the difference between the three of them. Simon Cooper cusses and raves about how much he hates the antiwar, peacenik, communist sons of bitches and wants to run them the hell off the island, but he does nothing about it. David doesn't like their politics, but he doesn't seem to mind them much and can be polite, even friendly, no grudges. John would of kept working to show that he can be tolerant but doesn't want anything to do with them, beer or no beer.

With a sharp knife, which she now holds, and a good potato, Betty can pare the entire skin off in one curled strip and drop it into the gurry bucket at her feet. She does so with the first, but gets only halfway with the second.

To her left out the window she sees Meadow Dawn, as large as ever in a shapeless garment of brown, coming slowly down Bridge Hill with a bulging Boy Scout knapsack on her back. Such names, Betty thinks. It was a meadow—a bright night meadow—where she and bold Ernest Morales first made love, and as a result Betty spent the happiest and hardest years of her life in exile in South Portland raising Sylvia, whose olive skin and jet-black hair would never have been accepted here on the island. At best, she and

Sylvia would have been snubbed and whispered after; at worst, they would have been driven off the island in tears by poisonous tongues. And now Betty is back (who would have guessed it?) and married to Gus Barter, her old friend and a widower, and though she sees too little of Sylvia, things are quite right in both their worlds. Safe. Sufficient. Well beyond blame.

The goat, who is not being watched, has been docile, chewing some stubby greens, but now begins to shake his head, slowly at first, then sharply, tangling his horns in the rope, gnawing on it, shaking wildly, his mouth wide open in what Betty supposes is bleating. At the fire, Willow hands his beer to Simon, finds a long stick on the ground, and whales on the goat's head and shoulders with a fury that subdues the animal but does not seem to faze the approaching Meadow Dawn in the least. When he returns to the group around the fire, wiping his hands on his trousers, Simon hands him his beer, and Autumn passes him a fat cigarette–a reefer, no doubt, Betty thinks, that has been making the rounds. Meadow Dawn drops her knapsack onto the ground, and Simon fetches her a beer from his trunk.

"Christine says they used old sails to build a tepee up on the land, their land. She says you'd be surprised at how big it is and how comfortable inside—a floor of spruce boughs, with sleeping bags and blankets on it. They painted the tepee with all kinds of bright colors—flowers and rainbows and Indian symbols and peace signs."

"Footprint of the American chicken," says Gus of the peace sign.

"Outside they have a covered kitchen, closed in by sail on three sides, with a table, shelves, and a wood floor, like those pioneer families you see in schoolbooks."

"Puritans, I suppose," Gus says. He finds *pickle* hiding backwards on a diagonal and circles it.

"We ought to go up there and visit, take something baked, a pie. They're going to get one of those little Swedish woodstoves, a Jotul, and put it in the tepee."

"In a bed of dried-out spruce boughs. Jesus wept. You want to see a fire."

Betty shakes her head: this is going nowhere fast. She clears her circle in the glass again to see that the hippie wagon train is moving on down the road, warmed and refreshed by their sojourn around the fire with the work-ers. David and Simon, whose fire has dwindled to ashes, lean against the back of Simon's Ford and watch the settlers make their carefree way homeward through the light drizzle. Simon draws two more bottles of beer from the trunk and hands one to David, talking while David nods, grinning in agreement. They are talking about Autumn, Betty is sure, and no wonder: she walks as if she is naked, like an Indian princess; she is untamed and beautiful, and she is afraid of no one.

Tart. They called Betty a tart when they learned that she was pregnant, then inferred by whom. Ernest was a Coast Guardsman, and to some that was bad enough; to others he was a Christly Mexican; to still others he was nothing but a nigger. They are calling Autumn a slut and whore and worse. The women hate her because she is different—she is unconventional, which makes her immoral in their eyes—and they are afraid of her, jealous of their husbands' and sons' eyes that follow her everywhere. Betty was beautiful too, beautifully proportioned and some proud of it, much the reason for their bitterness back then. They don't revile and hiss at the large one, Meadow Dawn, for living in sin and carnal slime in the tepee; they don't even mention her, or look at her when she passes on the landing. And Willow; well, he's for the men to despise, and envy.

Gus hears Simon's Ford growl to a start, then rev and rev, loud as a thunderstorm.

"Must be their dinnertime," Gus says. "Simon Cooper likes to go home for his lunch. She's there to cook up something for him."

"I think David likes to go with him."

"David likes it because she's there," says Gus, circling *hasty*.

"I don't think she minds setting an extra place when it's for David," Betty says.

"No, I don't suppose she does." Gus smiles at his puzzle, licks his pencil lead, and drains the cold dregs in his teacup.

✳✳✳

November 30, 1970

Dear Ruth,

Yes, it was my year for Thanksgiving dinner, and God, how I dreaded it. Gus saying the same grace and a few attempts at levity with old jokes; mashed potatoes and gravy, sauerkraut. Leah with the gossip from the post office ladies and made-up memories of Thanksgiving in Head Harbor when she was little;

canned peas and jello mold with fruit cocktail afloat in it. Betty all sad and wistful after her second drink about Sylvia not being able to come; boiled beets and pumpkin pie from a can. It honestly occurred to me to tell them that I was ill, which I believed I was when I thought of the dinner and the evening to come. How did Emily D. describe Thanksgiving? "Reflex Holiday."

So.

So I took the morning boat to Stonington (and while aboard, on a whim, invited David to join us—he accepted), hired Steve to carry me to Blue Hill, and spent the morning spending a fortune at Merrill & Hinckley, purveyors to summer people and the wealthy retired. Imagine: a rack of lamb, mint jelly, two bottles of red wine and one of Liebfraumilch for dessert, fresh asparagus, cucumbers, tomatoes, lettuce, parsley, and among other treats, fresh (well, nearly) peaches for a cobbler. I was so pleased with myself. I called Sylvia in South Portland and invited her, but she begged me not to beg her to come, which I did not do, though I probably should have.

But I needn't have. The meal was a great success. The lamb as pink as Betty's cheeks, and, as Leah said, everything tasted as fresh as though it had come from a September garden. But the "piece of resistance," as Gus is wont to say, was David; rather, it was David's presence. He and Gus teased one another—Gus called David's slightly ribald stories about their adventures fishing "damn lies" with loving disgust, and the atmosphere in the room was, well, downright jolly. We three females—mother, wife, aunt—could have shed happy tears to see Gus so pleased to have a close, young companion and David to have a man he feels right with. But more gratifying than the lighthearted air was the quality of our table talk with David present. Leah spoke not one mean word about the hippie girl, not a single sarcastic comment about the penny-pinching McGregors. And against any snide hint of Gus's about Myrtle's fears and phobias, Betty was an adamant defender, a compassionate neighbor friend. It was as though we were all talking on the CB, with all the island women listening in, and that resultant cautious tone, together with a merciful absence of any reference to the war or poor lost John, had us three Barter and Bowen women singing David's praises, deserved or not. I so wish you could have been here.

But every silver lining has a cloud. I begin to fear that there is going to be a price to pay for having such a pleasant neighbor. Last night was as clear and still as any autumn night one could wish for. The stars were so close and so many that they seemed indeed a firmament. The sea was so still and flat that it mirrored the sky. I sat on my perch on the cliff, out front all bundled up in wool coat and scarves and blanket, soaking up the silence, as quietly adrift as Gus's boat sitting on her mooring. Not a silence that would haunt, but one that softens this old soul. Then *crunch, growl, grumble, vrumvrum* down the damn cove road comes that Simon Cooper in his goddamn Ford and strikes me from behind with his glaring headlights, throwing my shadow, a little, stretched-out elfin form, across the water, and shattering my calm nocturne, making me think suddenly of Nazis smashing shop windows. He was going slowly, to be polite passing the house so close, on his way to see David, but I knew and was right to suppose, that when he came back in the wee hours, he'd be grinding and roaring, tearing up the night with his angry car.

But I complain; I'm sorry. I grow crotchety in my old age. I think how lucky you and I are to have our health and our families around us.

I'm reading my way through the novels left behind for the library by the summer people, but I doubt I will finish this cynical Indian novel that won the Pulitzer, especially having had such fun as you did with *The Reivers*.

Love always, dear one.

Maggie

***

When Simon passes Maggie's house on the dirt road and turns uphill toward the meadow and Ava's house, he downshifts to climb the short steep hump in the road where it rolls over the granite ledge beneath. The unnaturally bright beams of his headlights illuminate the gnarled top branches of the old oaks along the road; then, as the Ford finds a flat surface again, the beams drop slowly to light Ava's roof, then the kitchen door and window where David stands at the sink, blinking at the sudden unnerving assault of light and engine noise. He knows that it is Simon; who else would be out at 7:30 on a dark winter night; who else would have his car radio blaring Mick Jagger who can't always get what he wants. Drying his hands on a linen dishtowel, David opens the kitchen door and stands behind the screen to watch as Simon shuts down his machine, slides out of the door, and leaning back in, fetches out a half-gallon of Canadian Club and a large, green bottle of mixer. David smiles a little ruefully to think of the night to come—a night of booze and noise and endless incoherent war stories. But Simon, he well knows, is here to drink, to hell with what David feels like doing. God grant me the serenity to accept those things I cannot change, he thinks, with another half smile, put your head down and drive on.

Simon, a jug in each hand, negotiates the dooryard on his way to the kitchen stoop. He has reached the first level of a good buzz, about three fingers into the half-gallon, and he is eager to progress to level two, with company. He left Nancy, whom he affectionately calls Mother, at home on the couch reading in her Christly nurse's journal and in no mood for a drink or for his drinking. At level two, which is Simon's favorite, his mind is clear, his muscles, from his neck to his heels, have relaxed, and he feels good, playful—none of the bad shit has bubbled to the surface in his brain yet, and tonight he thinks it just might not, and if it doesn't he just might like to get a little rowdy, if that's possible on this fucking dead island.

"I thought you'd be in bed," says Simon, ascending the porch steps.

"No you didn't." David holds open the screen door.

"I was on my way down to Junior's. I saw your light on from the road."

This too is a lie; David knows it is not possible to see his lights from the road, but he doesn't say so.

"It's such a beautiful fucking night," he says instead. "Let's sit outside. I'll get a shirt."

"I can see my goddamn breath." Simon exhales a cloud. "Are you shitting me? Sit outside in the winter? Fucking summer people."

This is Simon's third or perhaps fourth nighttime visit to David's with a jug in hand. Once in October David escaped to the cabin. A week later Simon found his way up to the cabin high ground with a flashlight, and once he caught David in the kitchen as he has tonight.

In their brief shared history of serious drinking, the two men, without saying so, have each put up a few Off Limits signs that the other is willing to respect, or has so far. David will permit nothing demeaning about Gus or Maggie; nor will he listen to nasty talk about Southeast Asians, particularly females; the words *gook, slope, zipper-head, dink,* and so on, seriously piss him off. He waves away talk of his former fiancée and of his parents. He does not like to be called "summer people," especially by someone like Simon who is not from the island and has only wintered here once, but he has to suffer it, at least for now. Simon is not inclined to talk about his wife, though—or because—he suspects that David is interested, and that she might be too. Although he mentions it occasionally in a grim and offhanded manner, Simon insists that he does not want to talk about the fight in the Ia Drang valley. He doesn't give a flying fuck that it was such a huge and important battle—details of that experience are Off Limits. He is sick of trying to talk about Vietnam with people who have no fucking idea what he is talking about or, worse, aren't interested. He says he likes to shoot the shit with David because David has seen the shit; he knows what it is; he has felt the elephant sitting on his chest; he has felt the pucker factor, has been so scared it would take a sledgehammer to drive a pin up his asshole. Although—this will come out at level three or four if it gets that far—David may have been through a few ground attacks on his compound and an occasional running gunfight, he doesn't really know what full-scale battle is like, not really, with Americans dying, not just gooks.

David brings a plastic ice tray from the refrigerator to the kitchen table along with two jelly glasses pinched between his fingers. Simon puts a pack of Salems on the table and lights one with a Zippo that is emblazoned with the yellow-and-black rearing-horse insignia of the First Cavalry Division. David smokes Marlboros and lights them with a kitchen match that he scratches to life across the table bottom. Simon's pack of Salems reminds David of the noisy refrain of half-naked Vietnamese children crying "OK Salem" to any passing American, hoping for a free cigarette, or *"thich keo, thich keo,"* hoping for candy.

"That's good," David tells Simon, who is pouring whiskey into his glass. He holds his palm down as a signal to stop the pour, but Simon continues.

"Isn't it?" He pours until both glasses are half full, drops in a couple of cubes, and tops them off with ginger ale.

They touch glasses across the table. "To the boys we left behind," says Simon solemnly, then adds, "and to all the whores we never screwed."

Simon drains about half his drink, makes a show of popping his Zippo open by pinching the top and bottom between thumb and middle finger, lights his Salem, and shakes his head.

"I don't know, man. Some of those girls were pretty nice, the ones in Vung Tau specially; we talked about them, didn't we? But didn't any of them compare to this sweet hippie nympho we got right here on this island."

David agrees, thinking that Simon never clapped his eyes on Neang, thank God, and wondering if he has ever really looked at his wife.

When Simon announces that he has to walk the pink flamingo and lets himself out to stand on the stoop and pee, David brings a wedge of store cheese, a butcher knife, and crackers on a crude cutting board to the table. He cuts slices from the hard wedge, while Simon returns to pour them another one.

David tips back in his chair and listens from a distance while Simon tells the one about the time his battalion was traveling with a squadron of armored personnel carriers and was ambushed by North Vietnamese dug into a wood line along a dried riverbed. It was his company, not battalion, the last time he told this one, David thinks, but battalion does make more sense.

"They hit us hard from the right flank. A lot of the guys who were riding on top of the APCs, like I was, were hit, blown right off. We were already understrength of course; why else would the brass have given us that mission, and that first barrage—B40s, AKs, their machine guns, what were they?—it cut us up seriously, man."

"Probably Chicom 56s," David says.

"Yeah, well, this CO of the armored unit, I remember his call sign was Cattle Charlie One One, he wheels his APCs face into the fire, orders the infantry to unass the vehicles, and calls the world for air support, all the time us going across open fucking ground, just tall grass and shrubs and shit, walking behind the APCs for cover, their dual-50s roaring like Spooky himself. Goddamn, you couldn't hear individual weapons firing, but only a low grinding sound, you know, man."

David says he fucking-A-well does know and hopes to never hear it again. He cuts a few more slices of cheese and examines the old butcher knife, turning it over in his hands, admiring its heavy steel, shining edge, and simple worn handle fastened with brass rivets. He holds the knife in the air over the cutting board and lets it drop to stick into the board, shivering slightly as it settles upright.

"You don't have any dope, do you?" Simon asks as he lights a cigarette.

"No," David says. "Sorry about that."

"So we get right up to the wood line once, not a single fucking aircraft answering our calls, and they drive us back. They knocked out one track; you should have seen those fuckers scamper. The NVA were in deep bunkers made from palm trunks, man—you know how those fiber trunks can stop most anything—and they're not going anywhere. Three more times we try, Jesus fucking God. Finally, this sonofabitch Cattle Charlie calls his APC commanders and tells them to insert the infantry. I mean, shit. Armored personnel carriers can't take the wood line, so he sends in unprotected men in the open. There it is. What the fuck? Over."

Simon shakes his head, as does David in sympathy: doesn't he know it, the guy was probably OCS or West Point.

David thinks that the smoke from the menthol cigarettes smells like cordite, and his tongue feels dry. He cracks both kitchen windows open and fixes the door ajar with a stone doorstop. The night is quiet, though a slight breeze moves in through the open door.

"Like I said, what the fuck?" Simon raises his hands in a gesture of futility, runs them over his tight-curled blond hair, and crosses his arms over his chest, showing biceps the size of artillery rounds.

"Sergeant Turner, he stepped out from behind the APC, and I swear to you, man, he was instant spaghetti sauce, fucking lasagna. He held his hand up to protect his face, and I saw it, I swear, turn into a red spray. He went flying backwards, a fucking chunk of raw burger meat."

Here Simon pauses for effect. It was tomato sauce last time he told it, thinks David, and the radio operator who was hit. Simon is trying each time he tells the story to make it ring truer—going for the gut.

"So we stepped out behind him. There were seven of us behind that APC, and we just stepped out. I don't know why. I was sure I was going to get wasted right there, man. And we walked into that wood line, a whole battalion of troopers, spread out, guys going down everywhere, shit flying everywhere—some kid screaming for his mom, pissed off because she's not coming. Then suddenly it stops. Just like that. They're taking off; the fuckers are running. Holy God. I almost cried, I was so happy. I mean my mouth was full of cotton, and you know what, you know what I wanted more than anything right then? A fucking peanut butter sandwich, Skippy smooth on white bread, and a glass of cold milk. I swear, man."

They drift into a companionable silence, not saying, not even thinking, consciously at least, that it is comfortable being at a table with another man who knows the rusty taste of fear; how good it feels, how green and young and sweet it feels, to have been nearly dead and lived one more time.

David goes outside to pee. He walks to the edge of the meadow through the dew that is beginning to freeze and unzips under the stars, relishing the relief and the brittle night air. He breathes his own clouds of vapor in the starlight and remembers the few nights under the mountain when the temperature dropped to seventy degrees and the Khmer guards bundled up in poncho liners and hovered over a fire in a fifty-gallon drum, shivering and not at all amused by his shirtless teasing. He thinks that he could not have a better buzz on than he has now; he knows that he should stop drinking, and he knows that he won't. Inside, Simon is coughing, hacking, and wheezing. David thinks that if the man passes out, which seems likely, he will leave him in the kitchen where it is warm, give him a pillow, and cover him. He thinks that Nancy would rather he sleep it off here than risk driving home. This is David's last reasonable thought for the night.

When Ava's baby-blue teapot wall clock reads midnight, the half-gallon jug is down to two fingers, the ginger ale is long gone, the scallop shell ashtray is overflowing with butts, David is standing over the table dropping the butcher knife into the cutting board, and the two are making plans to go to South Portland to spend a weekend partying with Simon's high school friends, all veterans, and find a much-needed fucking truck for David to bring back to the island. It doesn't matter that David is broke, Simon explains for the fourth time; he can get him a used truck that he can pay for on time. He knows people. It's not what you know; it's who you blow. He didn't become the best scrounger in his battalion for nothing.

When Simon is as drunk as he is now, his center of gravity sinks, and he walks bowlegged, rocking from side to side with his beefy arms elbows out like Popeye the Sailor Man on a heaving deck: heavy menace. When he returns from his car with another pack of Salems, he remains standing by the stove, drink in hand, to tell the one about the black helicopter door gunner who caught a pregnant gook ("All right, all right, Vietnamese") running in the open in a free-fire zone.

"That 'groid,' he leaned out of that slick and opened up on her in three-round bursts from almost right overhead. You never saw better shooting, man. First burst sent her, what do you call it, somersaulting, then right while she was doing that he greased her again, and she started doing handstands— no lie, man, fucking handstands. It was beautiful."

Somewhere along the old road behind the house a barred owl hoots twice. David leans toward the window opening in hopes of hearing a reply, but he cannot as Simon has begun to tell the one about the time his patrol linked up with two CIA operatives to raid a Viet Cong village to take out a communist village chief. He describes how they assembled the villagers for questioning, and when no one would talk, they wrapped a strand of det cord around a palm tree and set it off, blowing the trunk in half, scaring the shit out of the villagers. But still no one would talk, so they took six of the most likely males, huddled them up, wrapped det cord around them—two turns—and then asked again where the village chief was. When no one would talk, one of the CIA guys detonated the cord and blew body parts into the trees, onto the roofs of the hooches, into the hair and clothes of the screaming women and kids, "a warm commie shower."

David is far more interested in hearing whether the owl will have an answer to his cry than he is in hearing Simon's stories, not that Simon notices or cares. The last time he told it they were out to capture, not kill, the village chief, and the spook blew up four, not six, men, not that it matters. David hears the owl call again, then again, but there is no response, and he imagines that the owl has flown away to try for an answer in another part of the island where there is not so much noise.

By the time the teapot clock's little hand is on the two, the jug is empty, and David is sitting cross-legged on the linoleum floor leaning against the counter next to the stove; an angular, curly-headed, thoroughly intoxicated Buddha, nodding in and out of Neverland. Across the room Simon is leaning forward onto his forearms on the table staring at the handle of the upright butcher knife and someplace beyond it. His face is set in anger, and he is breathing heavily. He lays his bulging forearm out on the table, hand palm up, and stares at the pale, muscular underside of his arm with obvious loathing, open and closing his fist.

"INCOMING!" he yells. David's lolling head snaps back and bangs against the cabinet, and Simon, standing now, laughs and slaps his thigh. He takes the butcher knife, holding it by the blade, handle up, and declares that it is time to go for a spin around the Christly island.

"Let's go, Harper. Let's *di-di*. You're halfway passed out, you pussy, and I am ungodly bored. We'll go around clockwise and stop at my house and get some beer—and maybe Mother, too. You'd like that."

"No thanks, man," says David. He rubs his face and thinks that cold water is what he needs. "You go ahead. I'm pooched."

"Pooched, my ass. You never heard that word till you came here." Simon lets fly the knife at the cupboard over David's head. David watches it tumble in slow motion, then covers his head with his arms before he hears it bounce off the cupboard and clatter harmlessly onto the floor.

"Candy ass," says Simon as he takes up his cigarettes and weaves out the door. The screen door slams, and David hears Simon laugh derisively—entirely victorious, somehow, and entirely alone.

David bows his head, shuts his eyes, and listens as Simon revs the Galaxie—forward then reverse, forward then reverse—to turn around in the uneven dooryard. As he listens, he sees the car rumble past Maggie's house in second gear. Then, still in second gear, Simon heads up the gravel hill to the crest, where he spins and then squeals as he guns it off the gravel and on to the tarmac lip to assault Bridge Hill at 3,500 rpms, then roar into the night, three deuces and a four-speed hell-bent for the west side.

With a little help from the countertop, David builds himself to his feet. He pumps cold water at the sink and rinses his face. He leaves the door and windows open to air the place out, then dumps the ashtrays and clears the table before he starts for the cabin in the dark. In the starlight, the meadow and well cover are shining with gray frost. David stops to listen but hears nothing, not even the sea, not the slightest breeze, only the tiny, distant high-pitched ringing in his ears. On the hillside, he stops at the twin birch trunks to gain his balance and let his eyes adjust to the darkness. While he climbs the hill, step by step, holding on to limbs and trunks as he goes, he remembers that Simon explained how he survived the massacre at the Ia Drang, but he doesn't remember anything but "massacre in the jungle." He assures himself that he will remember in the morning.

At the top of the hill, the forest thins, and he can see the cabin in its clearing and the cold, wide, lighted sea beyond. He is startled by a snort, then the thudding of retreating hooves as deer sprint for the darker forest. One night, David thinks, when there are no stars or moon, he will stagger right past the cabin and over the cliff, like old Amos is said to have done, for the final dive.

SIX

**There isn't anything wrong with Skippy except
maybe his lip. He's just shy is all.
—*Cecil Chafin***

Each of Gus's ears has an extra lobe that extends the ear considerably; when he is being thoughtful, he rubs his right ear's lower lobe
softly between his thumb and forefinger. He is doing this as he sits
watching the sleet skitter onto the frozen surface of the fueling dock outside
the store window. Baffled by the shifting afternoon wind, the boats moored
in the thorofare seem in constant, worried motion, sliding back and forth on
their moorings like nervous tethered animals. Their decks and washboards
and bait barrels glisten with ice, making the boats' outlines seem transparent
on the dark water. Gus is moored in the worn captain's chair by the kerosene
stove in the corner; his companions are bushel baskets of Idaho potatoes and
fat purple onions. Across the store, beyond the nearly empty bread shelves,
his mother, Leah, wearing her favorite blue cardigan over her shoulders and
her granny glasses on the end of her nose, is bent over some paperwork, or
other, at the counter, as she has been all of Gus's conscious life. His slicker is
draped to dry over one of the straight-back chairs next to him—it was raining
when he came in an hour ago—and today as nearly every day in the off-sea-
son he is clean-shaven and wearing a quilted flannel shirt and a clean, white

undershirt. Though his body is anchored in the old chair, Gus's thoughts have slipped their mooring and are adrift in a vague and pleasant harbor of memory.

"Gus," Leah says in a voice more suitable for a napping boy than a bereft middle-aged fisherman. "Gus, would you bring me out that box of ground beef in the cooler and carry it to the workbench."

Gus obeys wordlessly. With his knife, he cuts the twine that binds the box and returns to his seat. Leah pulls her apron over her head and ties it behind.

"I wonder, was it me that they tricked into biting into one of these purple onions saying it was a sweet plum, or was it John?" Gus asks.

Leah does not turn around but answers, "I've heard that story so many times I don't remember which of you it was. But I do remember the face you made when you tasted it, or maybe it was John, and the noise when you spit it out."

Leah does not much feel like talking just now; she wants to get the ground beef weighed and packaged and frozen to have it done when Mabel comes in to relieve her for the afternoon. But she knows that Gus finds comfort in remembering things from his boyhood years, from before the accident and loss of his Susan and the girls, from the time before he lived where there were stoplights and high-speed four-lane roads. And she is surprised to hear him mention John so casually . . . surely a good sign. So she says, as she wraps and tapes a half pound and marks it *lean* that she does remember the purple onion skin on his, Gus's, chin and shirt.

"And I remember your father made old Irville pay for a purple onion once, so it must have been you. Though it could have been Virgil he made pay, and that would have made John the victim. Perhaps it was the both of you. Irville and Virgil both sat in the captain's chair. Now you're the one sitting in the chair. Who are you going to play the onion trick on, your grand—"

Now she has done it, Leah thinks. Now he will lapse into one of his stunned silences. It must have been his mention of John that made her slip.

"It's all right, Mother," Gus says. "For some reason, today it's all right. Maybe Sylvia will bring her kids out here when she has them. She's Betty's daughter, but my stepdaughter, which means they'll be my grandchildren, kind of. I can trick one of them."

"Yes," says Leah, relieved. She thinks that Gus was telling the truth and that it is all right this time to be reminded of John and perhaps by grievous association of the accident as well–Susan buried with their unborn third child still in her womb. It might be David being here as Maggie has suggested: David who, much like Gus after the accident, came back to the island after the war–home for one, almost home for the other–to regroup, recuperate, recover, whatever the right word is. As she pats a mound of ground beef into shape, Leah wonders whether Gus or David has mentioned John to the other. Perhaps they have agreed not to, openly or with silence. It is not likely that John is the only friend that David lost in the war; he was there two years, in the army for five. Nor is it likely that David ever had a better friend than John: the two of them that last summer together here on the island,wearing their hair in ducktails like Elvis, wearing white T-shirts with a pack of Lucky Strikes rolled up in one sleeve, going around telling summer people they were twins. Big shots chewing Juicy Fruit. Stinking of Brylcreem and tobacco.

The door bangs open and Skippy, his checkered wool cap's earflaps tied snug under his chin, passes the counter on his way to the freezer and his daily ice-cream sandwich. He tucks his hands into his armpits for warmth, and he is humming through his nose, a sign that he is in good humor. Junior follows Skippy inside; behind him on the covered porch, David musses his curls to shake loose the sleet pellets and follows Junior through the door.

"Where'd you find those two?" Gus asks.

Junior sheds his jacket, shakes it out, and drapes it over the chair next to Gus's. David comes to stand with his back to the stove and light his cigarette and Junior's.

"On the road," says Junior. "Or I ought to say *in* the road. Trying to ice-skate down Town Hill in their shoes, for Christ's sake. Idiots. Like little kids."

David smiles. Gus smiles and shakes his head.

"Is the road so icy?" Gus asks. "It was rain a while ago; is it frozen so soon?"

"It's bad. It's real bad. I had to drive half on the shoulder, in the gravel, to come down the hill in first gear, for Christ's sake. It's black ice."

"I wonder how Aunt Maggie will get in," Gus says. "You know how she hates to drive on ice."

"She won't try," Leah says. "And here's why I want telephones down here. We could call her to see if she needs anything and you could take it to her."

"I should of stopped at the cove. I wasn't thinking," Junior says.

"No," Leah says.

When the four men leave the store an hour later, the wind has backed to the south and the sleet has turned to a fine, intermittent rain. To Junior this means that they will not have to stop to salt Town Hill on their way to make their visit, as the ice will melt soon enough with the wind southerly like this, carrying warmth in off the Gulf Stream. As they round the corner of the store on their way to Junior's truck, they are in single file, David taking up the rear. At the gas pump they find Maggie in a knee-length wool coat, beret, and green rubber gardening boots. As the old gas pump moans and whirs, she covers her head and shoulders with a plaid scarf and smiles, bemused, at the foursome as they pass.

"I didn't think you'd come over to town," Gus says.

"I almost did not, but I need kerosene and butter, and two of my magazines come on Wednesday. I think that if I linger here and at the post office for an hour or so, the road will have melted satisfactorily. Where are you fellows off to? You seem so purposeful."

"We're going to pay the hippies a visit," Junior says.

"Are you?" Maggie is surprised. "All of you at once? Just to be sociable? Up in the woods on this ice?" Maggie looks them all over, her eyes settling on Gus, then Skippy. "You'll be lucky if a tree limb weighted by ice doesn't fall on your head."

Skippy sucks in air, his eyes bugging. Gus notices that Maggie is smiling with the side of her mouth, which means trouble is coming, some form of teasing.

"Where will you get the torches and cudgels?" she asks. She withdraws the nozzle and replaces it on the pump.

"What?" Gus senses that he is being teased, but he does not know how. He climbs into the truck and scootches over next to Junior. Maggie takes her empty kerosene can out of her trunk and smiles good-bye at the truck as she turns the corner.

"I'll ride in back," David says. "Go on and get in, Skippy."

"What the hell is a cudgel?" Junior wants to know.

"It's a club," David says. Skippy laughs, then falls quickly serious. "What did she mean?"

"You know, in the horror movies when at night all the villagers gather with torches and clubs to go up to the castle and kill the monster or Igor or the mad doctor because they've heard stories and they're scared of them?"

Junior and Gus and Skippy say "No" in unison.

"Well, I think that's what she's talking about," says David. "She's teasing us and kind of warning us, too, I guess."

"Maggie never saw a horror movie," Junior says. "How could she?'

"She could of when she used to visit Ruth in Bangor. Easy," says Gus.

"Or she read the book," offers David as he shuts the cab door.

"Most likely," says Junior. He has forever been in awe of Miss Maggie Bowen, who was his teacher from kindergarten on, as she was everyone else's who grew up on the island. "She's been to college," he adds.

"David, he's been to college," Gus says.

"I went to college, yes, for a semester, three months." David shakes his head at himself. "All the other prisoners were already brainwashed when I got there, and by the time I had grown my hair long enough to fit in, I'd had it."

"Had it with what?"

"With being surrounded by the enemy, surrounded by enemies for two and a half years."

Skippy unties his hat string, rolls down the window, and holds out his hat to David.

"Here, wear my ha'," he says.

"No, thanks, Skippy, I'm okay. You wear it."

"He likes to show off them curls to the girls," says Gus.

Skippy, who loves a rhyme, laughs heartily, a belching chuckle.

David arranges himself on a bundle of oak laths in the bed of the truck, his back against the cab, his legs crossed, and his hands inside the opposite sleeves of his coat, like a Mandarin. When they have passed the town hall, moving slowly with two wheels on the irregular shoulder of the island road, Gus sees the little house on the road that the town has rented to the Coopers as part of the package to attract Nancy to the island to be the nurse. Simon is usually in the garage/firehouse next door, tinkering with his car or someone else's, but from a distance there is no sign of him today.

"Where's your stern man, anyway?" Gus asks Junior. "I bet he'd like to come along."

"He went off-island yesterday to raise hell with his pals in South Portland, as usual. Probably he would like to come with us and carry one of those torches Maggie mentioned. I'm glad he isn't here; there's no telling what that guy will do," Junior observes. He slides open the window behind their heads so that David can overhear their conversation.

"No," he says louder than necessary. "No. Simon, he's off-island. Nancy is here, though, alone in the house, I guess."

Gus smiles knowingly. Skippy wipes his nose with his sleeve.

"I don't know about you, Gus." Junior is trying to sound sincerely contrite, regretful, but he is not doing it well. "I don't know about you fellows, but when I drive slow by her house with David sitting up in back in full view, I feel like I'm trolling. Curls for bait; curls for girls."

Skippy puts his hands on his knees and chortles. He strains to see if there is any sign of Nancy in the windows, but he is disappointed.

David understands now why Junior opened the cab window.

"Oh, go to hell, Junior," David says through the window. "There's nothing. You just want to get me in trouble." And he shuts the window.

David travels backwards up the steep hill, watching the town below shrink to a landscape. He thinks that he likes the teasing, and he thinks that he likes just as much riding with these men. He is warm inside his coat; his cheeks are thrilled by the cold air; and though the glazed vista of the town and west side of the island is confined by haze on the water and a low cloud lying on the top of the mountain, he is astonished again by its splendor, amazed again at how the weather tones change so quickly and frequently. He is comforted by its familiarity.

On Lovers' Lane, limbs of young maples on both sides of the road lean inward, burdened by ice, forming an elegant arch. The branches that cannot bear the weight of the ice snap off and plummet onto the road, exploding when they strike in a crystalline outburst, strewing the gleaming road with thousands of tiny shards of diaphanous sea glass. The drooping shoulders of the spruce gathered on the edge of the cedar swamp seem forlorn and somehow silly to David, on whose own shoulders and sleeves the freezing fine rain has turned to frost.

How could he ever describe this sparkling cold to Neang, or to the others, who live in a land so hot that chocolate melts in winter? The only ice they know is in murky blocks, kept cold buried in rice hulls. Ice is a wonder in their climate, but it is nothing like this. Nothing. She'd find it so cold, and he, well, he finds it wonderfully warm to be swaddled in ice as he is.

The cab window slides open on Skippy's side and exhales onto David the warm aromas of tobacco, drying wool, soiled shirts, and laundry detergent. As though by its own volition, a Charleston Chew sneaks out of the window and slides to rest in the safety of his crossed forearms. Without a sound from inside the cab, the window slides itself shut again. David knows that Skippy knows that he will let the candy bar freeze, then smash it into slivers that he will let soften in his mouth before he chews them, a sweet gift of warmth. At the bend by the gravel pit the raspberry bushes have lain down their arms in supplication, and the truck slips past them quietly.

Sensibly, Junior does not brake going down Bridge Hill but rides scrunched as far over as he can get on the shoulder. At the foot of the sharp little hill, where his cove road joins the island road, David smells wood smoke and recognizes it as his own–his box elder–wafting uphill from the cove. And when the road opens to travel south down the east side, he can smell more wood smoke–spruce, and birch, too–drifting from Gus's parlor and beyond from Junior's, to mingle with the smoke from his own stove, and arising, ascend the mountainside to be assumed into the cloud that lies asleep atop the island and town.

✳✳✳

"Well?" Junior asks.

He is standing facing the front of his truck, warming his hands on the hood and watching Skippy, whose earflaps are lifted and tied together on top of his hat and whose head is cocked slightly toward the forest that rises from the road.

David is standing in the bed of the truck leaning on the roof of the cab. Gus is bent over on the frozen roadside looking for a sign of the path that leads to the camp, looking for signs of damage from shoes or boots to the icy, brown fern fronds and glazed sphagnum at the edge of the woods.

"They must be up there still, to home, if you could call it that," Gus deduces. "There's no sign . . . wait, here's their path. See where it goes up through the puckerbrush, but it's not . . ."

"Shush for Christ's sake. How can he hear?"

"There's a doe up there." Skippy points into the glistening forest on a rise to the south. "And a little one with her."

"What about up here, though?" Gus beckons to the path that leads straight up the hillside.

Skippy holds perfectly still, his chin lifted slightly, eyes closed. The drop on the tip of his nose has grown to a little icicle.

"Hanimals sleeping," Skippy finally says. "Dogs most likely, and another one I don' know that breathes real quick, snorty kind of."

"A goat," Gus says.

"Maybe. I suppose."

David, who has carefully stowed his candy bar behind a toolbox for later, is standing in the truck bed, hands in his pockets, examining the eyes and the faces of the three men before him for some sign of a conspiracy, an old and familiar joke being played out, of which he, undoubtedly is to be the butt. He has heard about Skippy's gift, that he can supposedly hear clams in the tidal mud and detect lobsters walking on the rocky bottom at twenty fathoms. David saw him push Marlboro filters into his ears at the shop party, forcing them in place with his thumbs, then covering his ears with his palms, his wounded mouth partly open. But sleeping animals at five hundred meters, a half klick away, through a thick forest?

"Can you really hear animals breathing up there, Skippy? Or are you just jerking us off?"

Neither Gus nor Junior seems surprised by the question, but Skippy immediately turns beet red from his collar to his cap line and looks at David apologetically, his rheumy blue eyes steady on David's belt.

"He can hear them," Gus says. "It's not bullshit. And it's not that far either. No people, Skippy?"

Skippy shakes his head no.

"Are you certain?" Junior asks. "Maybe they're asleep, bundled up inside the tent and inside sleeping bags. You positive, Skippy?"

"Who would be sleeping in the middle of the afternoon," Gus wonders.

"Hippies would," says Junior.

Skippy shakes his head again. He is avoiding David's eyes, and David promises himself that he will apologize to Skippy for doubting his gift; it's just so unnatural.

Gus leads the way, stepping carefully to avoid ice-covered granite, breaking a glassy trail up the mountainside. When they stop for a breather, Junior breaks a low limb from a spruce to use as a walking stick to help him along. David lights a cigarette. Every few seconds there is a shattering crash as a limb sheds it icy load or falls with it, each time from a different part of the forest.

When they come into a wide, open area that is nearly flat, Junior takes the lead with his stick to shatter the waist-high bayberry bushes, clearing the ice ahead, just as a point man clears the jungle with a machete, David thinks; but this time there are no bad guys waiting for them up ahead, only sleeping hippies, one of which David hopes to see sitting up in her sleeping bag, in a T-shirt, her arms stretched over her head in a soft, opening yawn.

A startled bark followed by a high-pitched, rapid-fire yapping surprises the climbers when they approach the flatter ground on the next rise. A goat bleats nervously, and Skippy ties down his earflaps. Junior, breathing hard, hitches his belt up under his belly. He mutters something, then he and Gus push ahead.

The tepee rises like a gray monument in the middle of a cleared, flat half-acre; it is perhaps twenty-five feet high and eighteen feet in diameter at the base, gray but gaily painted and sparkling with ice in the dappled light. Gus shouts, asking if anyone is at home, assuming, as are the others, that the hippies are inside the tepee, whose icy shell is intact. There is no response from the first loud query or from the second; with each, only more frantic barking.

The two dogs are straining at the ends of their chains and pawing up a foul stew of mud and feces, barking furiously, eagerly. They have come out from the cover of a spruce limb lean-to where a goat stands tied, bleating, its nose quivering. Gus shouts at the dogs to shut them up, but to no avail, so Skippy approaches the louder of the two, the brindled mongrel with pointed ears and bared teeth. Skippy talks to him softly, approaching with the back of his hand proffered. When the dog lunges at him, Skippy backs away to stand at the black, frost-covered fire pit and explore the scene from there. Junior threatens the dogs with his stick, and the mongrel skulks backward, but the younger dog, not much more than a puppy, his black fur matted with mud and burrs, a bald spot over his ear where a wound is healing, keeps yapping, his tail wagging, one paw in his muddy empty bowl. Junior raises his stick again, but Gus holds up his hand.

"Cut it out, " he says. "The poor goddamn things are hungry, is all; probably thirsty too."

"We ought to feed them," David says.

"How do we know they're not coming back on the late boat?" Gus asks. "Feed them what?"

Skippy approaches the low, rectangular sailcloth shelter next to the lean-to. He slaps the front panel with the back of his hand to knock the ice off and tucks his head in the flap, then disappears inside.

"We ought to look inside the tepee in case there's something wrong," says Gus, and tries again, not as loud this time, but clear. "Anybody home?"

A pinkish rainbow is painted over the front flap of the wide tepee; around its skirt is a pattern of orange fishes in a blue stream, floating nose to tail; at waist level and higher are huge, childlike drawings of pink flowers and moons and radiant suns–symbols of the Tao, of peace–and large, solitary letters in what David thinks might be Sanskrit.

"Rice." The sailcloth muffles Skippy's voice. "It's brown. There's a whole feed sack of it."

"Will a goat eat rice?" Junior wonders.

"A goat, he'll eat tin cans," Gus explains.

"No he won't." Junior is leaning on his stick; he can't stand ignorance. "He eats the paste on the label, you fool."

"He'll eat anything." Gus agrees.

"Me and Skippy will get a fire going and see if we can find a kettle of some kind," Junior says. "Why don't you and David find some buckets and fetch water to boil. There's that bog that Wayne's Creek flows out of not too far from here."

Junior points through the trees to the south. "You can't miss it if you stay on flat ground."

"What, and not look inside first? Jesus. Suppose they're in there and something's wrong," Gus says. "Suppose they're just not answering and waiting for us to leave them alone? Suppose . . ."

"Okay, okay," says Junior. "Go on ahead, then, and open that flap."

"Let me see that stick."

Junior throws the stick upright as he would throw a gaff from boat to boat. Gus catches it and stands looking at the tepee for a long moment.

To the right of the entrance flap is a fading yellow peace symbol the size of Achilles' shield. Gus strikes it with the stick, once, hard, and steps back to watch the avalanche of ice that falls in a sharp instant down the sides of the tepee. He steps forward, conscious that all eyes are on him, and gingerly lifts the flap, secures it, and leans forward to peer inside. As his head disappears, the others edge closer to the entrance to see. Gus is silent, his backside motionless; finally he says "Fooh!" and backs out.

When Junior and David look inside, they see empty sleeping bags and clothes, large, soiled, gaily decorated pillows all strewn over a deep flooring of spruce boughs and straw.

"It's a nest," says Junior with some disgust.

"Who the hell would want to live like that?"

"I wouldn't mind being him," says David. "I could stand it."

Skippy does not look inside the tepee, nor is he listening to the others, but seems far more interested in the distance as he plucks twigs from nearby trees for kindling.

"Anyway, it's only temporary. They're going to build a house," says David. "It's like the first settlers who came down here—when was it?—in the 1790s. Your ancestors must have started out just like—"

"Watch who you compare to who," Junior snaps, and turns his back on David.

While David hunts up two well buckets, Gus consoles the dogs and goat, explaining that food and water are on the way, but to settle down while they wait, as it'll be a few minutes.

The trees are dripping big accumulated drops of melting ice onto their caps and down their necks as Gus and David, each carrying a bucket, walk into the woods toward the bog, both hoping to find a path through the slippery tangle of puckerbrush and protruding granite edges. They have not gone twenty feet into the woods from the clearing when Gus stops suddenly and takes a step backward, away from something on the icy ground in front of him.

"Jesus," he whispers, and steps around, pointing for David.

It is a smooth brown coil of human feces under ice, a little wad of tissue on the side. David shakes his head and steps around it, thinking, as is Gus, that he, or she, could have at least covered it with leaves.

In a swath of strewn and broken granite made even more perilous to negotiate by the ice, Gus makes a noise and steps aside again, pointing as he had a minute before at another heap of human dung and tissue.

"It's no goddamn wonder it stank downwind this summer," he said. "You'd think they would have dug a hole by now. This stuff is fresh."

"That one over there isn't." David points to their right where five feet away there is another iced-over pile.

"What the hell?" Gus wants to know. "What kind of people are they? Why do they have to spread their shit all over the forest?" Gus's voice takes on an adenoidal tone like a teenaged boy's when he is this perplexed and angry. "Junior tells Myrtle about this and she's going to go henshit. Then you'll get your torches and cudgels for sure."

"Watch out, for Christ's sake," says David. "There's another one."

Surprised, Gus hops off to the side like a kitchen maid away from a mouse, his arms lifted, whacking himself with the bucket. His face is a mixture of abject disgust and bafflement, and David almost bursts out in laughter but keeps it in check.

"Who are they? Why do they live like this?" Gus cannot understand; one or two piles perhaps, but a profusion of them, a carpet?

"I know what they'd tell you if they were here," David says. "They'd say that it is natural, that the shit and the paper, too, are biodegradable, that it's even good fertilizer for the forest."

"Oh for God's sake."

"They want to commune with nature."

"Commune?"

"Be at one with nature, with as little between them and the natural world as possible. They want everything in their lives to be natural, uncorrupted by civilization and material wealth and luxuries. That's why they're down here on this island." David is talking to Gus's back as he follows him through a spruce thicket.

"How do you know all this?" Gus is on the lookout, sweeping the ground ahead with his eyes–sweeping a field in which the land mines are visible.

"Because hippies are everywhere, and because they all say the same thing," David says. "Some believe it; others are just saying it because they want to be accepted, to be cool. There are different degrees of seriousness: on one extreme there're the back-to-the-land people, the Nearing followers, like the McGregors; on the other there's this kind, and the ones who think of themselves as revolutionaries."

"The McGregors are clean and married, and they work and they don't take drugs and–"

"Right," says David. "That the bog he was talking about? Watch out on your left."

"Yes, this is it." Gus steps around another pile. "It's where they found old Leon froze to death years ago, or so they say. There's a deep spot right there."

"I guess it doesn't matter how clean the water is," David observes.

Gus stands still, facing David, bucket at his side.

"I'll tell you what worries me, what scares all of us, and you just said it. These people are everywhere, more and more of them, and for reasons I guess

I understand, though I don't think Junior does, they are attracted to this island. And these ones here are going to bring more of their kind down here until we are overrun by them, until our ways and our island are wiped out, until a guy like me who worked six years to save up for a pot hauler so's he wouldn't have to haul traps by hand anymore is replaced by a guy who lays around drinking and taking dope and screwing and collecting welfare from honest hardworking people. It'll be the end of us, of our ways, you watch. Not only that, but they are goddamn communists to boot and would see our whole government and country destroyed. I can't stand the thought of it, David. I can't stand it."

And you believe your only son who joined the military to live up to your stories of fighting the Battle of the Atlantic here on the island got himself wasted, and his sacrifice, if that is what it was, is a subject of scorn for these people who think him a pitiful victim of capitalism.

David kneels on a cushion of moss and tips his bucket to watch it fill slowly with ice-clear, iron-black bog water. When his bucket is nearly full he hands it to Gus, who gives him his empty one in exchange, watching intently as the second bucket slowly fills.

"I just wish to hell they would go away," Gus says, more to the familiar forest than to David. "That's all I want."

✳ ✳ ✳

All of his young life, during the summers, at least, David heard about the sledding parties in winter on the island, especially from John. When they were little, John made him jealous with accounts of zooming down Town Hill faster than any car, tumbling off to roll into the snowbank by the alders, sanding the runners of his Flexible Flyer for real speed, and of cups running over with plump marshmallows and hot chocolate. Even when they were cynical teenagers, John talked fondly about sledding: running other sledders off the road, heating big flat stones by the fire to make warm seats for the girls, watching caps blow clear off frozen beer bottles, and sledding prone with Clara lying on top of him, sneaking in a little squeeze when they rolled off.

The thermometer has been at or below zero for more than two weeks, and the sea has been a flat calm for almost as long. Though still open enough in the channel for the mail boat to pass through, the thorofare is nearly frozen over. In the coves and on the leeward side of the island, the shoreline wears a skirt of heavy salt ice, reaching out in some places thirty or more feet from land. The rare stretch of very cold weather has let the several snowfalls since Christmas settle, pack down, and stay dry. Last night the island was dusted with five inches of light powder, and no one plowed or salted the road during the day, so tonight the Town Hill and the road through town are packed perfect for sledding, and though there is no moon at all, the stars provide enough light for the dozen or more old and young who have turned out with sleds to race on the hill.

Gus is parked in the Willys at the top of the hill next to the lonely mountain ash on the crest, facing the town below and the black surface of the mouth of the bay in the distance. He has chocked all four wheels. With the motor running and the heater soft on his shoes and socks, he is listening to Lynn Anderson, who never promised him a rose garden, on the country music station in Brewer and watching the sledding. Beyond the bottom of the hill, he can see the fire in the steelyard and silhouettes moving around it; Fuddy, he sees, has parked Fat Albert inside the wide yellow circle of firelight by the swings. Gus watches Skippy and Junior's little grandson Cecil crest the hill in front of the Willys pulling a Flexible Flyer. Gus thinks it's funny that he almost never notices how pigeon-toed Skippy is, even though he sees him nearly every day. Skippy turns the sled around, sits behind Cecil, stretches his legs around him to work the steering handle with his feet, and pushes them off with a whoop.

From the hilltop, Gus can see only Skippy's silhouette as he and Cecil careen down the hill, lean into the wide turn, waving to the pairs of climbing sledders as they pass, and gradually disappear near the steelyard where Fuddy announces another successful run for Skippy by flashing Fat Albert's headlights and honking three times. When Betty and Mabel Haskell and Christine McGregor have arranged themselves sitting up on the Haskells' extra-large sled, Gus toots his horn to send them off. They squeal with delight as they begin the descent, then squeal even louder when Betty fails to steer them wide enough in the bend, and they sail off into the alders in a flurry of white powder and kicking legs. The man on the 7:30 news reports that a federal grand jury has indicted the Berrigan brothers and five others, including a nun and two other priests, for plotting to kidnap Secretary of State Henry Kissinger. Gus thinks that he is almost glad that John didn't live to see Christian leaders conspiring to overthrow the U.S. government, and he hopes ardently that Betty is wrong when she says that John can see what's going on down here from where he is now.

The vague bundled female forms that reach the top of the hill next are again, to Gus's surprise, Betty and Christine, who didn't make it all the way down, followed this time by David and Nancy Cooper pulling another Flexible Flyer. Gus he allows himself a sly smile as he watches David settle carefully onto the sled behind Nancy, knowing full well that David knows he is watching and knows that he is going to catch a raft of shit from Gus later for bundling up with Nancy Cooper while her husband is away on the mainland, not that she seems to mind too much.

When the sleds are aligned abreast on the edge of the hill in front of Gus, they push off at Betty's shout of *Go!* with whoops and yells. Christine and Nancy, who are riding forward on their sleds, stretch their arms to hold hands for the steepest part of the run, but soon are parted as Betty and Christine's sled pulls slowly ahead. Betty, the driver, has been making this run all her life and knows to steer to the left side of the road as they go into the wide turn in front of Charlie Bowen's, a maneuver that will increase her speed as she reaches the last hundred feet of the descent. Gus smiles to see her do so and thinks that he taught her that steering maneuver years ago, back before WWII, before they both left the island. Then he remembers that it was she who taught him the trick and smiles to think that she's so clever, and that she ended up being his wife who ever would of guessed it?

Nancy and David, who cannot even claim a close second to Betty and Christine in the race down the hill, manage to beat them to the congregation at the fire, where they reach over the little ones in snowsuits to warm their hands. The fire is a pyramid of blazing stove-length sticks of spruce that snap and throw sparks that fly upward to disappear in the rising smoke. It has been built next to the low, wide schoolhouse boulder—a favorite place for picnic lunches in fair weather—which has been swept clean of snow tonight to serve as a perch for the Lodge twins, who sit with steaming thermos cups in their laps, plucking soggy marshmallows with their fingers. On the far side of the fire, a group of adults and teenagers, bundled nearly beyond recognition, mills about the bed of Fuddy's truck, where Bernadine's portable radio plays country tunes and a half-dozen thermoses are gathered around a heap of frozen chocolate cookies. While Nancy and Mabel pour themselves cups of hot chocolate, David accepts with pleasure a cup of honey sweetened chamomile tea from Christine.

In Fat Albert's cab, Fuddy sits swaddled to the waist in an old army sleeping bag, sipping on something. He gets David's attention with a waving motion, and beckons him to join him in the cab. David declines the offer to sit inside with a shake of his head, but is happy to lean on Fat Albert's hood, which is plenty warm. Fuddy nods at David's cup and pulls a bottle of whiskey out from inside his sleeping bag, offering it with a tilt of the neck toward David's tea.

"It's Green River," he explains as he pours. "I grew up on this shit. Basil Bowen fed me it when I was still in knickers. It's just as bad now as it ever was, but you kill it with something and it'll go down. It's cheap and it works."

David thanks him and takes a drink, gagging once and dribbling a little firewater off his chin and into his scarf.

"Jesus," he declares.

"Told you," Fuddy says. "Here, let me top you off again."

"I don't know," David says, then shrugs his shoulders, thinking why not, and holds out his cup.

The cup is almost knocked out of his hand by little Cecil, who bumps into his hip as he runs by, mittens dangling from his wrists, pursued, not too heartily, by Skippy who is crying in his perfect loon imitation and laughing happily between cries.

Betty, Christine, and Nancy are standing with their backs to the fire, their hands cupped around hot drinks, enjoying the play of the firelight on the schoolhouse windows and the babble of voices all around them. Betty notices that the long tassel on Christine's hat is dangling too close to the fire and flips it over Christine's shoulder.

"I like your hat," Betty says. "It's some pretty; that pattern is a cheerful one isn't it? Pretty greens."

"It sure looks warm," Nancy says.

"Meadow knitted it for me," Christine says. "I should say Meadow Dawn, I guess; it matters to her that you use her full name."

"I wonder what her real name is."

"Eliot asked her, and she said Meadow Dawn is her real name. Watch out, a spark landed on your shoulder."

"You said she was having problems with stomach cramps, bad ones, before they left," Betty says. "I wonder if she's over them. Have you heard from them? Where are they? In Deer Isle?"

"No, I haven't heard from them. They've been gone two weeks, maybe more, to a commune up on the Burnt Cove road outside Stonington, a commune in a house, I guess. I'm feeding Gandalf, their goat. We gave Meadow Dawn raspberry tea for her cramps; I hope it helped."

"Do you think they'll come back when it warms up?"

"Oh yes," says Christine. "Certainly. They want to get started on clearing the land and building a cabin. I'll bet they're back well before spring comes."

David sets his cup, which now holds more whiskey than tea, on the truck bed and walks away from the firelight, past the schoolhouse, toward the water, following a path in the snow that several have used before him. On Bernadine's radio a man is singing about how proud he is to be an Okie from Muskogee, hinting at his hatred for hippies and antiwar types in general. As he walks away, David thinks that he is glad to be out here on the island, as far as one can get from the cultural upheavals and the venomous, simplistic, uninformed declarations by pundits on both sides. He wonders if the name-calling and blaming in the media, in the streets, on the platforms will ever end. Rather than follow the path into the alders, where others have stopped, he walks farther on, past Payson's boat, *Lucinda*, resting in her cradle, and down to the shore where the silence is complete except for the occasional low groan and crunch of the ice as the tide recedes and the ice settles onto boulders beneath and breaks apart. David wonders if it is as quiet in the camp at Ba Xaoi as it is here, and if there are as many stars in the clean sky above Neang's mountain as there are above this frozen landscape. He hopes she is safe in the village now that the Vietnamese have taken over the camp from the Americans, now that the North Vietnamese have begun to come across the border, now that the Khmer men have fled into hiding in the mountains, choosing to starve in exile rather than be murdered by Vietnamese on either side. Fat Albert's horn sounds another successful run by Skippy and cuts short another journey into sorrow and remorse for David.

Zipping up as he rounds the corner of the schoolhouse, David sees that it was not another downhill run that Fuddy was honking about, but something on the north side of the town garage across the road. Though some of the little ones are still sitting on the boulder by the fire with their parents, most of those who were gathered there are walking across the road toward Fat Albert, whose headlights illuminate a blizzard that is confined to the front of the truck. The heavy snow falling on Fat Albert beneath a clear sky makes David think of Joe Btfsplk–who had a perpetual cloud over his head–in the Li'l Abner cartoons.

"Where are they going?" David asks the twins.

"The lights," says one, her voice as squeaky as the snow.

"What?" He sees now that someone is on the roof of the town garage with a broom, sweeping snow into Fat Albert's headlights and onto the cab.

"It's the lights," says the other twin, who points, her mitten dangling, to the empty, black northern sky. "You can't see them from here. You got to get on the roof, and we're not allowed."

As David leaves the shrinking circle of firelight, he can see that a little wooden ladder stands in the bed of the truck, leaning against the garage gutter. Skippy is the sweeper; little Cecil sits on the peak of the roof watching him, calling out something unintelligible. A loon cries, and Cecil giggles. Bernadine and Fuddy are passing a heavy plank to Christine and Nancy, who are standing in the bed of the truck; they lean the plank against the garage and wait for Bernadine and Fuddy to bring a second one out the side door of the garage. The women are chattering gaily among themselves.

Christine sees David approaching and calls to him to come and lend a hand. Nancy, he sees, is climbing the ladder with one hand, the other wrapped around a bundle of blankets. David climbs onto the truck bed next to Fuddy, who is helping Bernadine aboard with a proffered hand. They slide one plank up to Skippy and Nancy who lay it across two roof jacks near the peak, onto which Cecil settles.

"How are they?" Bernadine asks.

"Green and blue and wavy as hell," Nancy says from above. "Wavy as hell and unbelievably cool."

"It's far fustin' out!" Skippy cries.

Bernadine ascends behind the second plank, a thermos in hand. When she gets on the roof, she turns around, her face lighted by Fat Albert from below, and says "Oh my! I never."

"She says that every time she sees them," Fuddy remarks. "She never."

"Perhaps because they are different every time, Mister Smarty Pants," says Bernadine, as Fuddy gains the roof. They lay the second plank over two more of the triangular roof jacks, forming a bleacher row near the top of the garage roof, a secure scaffolding under the black sky. When he reaches the top of the ladder, David looks over his shoulder to see the rippling edge of a ribbon of greenish light.

"Last one up shuts off the lights and truck." Fuddy knows damn well that David is the last one but doesn't want to be ordering him around by name. "And fetch what's left of that jug in the glove box, why don't you?"

David does. When he reaches the long plank row, the others are seated in line, a bundled audience. Fuddy pats the plank next to him for David to sit; David sets the bottle in Fuddy's lap and sits down to watch. At Fuddy's left on the end of the plank, Skippy is leaning over and down toward Cecil, and the two are rapt in an excited whispering commentary entirely their own, pointing at the waving lights and tittering. Tonight's show is a shimmering ribbon of ocean blue and soft green that seems to shed its lower layers in a fall of veiled light. Fuddy flatfoots about half the remaining Green River and hands the jug to David, who holds it in his lap while he gawks at the northern lights.

"Wow!" Christine, who sits at David's right in the center of the row, points at the lights. "Look! Pink!"

"It makes a fireworks show look puny, doesn't it?" Nancy, like the others, does not take her eyes from the northern sky; she is not talking to anyone in particular but into the night to all.

"It's too bad Eliot didn't come," says Christine, who does not mean it. "Too bad Simon isn't here either, I guess."

"Oh, he's happy where he is," says Nancy. "Look how quick that disappeared. Simon's with his pals—Scooter, Greek, Collard—his veteran buddies, at the A-Frame or Mad Mama's telling stories and dreaming out loud. If he was here he'd be complaining about his toes freezing." *If he hadn't already fallen off the roof and passed out in the snow.*

"Still," says Bernadine, "I bet you wish he was here."

"I do. Sure."

Bernadine notices that David looks across Christine at Nancy, who turns toward him for a long second.

"What did Simon call the lights last year, that last time we saw them?" Bernadine asks, as if she did not know.

"Roaring boring Alice," says Nancy and laughs.

"Betty will be sorry that they left early and she missed this. Oh my, look at that thin part there. I've never. She so loves to watch them."

"And all along I thought these roof jacks were just an unfinished shingling job," David says.

"Well, it was unfinished for a while, which is why Myrtle thought of this," Fuddy explains and accepts the jug from David.

"Look, that's a satellite. See, it's moving."

David remembers watching a satellite cross the sky while he was lying on the roof of the communications bunker in the compound. Chau Sinh, who in six months had yet to come to terms with the image of men on the moon, believed a pilot was driving the satellite. At the pagoda, sometimes in the dark he and Neang saw falling stars, whole showers of them, but never anything like this.

When Bernadine turns toward the sound of Fuddy's snoring, she sees that he has settled back for a roof nap, his head resting on the peak, the jug in his arms. She also sees David and Nancy exchange a smile behind Christine's back.

Bernadine thinks that she would like to get to know Nancy better; despite their difference in age–Bernadine is fifteen years older–they are a lot alike. Nancy is quiet most of the time, not because she is afraid of people or because she doesn't have something to say, but because she thinks that if she isn't careful she will say something foolish, something that might hurt someone else. And when her husband, Norman, was alive, Bernadine was always the meek one when she was with him, especially outside their house. Leah had Nancy and Simon to supper when they first came onto the island, and she said it isn't so much that Nancy is afraid of him, it's that she's afraid of what he will say or do; like Norman, he can't sit still, and you never know when he is going to erupt. Maggie called Norman Vesuvius. Bernadine and Nancy are long and thin; Norman and Simon are shaped like bulldogs.

"Do they go on all night?" David asks anyone.

"They say they do," Christine says. "Eliot has watched them all night, but I haven't yet. If he were here, he could explain them, what causes them exactly. He has the vocabulary."

"I'll bet," says David.

"I've got to go," Nancy says. "My toes are frozen."

Skippy rouses Fuddy, and with an arm holding Cecil in his lap, slides down to the ladder on his bottom.

Bernadine says she could watch all night if it wasn't so cold. She watches as Nancy stands up and wishes them all a good night.

"Have you ever seen anything so beautiful?" she asks the bench.

"Not me," says David.

Bernadine cannot see the color of Nancy's face in the dark, but she knows that the younger woman's cheeks are red and she thinks the shy smile that she gives David is not so darn meek, at all. Bernadine thinks that she will have to remember to ask Maggie what she sees between these two.

SEVEN

That McGregor, he's a cheerless bastard.
He ought to take a drink now and then.
                                    —Simon Cooper

In the only shaded corner of the cove, where the meadow and the stone wall running down from Ava's house meet the water, the bank drops eight feet from the meadow to the cove's only level shoreline. The exposed bank and a tumble of boulders as big as outhouses form a protected nook that the tide does not reach. Here Gus cradles the Betty B. for the winter. A rare storm surge might rise to three or four feet beneath her in the foul-weather months, but her cradle is well secured with heavy lines to the boulders and the trunks of birches that tend downward from the top of the bank. In winter the Betty B. is covered with taut canvas; in spring Gus opens her up to the air and sun to dry her for painting. This year there has been an unusual run of warm and clear weather, and as a result Gus has her painted and ready to launch by the day after Easter.

David is standing beneath the Betty B.'s stern waiting for Gus to appear at the top of the embankment with the peeled log rollers and God knows what else he has gone to fetch. While he waits, David uses a piece of driftwood for a trowel to dig in the layers of bleached clamshells that make up the top half of the embankment; he dislodges one handful at a time-looking for arrow- or spear- heads left in the midden centuries ago by the Passamaquoddy Indians who came to the island to dig and smoke a winter's supply of clams. John once found a spearhead here, and Gus, everyone knows, has the best arrowhead collection on the island thanks to this midden.

"Watch yourself." Gus slides one log over the edge, and when he sees that David has stepped aside, lets it fall onto the tidal flat. When the log tips back and leans against the bank, Gus lets go a second one.

"Why don't you hand up the ladder; then you can let loose the lines from the cradle. Here's Junior's truck."

Junior eases his Ford pickup over the edge of the cove road and onto the meadow. He does not need Gus to tell him where to position the truck; he has done this at least twenty times and watched it being done twenty more. He backs the truck down to the edge of the bank, coming so close that the vibrations shake loose a thin shower of shells from the exposed midden.

Gus is surprised to see that Simon is with Junior this morning. He had thought he was still off-island, and he hasn't seen him in over a month. Junior shuts down his truck, and Simon climbs out of the cab to chock the wheels. He is carrying an open half-gallon carton of chocolate milk that he sets on the tailgate while he secures the wheels. He is pale and has put on some weight, at least in the face. Gus thinks the man looks like hell warmed over, all bleary-eyed, dark circles, and splotches of beard.

"You're going to want boots," he says to Simon. "You look like hell."

"That don't come close." Simon manages a weak smile. He looks over the edge of the bank and salutes David. "Actually, it could be worse. I'm still half drunk. It was one hell of a going-away party; I don't even know how I got back to Stonington let alone on the mail boat."

"He doesn't dare go home like this," Junior says. He lights a cigarette and shakes his head in amused resignation. He leans back against the truck, one hand resting on the brim of his belly inside a suspender strap.

"You're not going to be much use to us, I don't suppose," Gus says.

"The hell. I can push and heave as well as anybody, probably better." Simon is wearing a University of Maine sweatshirt with the sleeves trimmed short and a V-shaped cut at the neck. He squares his shoulders and folds his massive arms over his chest. "I'm good for anything that doesn't take too much thinking."

"Well then, you've come to the right place," Gus says. He picks up a block and tackle and slings a coil of rope over his shoulder. "Betty fixed a whole basket full of ham sandwiches for us here. I'll get the tackle in place."

On the path to the wharf and fish shacks, Gus takes hold of the trunk of a small shadbush, in full pink bloom, and eases himself down the bank to scrabble over the rocks and secure the big wooden pulley to the foot of one of the wharf pilings. High above him two circling ospreys chirp to one another in a slow, sweet mating dance.

"The tide's just begun to turn," Junior says to anyone. "We got plenty of time."

Simon is drinking chocolate milk from the spout, his head tilted back and eyes closed; in his left hand he holds a cigarette. To Junior, Simon is something of a marvel; nothing seems to faze him, in any way. Nothing.

"Why don't you pay out the long line," Junior tells Simon, "while David helps me secure the front line on the crib. Then we're going to need you to help get the first rollers in place."

It is an eleven-foot tide. When it is full, if things go right, they will have the *Betty B.* in her cradle far enough into the water and the cradle weighted well enough with stones that the boat will float free and can be taken out to her mooring. David has never seen a spring launch; he is careful to pay attention and waits to be told what to do. Junior hands him one end of the hawser. He expects David to watch him to see how to tie it, and David does, tying a clove hitch and two half hitches on his side of the foot of the cradle. Simon, muttering to himself cheerfully, uncoils the long line along the shore to the pulley, waits while Gus takes it through, then starts back to the truck, uncoiling as he goes. By the time he has reached the truck, Simon's sweatshirt is soaked through, and sweat drips off the end of his nose. He sits on the tailgate and lights a Salem.

"I could squeeze out this shirt and get you drunk with one sip of this sweat coming off of me," Simon tells Junior.

"Thanks," Junior says. "I'll pass on that one. Rather than make me sick, why don't you hand down the rest of the rollers to David there, the planks too. I'll tie this off and bring down the lard. It'll take all four of us to prize the skids free."

Behind Junior and beyond his truck, Maggie is walking down the rutted road from Old Cove with a spray of loosestrife in her arms. She stops to watch for a moment, shuts her eyes, listening, then walks on toward her house.

"You want to be sick, you ought to take a close look and a whiff of those three pieces of hippie shit that came down on the morning boat. You would of mistaken me for Beaver Cleaver next to them," Simon says, loud enough for all to hear.

Junior hands a small metal bucket of lard down to David and points to the log roller that Gus has positioned in front of the cradle's skids.

"I thought they came back last week," says David.

"Not our hippies, for Christ's sake, new ones that came down to visit ours. All male types—beards and long hair and earrings and Indian clothes. One has his beard braided and tied off on the ends with little red ribbons like a fucking pirate captain. I think I've seen them before up around Deer Isle, or maybe they're some of the ones from Blue Hill they call the Dog Kids."

"Jesus wept." Gus lays a log parallel to one of the skids to use as a fulcrum and kicks it spitefully.

Simon feels a nibble of fear and anger from the older men. To set the hook, he adds, "They begged a ride off of McGregor over here to the east side. Christ, they had enough gear with them to stay for weeks. Months. Permanent."

Junior stands in stunned silence, the log for the companion fulcrum clutched to his chest as though someone were reaching for it to take it away. Gus freezes too, one hand outstretched for the lard bucket that David carries toward him.

"An invasion," Junior finally says. "They're going to take over."

David laughs, or begins to, until he sees Gus's face, his blue eyes wide and wild like a man surprised in his first ambush with nowhere to run. Gus looks up at the freshly painted white hull of his boat, then shakes his head once, hard, as though to clear it.

"I tell you the whole world has gone nuts," he says. Alarm has shifted to anger in his voice. "Grown people going around with hair down to their ass and dressed up like goddamn Indians; people with enough money to buy ninety acres of land and a big house and travel to Europe to study gardens are trying to be poor; people burning their draft cards and their bras, too, in public. Why would anyone burn her underwear on TV? Because they're nuts, that's why; brains destroyed by drugs and communist propaganda."

Simon reaches for his chocolate milk, feeling a little better with each of Gus's execrations. David lights a cigarette, knowing that this familiar tirade still has life left in it.

"And we get most of them out here. Of course we do." Gus's tone has changed color, from fire to dull gray. "This island, this rock, used to be a place with a few healthy communities, poor maybe, but happy enough most of the time to be together out here, not bothered by people and the government from the mainland. And now what's it become? A goddamn loser magnet, is what."

Junior, who has been adrift in Gus's skiff of sorrow, could not agree more. "God, I know it, dear. What would your grandfather Amos say could he see this island today?"

"Christ, if he had the choice he'd rather have the goddamn Germans invade and take over the island. At least they were clean. They believed in God. They ate meat." *And they would have had respect for those that fell on the field of battle. They wouldn't of said they died for nothing, wouldn't of mocked them and sneered at them on the radio and in their newspapers.*

Junior sets his log in place and steps forward to reach for the lard bucket that Gus has been holding in both hands. "Here, let me have that. You're so worked up, you'll melt that lard. You ought to go sit with Myrtle; between the two of you, you could cook up a way to get rid of these hippies once and for all, and you could get Simon here to do it for you."

Gus pulls the bucket away from Junior's reach and sets it down by the peeled log roller.

"The hell," he says.

He dons a dirty pair of gloves, fills each hand with a dollop of lard, and spreads it on the log, saying, as he has every year for thirty years, his voice becalmed now, that if you can't grease the skids, at least you can grease the rollers.

When Gus is done, and the lard and gloves are set aside, he and Junior, on opposite sides of the cradle, hold the fulcrum logs in place with a foot and worry the thick levers under the front skids. Simon leans on Junior's lever with him, and Gus says to David, "Maybe you could get behind me on this one." Which David quickly does.

"On three, but easy, slow; watch we don't tip it too much to one side and throw it over," says Gus. He counts slowly to three, when all four heave at the same time to raise the front of the skids enough for Gus to kick the greased roller into place beneath them.

"There." Junior removes his lever. "I hope it goes that easy with my boat tomorrow."

"Everything's going to go good," says Simon. "It's going to be a good season for all of us—two guys on each boat, and me with my forty traps and my own colors."

Gus watches the tide, which has lapped ahead only slightly, pushed by a freshening southwest breeze. On the far side of the cove, a gull carries a small green crab aloft in his beak, drops it onto the ledge, then lands beside it to enjoy a late breakfast.

"Those Stonington boys aren't going to like forty more traps on the east side here, especially ones with new colors. They might tie you off," Gus tells Simon.

"They do, and they'll fucking-A-well regret it." Simon squares his shoulders and balls up his fists.

"Let's not get worried. It comes to it, we'll face them down like we always have," says Junior.

"Face them down? Face them down my ass. What, like Davey Crockett grinning down a 'bar'? I'll tell you . . ."

"Right now, rather than tell us something, maybe you could get yourself set to help us get this thing into the water," Gus says. "David, if you would, you stay on the starboard side, Simon you on the port. Once Junior gets her going, you can move the rollers under her. I'll tend to the pulley. You need to watch out, David; if she begins to list to your side, you'll want to get a pole against her hull pretty quick. Then get the hell out of the way."

"Don't you worry, Captain. I'll be mindful."

When Gus gets to the pulley, he settles on a boulder and watches as Junior checks the line attached to the rear of his truck, lights a cigarette, signals to Gus that he is ready, and climbs into the cab.

Gus holds a hand up, palm toward Junior, and signals to him with a pushing motion to move ahead slowly, watching the lines anxiously as they go taut in the pulley and on the cradle. Gus continues to push Junior ahead slowly as he pulls the cradle toward the tide's edge. Simon has a second roller ready as the skids slip slowly over the first, and he slides it into place just as the boat and cradle settle onto it with a shudder. David looks up at fifteen tons of boat timber and engine as it lists for a second, then settles upright, thinking that he will mostly likely scamper out of its way rather than try to wedge a pole against the hull and risk having it slip and flatten him like a frog in the road.

Simon wipes his face with his sweatshirt and gets set with the next roller. He is wearing worn jungle boots, not rubber boots like the others, and he is up to his shins in the cold tide.

"Easy," Gus says. "Easy." His hand is testing the taut line. "Easy."

"All right, all right," says Simon.

Junior's truck coughs, then backfires, loud. David, who is watching the white hull above him, jumps at the noise, impulsively ducks, only to look back up sheepishly.

"Pussy," says Simon grinning.

"Fuck you, man."

"Green Beret, my ass." Simon is feeling better, enlivened by the cold water and the loss of so much ninety-proof perspiration.

"Scooter–the guy who sold you your truck–he asked about you, when you're coming back. I wish you could of seen him the other day at Davey Jones's. Can you hear this, Cappy?" Simon asks Gus.

Gus shakes his head no, lying. David slides another roll under the skids and steps back to light a cigarette and watch the progress.

"There was three of us and this candy-ass Coast Guard kid, some clerk. Scooter, all three hundred twenty-two pounds of him naked inside his coveralls, half in the bag at ten in the morning, doing shots and beers, tells this poor kid how much he loves his Louise. Oh, does he ever. He's almost in tears."

"You ready with one more?" Gus calls. "Another few feet and she should be in deep enough."

Simon is holding the log, awaiting Gus's signal. "That poor Coast Guard guy, he can't take his eyes off of Scooter's tattoo–the skull and crossbones with 'Fuck God' under it, remember? Only a marine. You gotta love him."

Simon looks to Gus, who nods and points for him to put the last roller in, which he does.

"Is this going somewhere?" David wants to know.

"Anyway, he finally convinces the poor bastard that he's got Louise in the car out front. Light me a cigarette would you? And we watch out the window while Scooter takes this guy to his car and opens the trunk and lifts out

Louise, holding her in his arms like he's carrying a bride. Louise, who is a fucking Guernsey calf!"

Up to his knees in the cove, Simon laughs so hard that he nearly chokes on his cigarette. David smiles and shakes his head slowly and looks at Gus who is doing the same.

Gus puts a pinky finger in each side of his mouth and whistles to Junior to stop where he is.

"Let's get this weighted good," he says to the young men.

As the lines go taut, Gus pulls his folded boots up to full height and steps out into the water to help weight down the cradle, thinking that old Junior Chafin has a stern man working for him who has a body like an over-sized dwarf, a mouth like the bottom of the foulest shithouse, a looker for a wife that he ignores, an appetite for alcohol of any kind like nobody's business, and on top of it all, a Jew name. Jesus wept.

With the cradle lines loosened, coiled, and secured on the wharf, the four men find upturned crates and oak traps to perch on while they unwrap fat ham sandwiches and watch the tide lift the waving rockweed and rise toward the keel of the *Betty B.*

Simon, who is sitting at the end of the wharf with David, has finished a second sandwich and asks if David has anything up to the house that they can wash the sandwiches down with.

"There's three beers in the refrigerator if you feel like walking up there," David says. "Help yourself. I'll just have some of that tea."

Simon puts his hands on his knees to push himself to his feet. He watches a gull on the near piling lift his tail feathers to make a deposit and says, "Face them down? What kind of bullshit is that? They cut *me* off and I'll blow them out of the fucking water. No Mexican standoff for me."

The exact words, David thinks as he watches Simon walk away; the exact words that popped into his mind that hot afternoon in—what was the hamlet?—Nam Qui. In that frozen instant, that crystalline, perfectly remembered moment of abject terror, words from some foolish cowboy movie he had seen as a boy popped into his mind when they all stood still staring at their own and one another's imminent slaughter.

There were perhaps a dozen that afternoon: boys and men from Chau Sinh's platoon. They had been patrolling the border, looking for signs of infiltrating North Vietnamese, quizzing Khmer woodcutters for any hint of enemy movement. It had been more than a week since they had seen or heard any sign of enemy activity; that peaceful stretch and the day's long march without contact had lulled them into a sweet complacency. They walked in single file and in chatting pairs, their M16s slung over their shoulders, one pair of young friends holding hands. When bold Socheat, the handsome dark one, caught up with them, having fallen behind to talk to a girl carrying water, he took David by the arm and turned him toward a wood line, pointing to a tall stork standing attentively over a water hole. Like David, who was the other grenadier, Socheat was shirtless, his chest crossed with bandoliers of grenade rounds and hung with amulets.

"*Si bye.* 'For dinner,' " he said. "Your shot, *Trung-si.*"

It was not a good idea to fire off a grenade round so close to the mountain so late in the day. David looked to Chau Sinh for approval, and when Chau Sinh smiled and nodded, shrugging his shoulders, David chambered a round, adjusted his elevation, and popped one off. The shot was perfect–not so close to damage the meat–and the stork crumpled. Socheat laughed and patted David on the back; it was he who taught David the skill of the grenade launcher. They watched from the paddy dike as three of the youngest soldiers raced for the stork.

Reap, who'd won the race, won also the privilege of carrying brother stork. Chom, who'd come in a close second, helped him arrange the huge, bald-faced bird for carrying, its leathery legs slung over Reap's shoulders and tied at the knees across his chest. To keep the stork's head from dragging in the dust or pummeling Reap's heels, Chom tied the head to its feathery torso so that brother stork kept a sightless watch on their rear as they walked toward home in the waning light, observing none of the rules of watchfulness, with the exception of Chau Sinh and Socheat and two others who unlimbered their weapons as they passed empty and desiccated houses on the old path under the northern shoulder of the mountain.

David was adrift in a walking daydream when he blinked to see that the soldiers ahead of him had stopped cold before a shadowed bend in the path and stood as stone still as the statues of the guardian *nagas* at the temple. Frightened by their motionless silence, David and the others came to a halt behind Chau Sinh and Socheat, over whose heads David saw a band of Viet Cong guerrillas, as many as they were and as still, halted, facing them clustered in the road, their weapons at the ready, both sides knowing full well that one round fired, one nervous jerk of hand or arm, would result in immediate suicidal slaughter, a mutual massacre. A Mexican standoff.

All David could hear was the breathing of two dozen men and boys, the breathing, and the rapid thumping of his own blood in his temples. David's knees softened, and every inch of his skin broke out in cold sweat. For a moment he thought that he would be glad if someone pulled his trigger and put an end to the fear. In the dark trees on their flank a night bird cried, and from far away another answered.

Chau Sinh began to turn slowly. The man in the conical hat and black pajamas in the forefront of the Viet Cong did the same in a silent, mirrored motion. Wordless, one after another on each side turned and, with their backs exposed to the remaining guns, walked slowly away. As David turned to his left he thought that he would faint but did not. With his back to what he imagined were six aimed assault rifles, he followed behind the staring empty eyes of brother stork. As he passed the last empty house, he felt the hot release of urine run down his leg and into his boot, and he saw the stork he had murdered smile victoriously.

"*Cadhui.* 'Pussy,' " it said.

✳✳✳

Tuesday evening
April 18, 1971

Ruth Dear,

Just listen to this: Sunday evening, after a long walk in a gentle rain, I went to the bookshelf with the intention of choosing a comfortable, familiar old friend for a read. I chose *Persuasion*; read happily for an hour, and upon closing the book, I thought fondly of how you used to try to "persuade" me to take comfort in Anne's ten-year wait for her man.

Then! Home the next day from the P.O., I opened your Monday letter and read that you, too, had returned to Jane Austen just a day or so before–after, for both of us, so many years. I suppose I shouldn't be surprised at such a coincidence: we have ever been so close, our physical distance notwithstanding.

I sometimes think that I have said all that I have to say, that I have heard all that I need to hear, that I have seen all that I need to see. Then, then spring comes–"this whole experiment of green"–and all my delight in life is reborn. Trillium! Spring beauty! Coltsfoot! Tender green tips of spruce boughs! Forsythia! Cedar waxwings! Skunk cabbage shoots! I think that this is the kindest April that I have known (but I'll bet I say that every year). Wouldn't it be so much simpler (and truer, though you hate to hear me say it) to say "God so loved the world that he resurrected it every year"?

Yesterday afternoon Leah stopped by and we decided on a whim to pay a visit to the McGregors to see their spring garden, which we've heard so much about. We found Christine and Eliot busy in the garden and Nancy Cooper, who had just come from a visit to the tribe on the hill. (Nancy and Christine, it seems, are fast becoming close friends, which we think is wonderful for both of them.) When we arrived, the women greeted us, but Eliot barely recognized our presence, nodding hello with a look that made us feel like intruders before he turned back to his work. One has to admire the man's industry-you can't help it when you see the fruits of his labor-but one can't admire his cold and cheerless demeanor, his soulless approach to his work and to others. While Christine told us all about the garden, and the four of us walked around it making appreciative noises, Eliot turned over the compost pile with a coal shovel. When Nancy asked him a question about his formula for fertilizer, he barely answered her, and Christine had to finish for him. When Christine asked him something, ever so deferentially, he did not even deign to answer her. Leah thinks that they are at odds over something and Christine is getting the worst of it; I think that Eliot is a nasty self-absorbed man, a mean-spirited ideologue.

But the garden! You would love it so. Orderly rows marked with stakes numbered in different colors; bean poles and trellises of woven twigs; raised beds for squashes, all kept weedless and somewhat protected from late frost by blankets of building paper with little holes cut for each planting. I want to go back in the late summer and take some photos for you; with the care they have taken with the soil and composting and fertilizing, it will certainly be a luxuriant sight. They even have separate sections for perennials: asparagus, rhubarb, berries, and herbs.

Christine insisted that we come in for tea, and we were glad that we did as she served us fresh scones heaped with blueberry jam (no butter, mind you–animal product) and honey-sweetened chamomile tea. Nancy was all aglow with plans for a community garden behind the schoolhouse; when Christine volunteered to help, Nancy squeezed her hand and Christine blushed with pleasure. When Leah asked Nancy about the girl Meadow Dawn, whom she's been nursing through some kind of internal ailment, Christine, we thought, became suddenly quite anxious and eagerly changed the subject. She showed us their careful schematics for a pond and greenhouse (stone base walls to absorb the heat!) and their reams of notes on the garden: every plant nuanced, counted, measured, weighed. Leah said

"How thorough!" I thought "How tedious." We three left at the same time, and Christine walked us out to where we'd parked in the meadow. We waved good-bye to Eliot, who rewarded us with a nod of his head. When Leah admired the little waist-high white fence that they had built around the Eatons' headstone and the daffodils planted on their graves, Christine became quite visibly agitated. I joked about the ghost story in which the Eatons rise from their grave and the girl laughed nervously. On the way home I decided that Christine is mercurial; Leah decided that she is bothered by more than one thing.

I've gone on too long; my wrist aches. Oh, I read about a new movie called *Ryan's Daughter* that is filmed most beautifully on the Dingle Peninsula in the west of Ireland. Have you seen it? I'd love to.

Love always.

Maggie

EIGHT

From what I have seen and heard of them and of their husbands, I think both of the girls could use a little tenderness in their lives.
–Maggie Bowen

In Maggie's first year as schoolteacher on the island, Skippy Groth was her only first grader and the youngest of her fourteen students. Of all the children in those early years, not counting her Leah, of course, Skippy was Maggie's favorite, not because she felt sorry for him, though she did, and not because she protected him from the nasty boys who tormented him about his cleft lip and his speech, but because of his sweet and affectionate disposition, and because, though she has never told anyone this, she felt then—and still does—a special, ineffable kinship with him when he withdraws into one of his spells. It is the same empathy that she has felt for David Harper since he came back—when she notices him alone in the meadow or on the path, standing still looking into the trees—though her affinity for Skippy is stronger by decades.

It took Maggie nearly a year of patient listening before she could understand what Skippy was saying as well as his parents and his half brother Fuddy did. It took her longer to learn to predict the commencement of his moods of which he has only two: fetal, afraid and mumbling; or curious, adventurous and entirely silent. Skippy has never been off the island and never will be. When he is frightened and withdrawn, he is safe in the familiar house in Squeaker Cove with Fuddy; when he is adventurous, he has the whole, wide island world where there has been nothing to surprise or frighten him for more than fifty years.

Occasionally, he becomes so adventurous that he drives around in Fat Albert without Fuddy, as he has done today. It is June 21, the summer solstice, the longest day of the year, and Skippy has been out and about since the first glimpse of dawn. He has heard that there is to be a softball game this evening, which he is eager to watch. Somewhere along the way–he does not remember where or when–little Cecil latched on to him and has been with him since. In the late afternoon, Skippy has Fat Albert in second gear and is urging it up the hill toward the ball field on the level high ground beside the church. The southwest breeze is stiff and steady off the water, a little on the chilly side for this time of year; in Fat Albert's doorless cab, Cecil, who is the sole third grader on the island, is wearing only a soiled cotton shirt, and shivers and hugs his little chest with spindly arms. Behind the wheel, on the western side of the cab, Skippy, in coveralls, long johns, and a fouled flannel shirt, sweats in the sun. The lips and teeth of both man and boy are stained a purplish blue, and both strain ahead beyond the alders to see if anyone has showed up for the game; they have seen a Stonington boat tied up at the town landing and expect to see the ballplayers who came down on it already at the field.

The only road access to the ball field and meadow and church beyond is a rutted dirt track that runs from the island road (paved on this side, the west side) past the Coopers' house and the town garage, then through a copse of alders onto the open grassy plateau. In the alders, Skippy downshifts to first gear and inches along, enjoying a vague erotic memory of a moonlit night here watching Betty and her Coast Guardsman make love. Out of the sun and wind, he has stopped sweating, and Cecil has stopped shivering. Instead their heads are thrown back and they are sniffing the air with their eyes half closed like hounds, turning to the left then to the right to savor the sweet smell of grilling meat and barbecue sauce. Skippy points to his left, toward Simon Cooper's backyard, and Cecil nods, yes, that's it, his mouth and eyes watering.

Over a pair of card tables of unequal height, Nancy has spread a plastic red-and-white-checked tablecloth that is secured at the corners with clothespins. In the center of the tables is a large stoneware bowl filled with Simon's famous potato salad, enough potato salad, David thinks, to feed the entire village of Ba Xaoi. Arrayed around the mighty bowl are smaller bowls of fresh greens, lobster salad, pickled pole beans, relishes, and a roundish loaf of homemade white bread. Beneath the tables is a battered aluminum cooler that holds a case of Pabst Blue Ribbon on ice. The savory waft that brought tears to Cecil's eyes as he passed comes from the venison steaks that Simon is turning over on the grill-a fifty-gallon drum cut in half lengthways, propped up on cinder blocks, and topped by a wire shelf scrounged from an abandoned refrigerator. The fire is low, hot flames from birch chunks that drip red coals through ventilation holes to smolder in the charred grass beneath.

Simon turns the steaks and slathers barbecue sauce over them with a paintbrush. He wipes his brow with the back of his wrist and flatfoots half a sweating bottle of beer. To David, who is sitting nearby in the wooden rocking chair carried out of the house, Simon raises his beer in salute: a toast to good food, good meat, and peace on earth, at least on the island. David returns the salute and smiles beatifically, his lengthening black curls aflutter in the breeze. The grilling venison steaks, he thinks, don't smell as good as beef, but by Jesus they smell better than roasting dog or grilled paddy rat.

Nancy opens the back screen door with her bottom and steps out into the yard carrying two more plates, silverware, and a large plastic bottle of Pepsi Cola. She is wearing a green plaid flannel shirt, cutoff Levis, and hiking boots over gray wool socks with red stripes around the tops. Her hair is braided in pigtails tied with green rubber bands that match her shirt.

"What's all that for?" Simon wants to know. His white T-shirt is besmeared with orange swipes of barbecue sauce.

"Skippy and Cecil just drove by, gone in to watch the game. I'm going to go see if they want to eat with us."

"Good idea. We've got enough." Simon waves his saucy brush toward the groaning tables. "Is Fuddy with them? He is, we'll want more beer."

"I only saw the two," Nancy says in passing. "I saw them this afternoon, too, at the store."

As Nancy walks by him toward the alders and the truck beyond, David is careful not to let his gaze linger on her beautiful bottom and thighs, thinking how fine and strong her stride is, how unlike the pattering of Neang's delicate, little footsteps.

"Junior said that Bruce and Melvin Hanson are coming down from Stonington in the *Ellamae* looking to play ball. God only knows what assholes they'll bring with them. Probably they'll really be looking for buoys to cut off on the way down here," Simon tells David for the second time this afternoon.

"Too bad they didn't come for dinner and the game; Junior and Gus, I mean. Betty likes to play."

"Those guys, you know they don't like to come over to the west side when there's going to be strangers here; they don't like to come when there isn't."

David lays his empty beer bottle in the grass beneath the tables with the other dead soldiers, takes a fresh one from the cooler, and returns with an inaudible sigh to his rocker where he surveys the scene before him. He thinks that he could not imagine a better place to be and how grateful he is to be so far removed in every way from St. Elmo College. Here on the high plateau of the high island, in the slanting evening sun and soft sea breeze, he finds himself a part of the tableaux he dreamed of so often, escaped to, on those frightful nights in the sweltering camp and later on the unkind campus. Here he is among men who are all veterans, if not of war, then of hardship and want of luxury. Here the women of all ages are comfortable with traditional gender roles, yet they are independent and unbowed. Here he does not have to pretend to be the ever so sensitive boy/man, or to act and try to look androgynous in order to get laid—not that he hasn't been guilty of that, even now. It is not the real world, but a corny aberration, the collegiates and academics would say; not the real world because here on the island there are no hungry and downtrodden. He lived among the oppressed and starving for two years and does not want any more of it, real or not. Here there is no enemy, no need to be alert and circumspect, no need to guard what he says. Here no one is judging him; here there are no sour, affected intellectuals, no righteous moralists, no radical simplistic diatribes, no blind hatred of the status quo. Here the men are veterans of fear: fear of drowning, fear of humiliation, and fear of losing their income. Here he doesn't have to talk if he chooses not to. Here, this evening, he sits and, tonight, he will sleep on the high ground—the high ground on an island off the coast of Maine.

"Just in time," Simon says.

Nancy emerges from the path through the alders arm in arm with a visibly reluctant Skippy who is helped along by her and towed by little Cecil who pulls at his free hand. Skippy is in coveralls; his thin red hair stands up on the driver's side of his head. Nancy is speaking to him with a voice she would use to talk a frightened puppy out of a corner; his face is turned away from her eyes, which are too close to his ugly mouth for his comfort.

Simon stands beaming, beer in hand, behind the platter piled with slabs of venison that he has set down on the table.

"Skippy's out and around, and with no Fuddy to be seen," he says. "Means he isn't talking, I guess."

"Can we have some ice for our soda, Nancy?" Cecil asks. He is tiny for a ten-year-old and so frail that his arms and legs remind David of Tinkertoy sticks. He stays within reach of Skippy while they survey the table, plates in hand. While Nancy fills plastic tumblers with ice and Pepsi, Cecil spoons a mountainous helping of potato salad onto Skippy's plate; when his plate is full, Skippy watches thoughtfully as Cecil piles the same onto his own plate.

"Here's a nice venison steak." Simon forks a slab and holds it forward. "It's from the doe your grandfather got last month; it's some tender for this time of year—you'll be surprised."

Both guests shake their heads no. Nancy offers them a buttered slice of bread and a helping of lobster salad.

"Me and Skippy don't eat lobbies," Cecil says. He sticks a spoon into Skippy's heap of salad and one into his own and leads the way to the back-door stoop where they sit to address their plates. Skippy eats with his head down to spare Nancy the sight of his chewing; Cecil eats with his head down to prevent spillage.

Simon helps himself to the biggest steak and sits down at the table on a bench facing the house, cutting the meat with a long kitchen knife. Nancy sits next to him, and David pulls his rocker up to the far end of the tables.

"You should eat some meat, you know," Simon says to Cecil. "You got to put some muscles on you; muscles come from meat, not just potatoes." He pronounces potatoes *budaydoes*. It annoys him that Cecil and Skippy won't eat his steaks. Cecil shakes his head slightly in reply. Simon swallows his beer and hurls the bottle out onto the lawn before reaching for another. Nancy looks at him warily.

"It's cooked perfect," she says of her steak.

"It's outstanding," David says. "And so is the lobster salad."

"We should go get Gus and Betty and Junior after we eat; it's such a perfect night for a ball game." Nancy thinks that the hurled bottle was a bad sign, and if Junior or Gus would come, their presence might preclude the bad night for Simon that seemed to be brewing, which would mean a bad night for everyone.

Simon points a skewered chunk of venison at David. "You ought to cut that hair. You're starting to look like a hippie queer." He shoves the meat into his mouth and chewing, smiling, says to Nancy, "Junior says he's starting to look like Shirley Temple."

Nancy laughs. "I like it," she says, and immediately regrets it.

David laughs too. "Junior also says that you're built like a Christly Aroostook County potato farmer." He does not say that Junior also said that Simon's face reminds him of a fresh-dug potato, just rinsed.

Simon laughs uncertainly.

"How the hell would he know what a potato farmer looks like; he's never been that far inland. What do you suppose he means by that? Built how?"

"Like a brick shithouse would be my guess," David says. "It's a compliment."

Simon is not sure; that Junior might be making fun of him disturbs him.

"Pass the relish," he says.

"Pass the relish, what?" Nancy asks.

"Oh 'scuse me, I almost forgot." Simon holds up a limp wrist, and says "Pass the relish, dammit." Which he finds some comical.

✳✳✳

In the soft, incipient shadow of the mountain and the woods behind them, Simon and David sit in the front seat of Simon's Ford in the McGregors' driveway. Both are nursing a beer and smoking. Simon has left the engine idling and in frustration shuts off the radio, saying that east of the mountain you can't get squat for reception. Beyond the McGregor house the sun still shines on York Island and skips across the sea to the horizon. Someone lights a kerosene lamp in the McGregor kitchen and turns the wick down low.

"He won't let her come out," David says.

"If anyone can talk her into it, Nancy can. They been like sisters lately. She's been worried about Christine but won't say why; something about Christine being frightened."

Simon revs the Ford a little, just enough for those in the house to hear. "Junior would of liked to come," he says. "If it wasn't for Myrtle, he would of." Simon tries to shut the ashtray, but it is too full of stained filters to close. "You think Gus and Betty will?"

"I do. Betty's a pisser. Once she gets Gus out of the house, he's happy she did. I'll bet they come," David opens his door and leans over to roll the ash and the last of the tobacco off his cigarette onto the gravel, and fieldstrip the filter.

Watching David, Simon wishes he had the guts to dump his ashtray in McGregor's driveway, then wonders why he thought of such a thing at all. He peers through the windshield at the tiny Eaton grave plot at the edge of the meadow, then turns his headlights onto it, illuminating it with a span of dull yellow. The daffodils in front of the headstone have gone by; their leaves are bent over and tied together, and among them grow bunches of daisies. The white fence and headstone throw long shadows from the headlights.

"Did Gus by any chance ever tell you a story about this grave?"

"He did," David says. "And he made me promise never to tell anybody about it."

"Junior made me promise too. Dead dogs and a couple of fucking crawling ghouls all shredded up. Christ God." Simon switches off the headlights. "Maybe the McGregors know the story, too, and that's why they keep the plot up so nice, kind of like a what do you call it?"

"Shrine."

The kitchen door opens, framing two women in the soft backlight. Nancy follows Christine out the door, and when it closes behind them, they start slowly toward the car talking quietly and earnestly, shoulder to shoulder.

"Here they are." Simon flicks his cigarette in among the trees; its red tip glows in a tumbling arc before it explodes against a limb.

"Let's go play ball."

✳✳✳

The natives are the first to arrive at the ball field—not because they are necessarily more punctual than the summer people, but because they eat their supper at five o'clock while the summer people are sipping cocktails, and they do not linger over wine and cheese after their meal.

It is a little after six, the dishes washed and dried, when Bernadine, Bill, and Kimberly arrive in Bill's new, blue Chevy pickup. Bill, who would have preferred to drift into an after-supper nap in the porch rocker, parks in the lee of the willows on the western edge of the field beyond Fat Albert, drops his tailgate, and perches on it, legs crossed, to watch Bernadine greet arrivals with her glove and softball at the ready. Bill nods at Skippy, who is nodding toward his own nap, kept awake by the bump of his forehead on Fat Albert's steering wheel.

Bruce and Melvin Hanson have left the *Ellamae* tied up at the town landing and have caught a ride up to the ball field with the Coombs brothers. All four men are in their early twenties and single; all four are considered crackerjack young fishermen, and all four are related somehow to one another, though one pair is Hansons from Stonington, the other Coombses from Barter Island.

The early evening breeze is southwesterly and stiff enough to ripple the tall timothy in the far outfield, but it is not stiff enough to dispel the reeking cloud of oily smoke that rolls up from the rear end of Piggy Neville's old, gray Ford as it coughs through the alders, comes to a shuddering halt near home plate, and disgorges three disheveled shouting boys onto the field. Piggy's wife, Lucille, joins Bernadine, while Piggy saunters over to Fat Albert to see Skippy, or rather to see if by chance Fuddy has left a sup of something in the glove box.

Minutes behind, Gus and Betty pull onto the field in the Willys. Gus lets Betty out at home plate to help Bernadine organize things and joins Bill on his tailgate. Bill is a Turner, a west-side island family who moved down to the island from Deer Isle after the Civil War; Gus is a Barter on his father's side, a Barter as in Peletiah Barter, the first white man to set foot on the island in 1790-something, Barter as in Barter Island. They have known each other since they could walk, but since leaving Maggie Bowen's schoolhouse they have been estranged friends because of families and geography, both on shore and at sea; what matters is that they are natives, by Jesus, and that they are the two senior male natives in sight this evening. They exchange mumbled greetings, a few habitual remarks about the scarcity of lobsters, then, like synchronized swimmers, cross their right legs over their left in unison and lay their hands to rest in their laps, to wait for the women to get things going.

Gus observes that someone has taken down the tattered Stars and Stripes that rode out the winter on the spar behind home plate and tacked a new one up, adding that it looks some nice. Bill makes a noise in his sinuses in reply.

The sun breaks from behind a cloud and the white spire of the church beyond center field lights up in gold as the three Breeze girls, the English grandchildren of Beth Breeze who owns the Stillman cottage, come walking out of the alders. The girls–Tig, 13; Bing, 10; and little Bug, 8–are cherished by the island women (and the men, too, if they would admit it) for the seraphic range of their voices in the church choir. The two older girls walk ahead, while Bug, the least confident about this game of softball, follows behind in pink cutoff Oshkosh overalls and tennis shoes of the same light blue as her sisters'.

Behind them, a distant shivaree of laughter, honking, and high-pitched speaking in tongues from the far side of the alders announces the approach of the Bowditch clan, who own and in the summer nearly fill the old hotel on Point Lookout. They appear in their Model A Ford, which overflows onto the running boards with adults and teenagers, and which pulls behind it a flatbed trailer full of little Bowditches wearing ball caps and thumping mitts. Behind them, the red-faced, red-haired, jolly Charlie Pratt, the naturalist from Manhattan, and his son, Mike, a three-foot replica of his father, pedal onto the field, their mitts dangling from the handlebars of their Schwinns.

David and Simon each have a handle of the aluminum cooler and a beer in their free hands. They are following Nancy and Christine, who are lost in hushed conversation and stop to sit under the old apple tree behind home plate. The young stern men walk on to set the cooler down on the grass at the feet of the captains on the tailgate, and Simon offers them a beer, which they decline.

"You boys pretty well oiled, are you?" Bill wants to know.

"No, not really," David says.

"Not yet, he means," Simon adds.

"Bernadine wants you to come choose up teams." David tells the captains as he puts an unfinished bottle of beer into the cooler.

"We'll be there in a minute," Gus says. "Soon as they get the bases set out. I wonder who put that new flag up."

"I did that." Simon is proud of himself. "Didn't Junior tell you?"

"No, I guess he didn't," Gus says.

"Why *ever* would he?" Bill sniffs, his tone just shy of scorn.

"Well, I . . ." Simon, stricken, ducks his head and turns abruptly back toward the game.

Gus glares at Bill, who notices neither Simon's humiliation nor Gus's reproachful look.

Perhaps it is David's familiar, tilting walk, or the sound of a softball slapping into a leather glove, or the skipping sunlight, or the excited babble of voices of every pitch amongst the players, or the new flag, or all of it taken together: Gus does not know. But he sees clearly his boy, John, in white T-shirt and jeans, thumping the plate with the bat and taunting the pitcher, his bare arms sunburned to the shirtsleeves, his mouth wide open and laughing. Gus fights to will the sight of John back into darkness, back to sleep, before it hurts him further.

David and Simon stand in the grass, apart from the scramble of children and women hovering impatiently around home plate.

"It's no wonder the flag gets tattered so quick; there's always a breeze up here, and this high up there's more wind than on open sea, I'll bet. Good move to put up a new one."

David cups his hand around his Zippo, lights two cigarettes, and hands one to Simon, hoping that his comment and the gesture will be a little balm for the sting of Bill's question.

"Up to Orono, when I went to pick up those forms for Nancy, I saw some students drive down the American flag and run up the Viet Cong flag. Like you said, surrounded by enemies."

"The mommy-shooter's flag," David says. "The lead-them-away-never-to-return flag."

"The treasonous sons of bitches." Simon spins his empty beer bottle in the grass and it comes to rest pointing at home plate where Bill and Gus stand ceremoniously before Bernadine. She has hushed the crowd (all save the gamboling little Bowditches) and is poised with the bat.

"Before you choose up, I want to remind these fellows," she looks at the Hanson brothers, the Coombs brothers, and Simon and David, "that this is a friendly game, a family game—you see these kids—it's not a game to show off how hard you can throw or hit, or how good you are. No balls or strikes; everybody gets a hit. Everybody, every time at bat. Okay?"

She tosses the bat to Bill, who catches it with one hand high on the handle and holds it out to Gus, who wraps his hand around the handle above

Bill's and the two go hand over hand to the knob, which Bill covers with his palm to win first choice.

Bill chooses a Hanson, Gus chooses a Coombs, Bill chooses another Hanson, Gus chooses the other Coombs, thinking that only a west-sider would choose Stonington men over island boys. Bill chooses Simon, Gus chooses David; the six young men exchange haughty looks. Bernadine and Betty give the men warning signs that all six can understand, and the game is on. When the last Bowditch child and little Bug Breeze have been chosen, Gus's team takes to the field. The swallows skittering over the infield make way for the players and shift to the far outfield, above the tall timothy.

It is the third or fourth inning—no one seems to know which—when Christine, who is poised to pitch, hesitates, surprised by something behind the batter and his teammates around home plate. While Bill's team watches from the field and Gus's team turns to see, the three bearded hippies that Simon saw on the mail boat days before walk in from the road, cross the edge of the field in single file, apparently headed toward Fat Albert, where Skippy sits behind the windshield. The three wear black leather vests, jeans torn at the knees, fat, black leather wallets attached to their belts with chrome chains, and leather headbands to contain their unctuous locks. The two in the lead are smoking cigarettes, the third carries a fifth of Bacardi rum; they walk slowly, dreamily, defiantly, and stop to loiter next to Fat Albert. Skippy seems not to notice them. Christine waits for the batter's attention and lobs a slow one over the plate.

The last of the evening sunlight is flickering on the tip of the church steeple like the flame atop a tall candle when Betty Barter hits a healthy line drive directly at Christine on the mound. Christine ducks, the ball flies through David's legs, and Betty reaches first in plenty of time. No one has been keeping score, but the excitement is shrill on the sidelines as the bases are loaded and Cecil approaches the plate. David shouts at the outfielders, among whom the little Bowditches are playing tag, to *Back up! Back up!* Cecil puffs out his chest, takes a mighty practice swing, and steps up for what will probably be the last hit on the darkening plain.

Cecil takes the first pitch and drives a grounder between David and Charlie Pratt, who purposely run chest first into one another like two stooges. Delighted, the sideline fans are screaming to Bing on third to run home, which she does. Charlie takes the throw from Gus and feigns confusion, allowing his son Mike to round third for home, then overthrows first base after Cecil has passed it, facilitating a grand slam and a grand finale for the game and the evening, an outcome that is cheered wildly by Bill's team at bat and booed heartily by Gus's thirteen stalwarts in the field.

✳✳✳

Simon and David are sitting on the Coopers' back stoop, smoking and drinking beer in the last light, listening and not listening to the soft conversation beneath the splash and clatter of dishes in the kitchen. A June bug strikes the screen door behind the smokers; when it falls on its back onto the stoop and struggles kicking to right itself, Simon crushes it with his fist. David has decided to walk home tonight, rather than ride with Skippy as planned: he wants to walk off the huge supper that still sits heavy in him and the postgame beers that have bloated him. He releases a prodigious, beerful belch that earns him a pat on the back from Simon and evokes a "Simon, for God's sake!" from Nancy in the kitchen window. As he builds himself to his feet, David sees a figure pushing through the alder thicket toward them from the direction of the ball field. Simon makes a noise of surprise as Cecil emerges from the shadows on the run and nearly falls forward onto the pair on the porch, panting and prattling something about Skippy.

"Set still and shut up for a second, will you?" says Simon. "Get a hold of yourself. We can't understand you."

The fearful tone of Cecil's babble brings Nancy and Christine to the other side of the screen door, where they stand shaped by the lamplight.

"It's Skippy!" the boy says. "He's crying and making slobberin' noises. I never saw him so scared. You got to do something. He's hiding under Fat Albert. Oh please."

"I'll get a flashlight. Wait for me," Nancy says.

"He's all curled up, and he sounds like the sheep on York Island at night. Aw shit, I'm scared."

"Here, go this way." Simon catches Cecil by the arm before he can plunge back into the dark bushes and guides him around toward the road leading to the ball field. David, Christine, and Nancy with a large lantern flashlight, hurry along behind them.

"Is he hurt?"

"They did something to him, them hippies." Cecil is breathless, shrill.

"They hurt him?" Simon brushes aside a low branch that slaps back and catches David in the face.

"He said something about chewin' gum."

"He talked? Here, slow down. Damn."

A low, sustained moan comes from the shadowed field ahead, a muffled bleating cry like that of a motherless calf.

"Jesus help him," Nancy says.

"He said 'bobber asses.' 'Bobble asses,' he says, then he says chewin' gum."

Nancy shines the light ahead at the shape of Fat Albert's cab and bed and then on the dark, hunched figure beneath it.

"Nuh! Nuh-uh-uhh!"

"My God," Christine whispers.

The four stand beside Fat Albert, bending down to see Skippy underneath. Cecil slides under the truck to put his arm over Skippy's shoulder and whisper to him. Skippy mewls again and kicks once from the fetal position that he has curled into, knocking an empty can of blueberry pie filling and stained spoon out onto the grass. Nancy does not shine the light directly on Skippy's face, but in the half-light they can see that his nose is running a torrent of pale mucus onto his cleft lip, nearly drowning him, and that his eyeballs are straining out of their sockets as if trying to escape the horror in the brain behind them. A huge dragonfly, a darning needle, sits motionless on the front tire watching over Skippy, its transparent wings shimmering in the thin light.

The sight of Skippy's twitching, curled form and the sounds that come from somewhere inside him awaken in David a shapeless horror and dread that make him want to run away.

"Bobble asses? Chewin' gum? You don't suppose–" Nancy starts.

"Blotter acid," David says. "The sons of bitches gave him blotter acid and told him it was chewing gum. Oh my God."

"Simon, get Fuddy."

"He'll go crazy," Simon says quietly. "Goddamn them." He drops to his knees and reaches out to lay a hand on Skippy's shoulder. "Don't worry, old dog; you're going to be all right. We'll take care of you."

David, shaken in a way that is familiar but somehow foreign, too, watches Simon, thinking that he is cool, in control. He has his shit in order, and so do I, David thinks. He buried himself under the dead at Ia Drang; it will take more than a primal howl from the village idiot on a bad acid trip to rattle Simon Cooper.

A voice not his, a sound not human, escapes from deep inside Skippy, a bleating, heartbreaking, distant cry.

"Oh, sweet Jesus," David says. He thinks that he has heard this cry before, sees for a second an old man squatting over a torn child, rocking on his heels, keening.

"Here." Nancy hands the lantern to Christine. "You stay here with him. I'm going to get a washcloth and a towel. Simon, go get Fuddy. Please. Now."

"We're going to get Fuddy, and he'll bring you home. It'll be over real quick, Skippy. You wait here with Cecil."

Simon swears under his breath and turns to jog toward his car. David, whose fear is changing into anger, follows close behind him.

But when Simon revs up his Ford and backs out onto the road, he turns toward town rather than toward Squeaker Cove.

"What are you doing?" David asks.

"Those fuckers went with the Hanson brothers on the *Ellamae*, back to Deer Isle. They might still be tied up here. I'm going to kill them; I swear to Christ I am going to kill them."

"There's five of them."

"Don't you worry. I'll take care of four. I want those three hippies; I'm going to stomp them to death. Did you hear that noise? Did you hear Skippy?"

"Did I hear it?" David lights a cigarette, his hand shaking. "Jesus, I can't get rid of it. But those guys are gone by now; we ought to get Fuddy, catch up with them later when we can."

But Simon pays him no mind. He throws the Ford into third gear and hits sixty-five passing the post office, then the solitary light in Leah's parlor window. He brakes and downshifts, fishtailing through the town parking lot, and rolls down the ramp onto the town wharf, his headlights revealing the *Poozie* and *Danita* as they prance on their moorings in the wake of the *Ellamae*, whose running lights they can just barely see in the distance. The Ford still running, Simon gets out and stands on the wharf, shouting, his hands cupped at his mouth, ordering them to turn around, screaming, cursing them for cowards, shouting desperately, his voice breaking finally. He drops his hands and falls silent, his back to David, watching the boat's lights disappear behind Kimball Island.

"Come on, man. We got to go get Fuddy." When Simon does not respond, David opens his door and sees in the thin light from inside the car that Simon's shoulders are quaking, that he is sobbing. David shuts his door to give the man some privacy.

"I can't tell you." David thinks he hears Simon say. "God knows, I can't tell you."

* * *

When Fuddy has taken Skippy home, Simon and Nancy take Cecil and Christine home, and they drop David at the top of the road into the cove, not to disturb Maggie by driving in and out. David stands in a splay of moonlight on the road and watches as Simon roars up Bridge Hill toward home. He smiles to think that Nancy is telling Simon to slow down, dammit, slow down.

At the bottom of the cove road, just past Maggie's, where the meadow opens up and the cove and sea lie open beyond, David emerges from the shadows of the oaks into the light of the crescent moon that rides the sky above the cabin on the distant, dark cliff.

He can tell me, David thinks, going back to Simon sobbing in the Ford. At least when he is drunk he can. The other night, he described the sounds of the North Vietnamese bayoneting and shooting corpses and wounded all around him. The guy he pulled over and covered himself with was a spade, a brother, who smelled of puke and Johnson's fucking baby powder, of all things. Not true that you can fire off a round to dislodge a bayonet stuck in a chest, at least not with an AK-47. In the kitchen that drunken night, Simon said he had the presence of mind to take off his wedding ring, lest one of them cut it off and make him scream his last scream. Their "fucking gook voices."

From the moonlit meadow by the well in front of Ava's house, David steps back into shadow as he begins the path through the trees to the cabin and the clearing. The little moonlight that flickers through openings in the canopy above is enough to light the way on the path, though he no longer really needs it. The moonlight on the steep path reminds him of the first night he had tried the path in the dark; reminds him that he had used a flashlight to light up the path and remembered then, and now again, that he had given the order that other night long ago to light up the village.

The evening after he carried the shot-up children in the back of his jeep, he sat with Neang by the pagoda as usual and tried to explain what had happened. She pretended to understand what he was saying; they both knew that she had heard all about it already from the Khmer soldiers who were with him. She knew it was his fault even if he did not pull the trigger, any trigger. "Light it up," she knew he had said. She did not have the language, the words, to comfort him, if she had wanted to. When he began to cry, quietly, she was embarrassed for him, and for herself to be alone with a man who was crying. She did not speak, nor did she even turn toward him, and though he had stopped crying, she rose and left without a word.

When David steps out into the moonlight in his own clearing at the cabin, he finds that the wind has shifted, that he is in the lee of the trees behind him, and that the sea beneath the cliffs has gone flat calm in the thin, milky moonlight. He fills his lungs with sea air, thinks to sit on the rocks and have a last smoke, but decides not to. Instead he lights a lamp and sits on the porch to unlace his shoes, safe on his own high ground.

"Lord," he says aloud, his first prayer in peacetime. "Lord, let Skippy get over the acid trip. Let him come out of it in his own bed at home and not remember any of it. Not any of it."

NINE

It's not just the people; it's the island itself—the sea, the sky, the quiet, the easy pace they call "island time." I've never felt so at home, so safe, and it sounds silly but it's true, so liberated.
—Nancy Cooper

Last Halloween Nancy dressed in a tall, pointy hat with a fantastic wide brim and a cape made from a sheet dyed black; she wore a nose with a hairy wart and matching chin from the schoolteacher's make up kit. Nancy rode her old, black Raleigh bicycle into the schoolyard during recess, with a stuffed dog in the wicker basket, cackling madly, and croaking, "I'm going to get you—and your little dog, too," sending the little ones squealing and scampering for cover, all giddy with fright, save Cecil, who sat on his swing seat smiling wisely.

Today, as she pedals past the schoolyard on the same bicycle, the playground is empty—school is out for the summer—but she remembers Cecil on the swing in his cowboy costume, blazing away at her witch with cap pistols. She hopes that she will find Cecil with Skippy when she visits Squeaker Cove this afternoon, as the boy is balm for the man.

An early morning fog has burned off, and the lobstermen have all gone out, though most got a late start. Somewhere down by the town landing, boys are setting off the last of their firecrackers saved from the Fourth of July. The sun has risen above the high spine of Barter Island and spreads across the bay, lighting white sails that tack in the increasing breeze on Merchants' Row. Nancy's bike has three gears, but only one of them works—Simon swears he will fix it—so she has to stand on the pedals to gain the top of town hill; when she does, she is perspiring, but she soon cools off as she coasts down Lovers' Lane in the shade of the mountain, happy to be out of the smoky house and shut of the ripe stink of stale alcohol on Simon's breath.

Today she is not a witch but a nurse; there is no stuffed dog in the wicker basket that is tied to her handlebars with clothesline, but instead her nurse's kit bag, a lobster salad sandwich, and a nice apple, a Granny Smith. Her plan is to visit Meadow Dawn and see how close she is, then to look in on Skippy who has not left the house since his fearful experience. She might even take a dip in the pond and wash her hair if there isn't anyone at the secluded deep end where she can swim naked. She'll ride slow past Betty's on the way home and maybe be seen and get asked in for tea. Soaring down Bridge Hill, she swerves to miss a squiggle in the road and wonders why a green snake turns blue after a tire has flattened it.

Nancy sees no one, not Betty in her yard, not Myrtle in her kitchen window, not a passing car or truck, as she pedals down the east side of the island; no one until she sees somebody in red plaid at the edge of the road and realizes that it is Christine emerging from her wooded drive wearing a blue head scarf and carrying a soiled paper bag. Nancy's hand brakes squawk as she comes to a stop. When her brakes are silent, and before she can greet Christine, Nancy hears a distant, persistent yipping on the hillside and takes a second look at the paper bag of leaking table scraps in Christine's hand.

"They're not here?"

"You didn't know?" Christine asks.

"No, I was coming to visit Meadow Dawn. Did her contractions start?"

"They did, but then they stopped, and that worried her some. So they went to the midwife in Deer Isle. On the late boat last night."

"Did they start up again before she left? How did they get to the boat?" Nancy wonders aloud.

"I don't know. Willow talked to Eliot, I guess. I wish I did know."

"I wish I had the confidence to midwife for her like she wanted, like they all wanted, but I just couldn't. I mean, hygiene." Nancy has argued this with herself several times.

"You got them to dig a latrine." Christine holds the soggy bag up to inspect the bottom. "Want to come up with me? That's the puppy, Glamdring, making all the noise; he's a growing boy, poor thing."

Nancy lifts her bicycle over the narrow drainage ditch and lets it settle into the leaves and limbs of a mountain maple until it finds a leaning rest. She says she'd love to go along and hangs her kit bag and lunch from a nearby branch.

On the way up the path through the interrupted fern, Christine explains that Eliot has lapsed into one of his icy, silent, angry moods over her having to feed the animals again. Each of the McGregors is allowed two hours of time from their daily regimen for rest, reading, or meditation, and Eliot hates to see Christine spend hers caring for animals that are not only neglected but of no use whatsoever to anyone, a waste of scraps that could be added to the compost pile.

"He's even icier now, after what those three guys did to Skippy."

"That's understandable; he's not the only one down here who's pissed at those guys. I think Skippy will be okay, though," Nancy says.

The hermit thrush in the dark spruce to their left stops tweedling when he hears them approaching.

"It's not so much for Skippy's sake that he's angry, I guess. He says he can't imagine that a brief chemical interruption could make much difference to a mind as feeble as Skippy's. It's more that those three creeps were staying with Willow's family, who are here because we agreed to sell them the land. Eliot thinks that that makes him look bad."

When the animals hear their footfall, the goat Gandalf begins to bleat, his upper lip quivering, and the scabrous puppy lunges eagerly toward Christine and her damp sack, only to be caught in midair by his rope and brought down onto his side in the dirt. When Christine swats at a circling deerfly, the puppy cringes.

"If you'll start a fire, I'll get the rice and water. They seem hungrier than ever. I wish we could let them go."

"Let's take them for a walk," Nancy says. "Let's go up to the top of the mountain. It's such a clear day we'll be able to see everywhere. I wish I had brought my lunch with me."

"What if they run away?" Christine is behind the canvas kitchen wall filling the kettle with rice.

"After you've fed them? They know you from feeding them. They won't run away from you. If they do, I'll take the blame."

✳✳✳

On the bare mountaintop, Christine and Nancy clamber up the perilous sides of the stone cairn to look out over the scrub pines and sit in the midday sun with all of Penobscot and Blue Hill bays before them. The dogs scramble to climb onto the cairn with them, but cannot get a foothold in the loosely piled stones; instead they lie on the smooth granite ledge and soak up the warmth of stone and sun. Atop the cairn they can see Mount Battie and the Camden Hills, Blue Hill, which today *is* blue, Mount Desert, Cadillac Mountain, and all the far islands to the north and east. The surface of the sea that surrounds them is sprinkled with boats and sails, save the distant eastern horizon, where only a vague shimmering freighter and one of the Camden windjammers can be seen. After a half hour of only looking, barely talking, Christine says that she must go, and they start downhill through the pathless woods, heading for the tepee and then the road.

On the way down through the forest, they veer gradually to their right to avoid a thicket of spruce and find themselves, the skittish dogs at their heels, in a steep expanse of knee-high puckerbrush and bayberry. Christine looks up at the sun and says that they have drifted too far to the south, so they push their way through another spruce thicket and within fifty feet find themselves in a clearing of sorts on flat ground. The clearing is man-made, a long acre at least. The trees have been cut and dragged into the forest at the edges; their stumps are scattered among outcroppings of granite, patches of sphagnum and cushion moss withering in the sunlight, and hundreds of tidy little mounds of fresh topsoil and compost from which grow little green plants no more than a foot high. All around the edge of the field is a border of what appears to be brown paste that the dogs sniff and back away from, sneezing.

Nancy bends over to examine the border that is three inches wide of what was once powder before rained on. She takes a little on the tip of her finger and sniffs it, wrinkling her nose, then holds it under Christine's nose.

"What is it?" Nancy asks.

"It's to keep out the deer and rabbits. I forget the name of the product, some cutesie commercial repellent. They probably made their own: soap, beef blood, camphor, and castor oil. This smells heavy on the mothballs, don't you think?"

Nancy steps over the border and walks a few feet into the clearing, surveying the plantings appreciatively.

"They've done some clearing after all," Nancy says. "Tomatoes?"

Christine is standing at the border, immobile, unwilling to cross, her hands in her coverall pockets.

"I don't think so," she says, though she knows.

Nancy is leaning over one plant. "Nope, not tomatoes. Marijuana. I should have known. Did you know? Did Eliot?"

"Certainly not. Willow would know damn well that Eliot would disapprove and probably even turn him in or make him pull it up. Why else would he hide this patch up here so far from the path, and, it's my guess, not even on our land or theirs."

"This is more than just for their own use. This is a cash crop." Nancy has her hands on her hips; she shakes her head, thinking that the three guys who drugged Skippy are probably Willow's off-island dealers.

"Are you going to tell him?"

"I don't know," Christine says quietly. "I guess I must, but I'm afraid of what he'll do and then what they will do. What do you think, Nancy? What will you do?"

"I don't know that I will say or do anything unless you do. I'm going to visit Skippy. Let's take the dogs back. And let's take some of this dried moss for a bed for the puppy."

✳✳✳

One of the boats that Nancy and Christine saw from the mountaintop earlier was the *Betty B*. As the morning fog began to burn off two hours before, David stood on the wharf in the cove with Gus and chided his captain for waiting so long to be sure it would burn off, waiting while they could hear other boats rumble past in the thinning fog, even see one finally as it passed the mouth of the cove. By early afternoon they have hauled the four southernmost strings of ten in the deep, bowl-shaped area called the Turnip Yard, where they see and hail Junior and Simon. It is too early in the season for the shedders to start coming, and late enough in the season that most of the lobsters are still holed up in their little protective caves while they shed their old shell for a soft new one. Though they are getting a few lobsters in the thick kelp along the edges of the channel, they are coming up empty in the channel where the bottom is mostly sand and eelgrass. Gus is salty this afternoon–he hates to get a late start, David's carping on the wharf galled him, and they aren't even averaging a half-pound a trap.

The southwest breeze increases with the coming afternoon tide, so in the channel Gus cuts the *Betty B.* back to idle, motions David to take the wheel, and goes aft to put up his staysail, muttering that his Christly arches ache like sin. They work the second string in the channel methodically, speaking little. When each trap comes up on the washboard David plucks out snappers, crabs, and urchins and pushes it forward to Gus for baiting and pushing back overboard. Gus runs the bait needle through a sculpin that David has left in the trap for him, adding it, thrashing, to the dangling bait bag.

"Fuddy put Skippy up against the side of their old barn and painted his outline on the wall, three of them, black outlines with red hearts painted in the middle," David says as he pegs a keeper. "Skippy sits in the rocker on the front porch with their .22 revolver, and he and Cecil shoot holes in the hearts and the heads of the silhouettes of those guys."

"Sounds familiar," Gus says.

"How's that?" David pushes a trap forward.

"Years ago, it was during the war, old fat-ass Basil Bowen lived down there with Fuddy and Skippy. There was a stranger wandering around on the island, hiding out, and people thought he was a German spy or something. Basil outlined Skippy the same way on the barn door, and they did target practice on his shape long enough to blow that door all to hell."

David laughs. "They've blown a hole in the heart of one of these ones."

"How do you know all this? You been down there?"

"No, Nancy told me. She visited Skippy day before yesterday," David says.

Gus pushes a trap over. "It's too bad she's married, innit?"

"Yes it is, goddamn you." David should have known better than to mention Nancy.

"Goddamn *me*? I didn't have anything to do with her being married."

"No, but you've got everything in the world to do with rubbing it in. Not only married, but married to a friend, a veteran, a brother."

Gus smiles, deeply satisfied. His tone is one of sincere concern. "I don't know as I like the way she looks at you."

"I do. You would too, if it was you."

"I suppose I would," Gus admits.

As they pass the mouth of the cove and draw near the York Ledges, the seals that are sunning themselves on the rocks slide one and two at a time into the water to swim curious and impatient in the kelp. Between strings, David sits on the transom and looks over the port side at his cabin and the cliff that drops off from it, where Gus's grandfather fell to his death; the cliff that he, David, has scaled a hundred times. From the water, at a little distance, the cabin seems higher and the clearing he has done around it more expansive than it feels when he is on land. Today he notices a gull bobbing on the surface at the foot of the cliff and another twenty yards to the north, something he hasn't seen before. Then he realizes that the floating white objects are not gulls, but buoys, somebody else's buoys in Gus's waters. He goes forward and taps Gus on the shoulder and points. Gus says, "What?" then lifts his clip-on sunglasses and stares.

Without a word, Gus looks around to see if there are any other boats in sight, then turns toward shore and runs in to the buoys, where he slows down and takes the first one up with his gaff. The buoys are brand-new Styrofoam, freshly painted white with a red spindle. As Gus hauls ten feet of the toggle line on board, David watches quietly, surprised and respectful of Gus's silence. The air is warmer close to the cliff and smells of land.

"Is it the Hansons?" David asks.

"It is. It's that Milo Weed. I'm going to tie off two loops, a turn with a half bow in it. Take that oar and watch we don't strike those rocks."

"Will he know what it means?"

"Of course he will. He's a fourth- or fifth-generation Stonington man, a fifth-generation criminal. He's got twenty-four hours to get out or get cut off. He's just seeing if I'll do it. His father did the same damn thing."

When he has tied off the last buoy in the string of ten along the shore between Deep Cove and his own cove, Gus flings the buoy into the water just beyond the Sheep Ledges with an angry flourish.

"There," he says. "The goddamn prune."

"Prune?" David asks. "You call him a prune?"

"Yes; that's what he is, all of them, goddamn prunes."

✳✳✳

On the evening before a trip off the island, it is the McGregors' custom to sit together before supper and review the schedule for the morrow. Only one of them will go, to save mail boat fees, and tomorrow it will be Christine's turn. She will borrow Simon's pickup, which is parked in the Stonington town lot, the keys under the floor mat, and go to the food co-op in Blue Hill; to White's bookstore, where their copy of *Ten Acres Enough* is finally in; and, on the way back, to Beasley Lumber for six bags of Portland cement. They review the precise list of foods that she will buy at the co-op, a month's supply. The list includes number of pounds, projected price, and alternatives if, say, buckwheat groats are not available. It is the third draft of the list, printed in caps with a very sharp pencil in Eliot's hand; the foods are categorized in thinly ruled columns.

"You should make it back to the noon boat with no problem," Eliot observes. "But in case you don't—you might have to go to Bucksport for the cement—you might want to take a lunch with you. You don't want to have to buy something processed."

Christine laughs. "I'll have thirty-two pounds of organic foods with me; even so, I'd rather go without than eat processed food; you know that." Christine pauses, a little tentative. "I think we forgot to budget three dollars for gas for the truck."

"Ah." Eliot uses his upright pencil as an exclamation mark. "Good for you. We'll still keep the withdrawal to three hundred."

"Oh, of course." A husband, she remembers with gratitude, is a steward, one who manages thriftily and with care, who provides, and, interestingly, who tills the soil, cultivates.

At supper it is the McGregors' custom to abstain from frivolous conversation and explore elevated topics—topics such as world politics, gardening, current events, books they are reading (classics of economics and social philosophy), or recent UFO sightings. Together they clear the worktable in the main room, and while Christine prepares their simple fare, Eliot lights a lamp to set between the windows. Even in summer, a lamp is wanted at six o'clock as the sun is down behind the mountain ridge and it is growing dark inside the house. Yesterday was their weekly fast day, which, as always adds relish to their meals today. Christine sets their individual wooden bowls, chopsticks, and spoons at their places and brings forth a wide tray on which sits an assortment of bowls, wooden and ceramic, filled with their four courses:

rolled oats, uncooked, with a bit of peanut oil and sea salt; fresh salad greens from the garden; and applesauce, whole grain bread, and herb tea.

Eliot eats his oats with his spoon, chewing thoughtfully, while Christine begins her meal with greens and bread and tea, as is her wont. Eliot admits to a little surprise that *The New York Times* and *The Washington Post* have won their case before the Supreme Court and will publish all of the Pentagon Papers legally, proving, if proof be needed (he examines a heaping spoonful of oats), that Robert McNamara is a war criminal.

"And one who will never be brought to justice." Christine finishes her salad and scoops applesauce into her bowl. She adds that she is hopeful that Nixon's coming visit to China may be the beginning of the end of the war; it just may be.

The table cleared, their bowls and utensils scalded clean in the kitchen sink by Christine and wiped dry by Eliot, the McGregors read at the table for a half an hour or so until Eliot, looking out his window onto the water, suggests that the evening light is just about right, and Christine agrees, setting her book aside.

"I'll walk out to the road, and you can walk the shore," Eliot says. "It always seems overly cautious to reconnoiter each time, but I guess it's better to be safe, eh?"

"I think so," Christine says. "We could wait until it's completely dark and be sure; we don't have to see, really. How many are in the envelope? Twelve, I think."

"Fifteen." Eliot is unequivocal.

"Oh," Christine says. "I thought it was twelve. We can check the ledger."

"There's no need."

Eliot takes his cap from the rack and steps outside into the gathering dusk. Behind him, Christine shuts the door, then pauses on the stoop.

"What?" he asks.

"I'll get the snips; we'll want–"

"No." Eliot is impatient; he attributes her apparent agitation to her "humors," as he calls them. He leads the way across the meadow and stops at the little gravesite to open the white gate and hold it for Christine, who follows slowly toward the shore.

Without a word, they walk on either side of the bed of daisies she planted over the Eaton graves and take up positions on either side of the wide headstone. As one, they bend down, take hold of the thin granite head-stone near the base in which it rests, and when Eliot counts to three, they heft the flat marker and lean it against the fence. Eliot kneels behind the stone base, digs his fingers in at the edges facing Christine, who is on her knees too, and lifts the narrow base enough for Christine to reach into the rectangular hole beneath and take out the little black strongbox. While Eliot holds up the slotted base, she opens the strongbox and removes from it a dark, zippered canvas bank bag. Without a sound, without a breath, Christine faints, falling backward into the daisies, the bank bag still in her hand.

Eliot barks. He lets the stone base down over the hole and crawls to Christine who lies on her side in the darkness, only her shoulder showing above the tops of the daisies.

"Christine, Christine, oh Tina honey," he says as he holds her head in his arm and pats her cheeks. Her face is ashen, nearly blue, her lips are parted slightly, and almost immediately, she stirs and looks up at her husband, her eyes widening in horror as she awakes.

"What happened, honey? Are you okay? Good God, you scared me. What's wrong?"

Christine cannot speak. She is certain at this moment, as she sits up slowly in the daisies, that she will never speak again. Not to Eliot. Oh no. She feels for the canvas bag at her side and hands it to Eliot, then looks away, toward the sea, toward the wide, disappearing horizon.

And Eliot knows instantly, without unzipping it, that the bag is empty, or nearly so. He unzips it and finds that there is nothing in it save the manila envelope, and it, too, is empty. One hundred and sixty-five hundred-dollar bills—$16,500—gone. Every penny of their savings, of Christine's inheritance, gone. Stolen. Eliot slumps to the ground next to Christine, fighting back a rise of vomit in his throat. For a long moment he sits with her in the daisies in silence, his mind crowded with images, broken thoughts, fear that he will never have the cement for his pond dam.

But then he is on his knees, feeling once more inside the zippered bag, inside the strongbox, and lifting the stone base to feel inside the little rectangular hole, his face nearly down in the hole to see in the increasing dark, for he is certain that there has been a terrible mistake of some kind.

"You must have told someone," he says. "Who did you tell? Maybe someone is playing a trick on us."

Christine does not answer. She has pulled her knees up to her chin; stunned to silence and shivering slightly, she hugs her legs for dear life.

"Someone must have seen us moving the stone." Eliot is on his knees scanning the darkness all around. "It had to have been two people. No one on the island could lift this headstone alone. Not even, well . . . Those three guys, the ones who drugged Skippy. But no, they weren't on the island when we last opened the box. Oh, God."

TEN

Even though every single soul on this island, man and woman
alike, lives in a glass house, still there are some
who are always ready to throw stones.
-*Betty Barter*

July 8

Ruth Dear,

No, the creatures who slipped poor Skippy a mickey have
not returned, nor do we think they will. Junior asked the Deer
Isle police to pay them a visit and make it clear to them that
they are not welcome down here, and so far, so good. But that
foul incident, which I called an aberration and dismissed as a I
try your patience. Sorry. Someone robbed the McGregors,
robbed them of a substantial sum of money. Their ideology, if
that's what it should be called, will not permit them to use
banks, nor accrue interest; they apparently kept everything they
had buried on their property. No one seems to know exactly
how much was lost, but, as Betty says, it only takes two minutes
with the McGregors to infer that it was a serious loss, a loss,
some think, of all they had. Christine is devastated; she is
unspeakably forlorn and inconsolable. He, Eliot, is enraged, tormented. Leah said this afternoon that it is as though Christine

was raped by someone they both trusted, and perhaps that is not too far off the mark.

At times like this one doesn't know what to believe, or whom. Down here we know each other so well that we each know what the other wants to believe—a few, for instance, are absolutely convinced that the hippies (who left the island the day before the robbery was discovered) are the thieves—but no one knows anything for certain. The only thing certain is that this time as in so many other times in the past we will never know all of the truth. I don't know what I believe, but I do know what I hope: that the money is recovered somehow, that the McGregors will stay on the island, and that the hippies and their friends will not return.

You were right when you said in your last letter (or was it the one before?) that I seem to be growing quite fond of Nancy Cooper. In the P.O. today, while Lizzie sorted the mail, I sat with Nancy thinking how much she has changed in the two short years that she has been down here. The timid, rather flighty city girl who trembled in her husband's shadow now walks upright; she is as bold as Betty ever was, yet she is soft-spoken and modest. (I say modest even though she quite obviously no longer wears a brassiere and in summer is sometimes seen wearing only a T-shirt.) The better she gets to know us, the more caring and competent she has become, especially with the shut-ins. We all attribute Isabel's recovery and health to Nancy, who every afternoon walks with her to the store and back. I fear she only barely tolerates her howling husband, poor girl.

Tonight I'm retiring early with a hot water bottle for my back—still brittle from gathering sticks and twigs in the yard after the big wind.

Love always,

Maggie

PS: Nancy told Leah that she will ever be indebted to me because I "turned her on" to Isak Dinesen and Virginia Woolf.

✳✳✳

Maggie is reading in her chair under the light by the west window when her chin pops up, pointing at the far wall, and she shuts her eyes, listening. She makes a noise in her throat, which, if articulate, would say "Oh my. Oh my," in a rueful tone for David's sake.

David is just finishing his dinner dishes, wiping the last knife dry, when he hears the same noise and looks up at his reflection in the window, praying that the Galaxie will not downshift to turn into the cove road. But it does.

It is the third day of fog, July fog so thick that no fisherman has gone out to haul his traps, not even the men with loran. The captains are anxious, testy; the bait in their traps is dwindling, nibbled and washed clean of oil by the current, and the lobsters that are trapped are tearing each other to shreds—"acting like humans," as Junior likes to say. The stern men welcome the break as a time to catch up with little stuff left undone, or as Simon has been doing, to build new traps and paint new buoys.

David stands at the kitchen's screen door watching the headlights swing around the turn and sweep through the fog above the cove and meadow. The mesh is soaked with condensed fog: every little square a pane of water. David flicks the screen with a forefinger, dousing the doorstep yet again.

"Junior's back. On the late boat." Simon sets a jug and ginger ale on the kitchen table while David fetches glasses. "He stopped by on his way home."

Simon curses the fog while he pours, curses it in a kind of friendly way, with clumsy mumbling.

"What'd he say?" David drops ice cubes into the glasses. He adjusts the reflector on the wall lamp over the sink to shed soft yellow onto the table.

"The hippies didn't even slow down in Stonington. C.J. Marshall gave them a ride up to Blue Hill and left them off at the hospital."

"Whatever for?" asks David.

"Well, she's pregnant—Meadow Dawn, the big one, is. Didn't you know that?" Simon did not know until an hour ago, but he acts as if he has known all along and is surprised that David was unaware.

"I'll be damned."

"C.J. said she looked like hell. She said the girl's cheeks and arms looked like marshmallows, puffy and white and spongy. She couldn't tell how pregnant she was, nobody ever could, her wearing those sack dresses."

David hopes that Autumn is not pregnant too; what a shame that would be. He scratches a match on the underside of the table, lights a cigarette, and shakes the match out—shake, don't blow; only sissies blow matches out.

"But they didn't go in the hospital, none of them. Junior got the hospital to check their records to make sure. They never went in. They didn't go to see the midwife either. The clerk in the grocery store says she saw them and sold them bread or something. But nobody else did. Junior swore out a warrant for all three of them statewide for questioning. They must of got a ride hitchhiking."

"I bet they're gone for good, and they left the animals and all that gear behind." David tilts his chair back slowly until it rests against the wainscoting.

"We should of burned those fuckers out of there last fall and run them off the island then. You and I should of taken off after them three days ago, the minute we found out what they did. We could of caught up with them. We've had experience hunting humans, eh?"

"You don't know for sure they took it. How much was it, anyway?"

"They told Junior, but he's not allowed to say. What he did say was that you'd never guess how much it was, ever. Who the hell else would of done it? Why the fuck did they take off like that?"

"I'll bet Nancy knows," David says.

"No, she doesn't." Simon shakes his broad head, his eyes downcast. "Or at least she says she doesn't. She probably does, and if I'm right, that's not all she knows and is holding back. It pisses me off, but I try not to let it get to me. I mean, she's just being loyal to Christine, who's all secretive about this shit for some reason."

Simon stands over David and pours him another while David holds the glass on his knee. "You get any traps done? I got three built and rigged."

"I put up a cord of wood from those spruce logs. I haven't bought any gear for traps yet, you know that. I hope to get twenty-five done this winter."

David notices that the hard lines in Simon's face are softening and knows that Simon is pleased with himself as he sometimes is when he has had a few but not a few too many.

"Junior says he's impressed how many traps I've built and put over already; he says he'll probably have to look for a new stern man soon because I'll have my own boat. I've got to pee." Simon goes through the screen into the dark fog; his gait has a gentle roll to it when he is feeling this good. David just wishes the feeling good could last for Simon, but he knows that it almost never does.

Standing in the gray, black dooryard, Simon pees in the gravel. There is a slight breeze, not so much a breeze as a push from the west, which he thinks might blow the fog out to sea by morning. When he told Nancy that Junior was impressed, she kissed him and said, "Well, so am I." He zips up and hears a vehicle out on the road, heading toward them. He recognizes the sound of the McGregor pickup; when he steps back through the door, he thinks that it is probably Christine going to see Nancy, the first time she has been out since the robbery that he knows of.

***

The half-gallon jug of Black Velvet that was nearly full when Simon first placed it on the table is now down below half. The ginger ale is long gone, replaced by a Depression glass pitcher of well water. A recent spill on the brown surface of the table has taken on the shape of Indiana, perhaps Illinois. Simon has just finished a coughing fit after telling the one about the helicopter door gunner stitching the pregnant girl, and David is mildly grateful for the new twist that includes a noisy description of the gunning into gore of two sorry assholes in a sampan.

"You saw shit like that," Simon says.

"I saw door gunners firing a few times, but I never saw what they hit. They always shot into the canopy."

Simon nods. He is watching the thin white ribbon of smoke that rises from his cigarette.

"You know what gets me about you?" he asks, not looking at David. "What's been bugging me for months?"

"No. What?" David does not want to show his sudden anxiety.

"Why you extended. Why you took a second tour over there. It couldn't of been for the re-up bonus." Simon looks up at David and smiles. "Not for some slope chick."

"Fuck you, pal." David is deeply relieved; he flatfoots the rest of his drink.

"No, really," says Simon. "Why did you?"

"I told you. I thought I could help them, the troops and families in the camp, the people in the village. As long as there were Americans there, the Khmers stood a chance against both kinds of Vietnamese. And I knew them, their language and customs; a replacement would have had to start from scratch." David will not say that he loved them, his soldiers and, yes, Neang; he will not say that to Simon Cooper.

"You expect me to believe that shit?"

"My fiancée didn't," David allows. "I don't know why you should."

Simon shakes his head in disbelief, smiling at some great irony.

"Fucking sensitive Green Beret," he says.

A green moth the size of a warbler flutters into the soaked screen and falls away, leaving an imprint of fine dust on the wet surface. Simon pours them another one, and while he does, David thinks that the more Simon drinks tonight, the sharper his edge gets; the more he himself drinks, the duller he gets–not that he had an edge to begin with.

"And you know what else?" Simon asks.

David is leaning over his forearms on the table; wary, he sits back in his chair. "I guess I don't," he admits.

"I never heard you tell a story. It's aggravating is what it is. Oh, you mention night ground attacks and leeches and patrols and ambushes and eating rats, but you never tell a story, you know what I mean?" Simon is suddenly very serious.

"I don't know. What's to tell? That I was scared the whole time I was there? I'm not good with stories. You're the storyteller. You're the man with the war stories, I only . . ."

In two motions linked by lightning speed, Simon pushes himself up with his left hand flat on the table and drives his right fist into David's amazed face. David has been hit before, but never like this, never by a fist wielded like a stone club. Upended, his feet strike the table, his glass shatters against the wall, and his face explodes in pain. Like the rocket round that landed just inside the stone wall, with an explosion so bright and loud that it blinded him and launched him in the air, flailing like Spiderman. Before he can pull himself to his feet, saying "What the–", Simon hits him in the temple and sends him down again.

"Mister Fucking Humble Hero," says Simon, as he catches crawling David in the ribs with his boot. David rolls over, spewing vomit, but manages to catch Simon's foot before it can kick him again and pulls him down, striking him once, twice, squarely in the nose, his head against the wainscoting preventing any recoil. Simon howls, drives his fist with all his strength into David's face, then stands over David, breathing hard, shaking, waiting for David to rise. When he does not, Simon takes his jug, tosses the table across the room with one mighty sweep, and lurches for the screen door, cupping his battered and bleeding nose with his free hand.

✳✳✳

Maggie lies on her back in the dark of her bedroom, eyes closed but wide awake. She thinks that she can feel a little warmth from the slight riffle of air that is coming through her western window and thinks, too, that she can smell land in the same air. She hopes that she is right and that the fog will be gone out to sea by first light. She hears Simon's big Ford start up and grimaces in expectation of a roaring assault on the road past her house. But she is surprised to hear that he is driving slowly, barely accelerating, as he comes down the road from Ava's toward her. When he does pass the house, he creeps by quietly and takes the hill in the same considerate manner. She looks at her bedside clock to find that it is 10:15 and thinks that perhaps these are good signs, that his quiet and early departure are signs of his beginning to slow down, calm down, spare himself and all the rest of the island his reckless and terrible abandon. Around her, he has always been polite, even a bit bashful, as he was in the store the first day of fog when he wished her good morning and held the door for her, his full cheeks pink in the morning chill.

✳✳✳

Nancy hears Simon moving in the dark morning kitchen. She hears his dinner pail opening and the thermos being snapped into the lid. It is not yet five o'clock, but a hint of dawn light frames the bedroom window. She remembers that it was just 10:30 last night when she heard him drive up, and she thinks that she ought to tell him how glad she was to hear him come home early.

She stands in the doorway between the bathroom and the kitchen, her arms hugging her chest for warmth; her hair, sleep tangled, is tucked back behind her ears. He is turned aside and has not seen her; she thinks to scare him for the fun of it, but instead she watches in silence as he holds a teaspoon over a glass half full of orange juice and with trembling hand pours whiskey slowly into the upturned spoon. When two fingers of whiskey have spread and settled on the surface of the juice, he pounds the whole glass, the whiskey chased down, his mouth washed sweet by the orange juice. He shudders, and when she steps into the soft light, he turns toward her.

Nancy gasps and takes a step forward. He holds up a hand to stop her. His face reminds her of the hideous owls in *The Wizard of Oz*. His eyes flicker inside deep, purple black circles. His nostrils are stuffed with blood-soaked tissues that have hardened into bloody-brown flares.

"Did you fall down?"

"Hell no, I didn't fall down." Simon sounds like he has a bad head cold. "Mister Curls and I got into it a little, is all."

"A little? My God, Simon. What does he look like? What were you fighting about, with David of all people?"

"It was a friendly fight."

"Damn," she says softly. "Goddamn. Let me look at you."

"No, I'm all right. I'm going to haul." He closes and latches his dinner pail.

"You're *not* all right. Let me look at that nose; you're going to need to get it X-rayed. I'm going to clean it up and see–"

"You're not, goddammit." He turns aside again, takes up his dinner pail, and pushes past her. "Go take care of him, why don't you? He needs it worse than me."

"What were you fighting about? Tell me." Nancy is afraid of the answer, but she insists, not knowing or thinking why.

"Ask him." Simon lets the screen door slam behind him, which he knows she hates, and drops his dinner pail inside the open back window of the Galaxie.

Nancy stands in the front-room window and watches as he backs out onto the tarmac and without looking back lays a patch of rubber in second gear, with a high-pitched angry squeal from his tires and two little clouds of stinky smoke.

As she pedals down Lovers' Lane, her hair gathered under the back strap of her Red Sox ball cap, her nurse's kit slung over her shoulder, she sees Gus's Willys coming toward her. She stops and waits by the cedar bog, behind which the forest on the western slope of the mountain is still shrouded in darkness. It will be light in the cove now, she thinks, as Gus pulls to a stop in the middle of the road, his arm leaning out the window.

"I was just coming to get you," Gus says. His face and voice are both flat and calm, and Nancy breathes a little easier.

"How's Simon? David's going to have a headache for a while, one hell of a headache."

Nancy shakes her head in dismay; Gus agrees with the same gesture.

"His nose is broken," she says. "I'm glad I ran into you. Would you drive over and catch them before they set out and tell Junior that Simon needs to go to the hospital; he needs to have that septum X-rayed."

"Septum?"

"Nose."

"Maybe David needs to go, too, but I doubt it. I picked a sliver of glass out of his cheek but there's more of them. He needs to be cleaned up and maybe a couple of stitches to put his ear back together. You do stitches, don't you?"

"Yes." She sees the first light skip across the top of the maple behind him. "I'm not too good at it, though. Is it his earlobe?"

Gus reacts to the word by caressing his own earlobe between thumb and forefinger. "I wouldn't worry about how good it's done; if it scars he can say he got it in the war."

"Is he awake?"

"He was when I left. You go on. I'll catch up to Junior, don't worry. Wait till you see his kitchen. It looks like the war got carried down here to the cove."

"I guess it did in a way," she says sadly.

"Furniture all stove in, dishes smashed, blood everywhere. Jesus wept."

In his rearview mirror, Gus watches Nancy as she pedals to gain speed for the hill and thinks that he can certainly appreciate why two guys would fight over a woman like her. He would of at that age; he probably would of.

❋ ❋ ❋

As Nancy is leaning her bike against the ledge in front of Ava's, a clashing racket of breaking crockery startles her. She looks up at the kitchen door, frightened, as the sound reverberates on the surface of the cove behind her. She sees Maggie in her morning robe on the kitchen stoop; Maggie has dumped a dustpan full of broken dishes into the big galvanized garbage can. Her furrowed frown relaxes when she sees Nancy.

"He has retreated up to the cabin," Maggie explains. "He said something about withdrawing to the high ground. Why don't you go on up? I thought to follow him and at least clean him up some, but he asked me not to. He is ashamed and hurt. How is your husband?"

"I hope Junior will take him up to Blue Hill; he ought to have his nose X-rayed."

"Oh my," Maggie says. "Oh my." *First fornication*, she thinks, *then thievery, and now drunken brutality. Who are these people? Is this the brave new world?*

Is the ceremony of innocence drowned? She goes back into the kitchen and says through the screen that the water is heated and that Nancy take the kettle up with her, as she will want warm water to wash him.

Kettle in hand, Nancy knocks lightly on the back door of the cabin, then lets herself into the little kitchenette. She sets the kettle on the stove and says into the front room, "David, are you awake?"

"Yes," he answers. "You can come in."

The windows in the front room that face out to sea are ablaze with the horizontal rays of the rising sun. Nancy squints, expecting to see him in the big, cushioned rocker by the hearth, but he is in the little back bedroom. She blinks to adjust to the darker room and finds him propped up on pillows atop the quilt on the wide bed, barefoot and bare-chested, wearing only his splotched blue jeans. She has prepared her face for the sight of his, but as she gets closer to him, she almost gasps. Instead she swears.

"Goddamn you guys. You could have killed each other. Good God, look at you."

The left side of David's face is puffed out and glistening like an eggplant, his left eye swollen shut. In the darker bedroom she can see that the bruise has changed in color to a purplish yellow and that his left earlobe, black with dried blood, is indeed split. His right cheek is cut in several places, and his right hand, which rests on his bare stomach, is cut and bruised.

Nancy sets her nurse's kit on the bed and takes the porcelain pitcher from its basin on the bureau.

"I'm sick of this drunken shit," she says.

She holds the pitcher with both hands as if it is full and turns back, outlined by the sunburst in the doorway. She begins to say something, but holds it back; instead she shakes her head once violently as if to cast loose something clinging to her.

When she returns, David's eye is closed and he is drifting into sleep. She fills the washbasin and soaps a washcloth; he awakens with a start and a childlike yelp of pain when she begins to wash his face.

"I'll go easy," she says. "I've got to soak the blood off to see what damage there is, though I can see plenty now."

David shuts his eye as she applies the warm washcloth.

"You have to lie still," she says. "The washbasin is on the bed next to you. Turn your head this way, and tell me . . ." She hesitates. Should she ask was it us, was it me, or was it what he could see and feel between us?

"Tell me what started it," she says. "What set him off?"

David opens his eye to look at her, then closes it again, smiling.

"I started it, actually. I knew he could kick my ass. I was hoping that when he did, you would take care of me, like this."

"That's not funny." She makes him wince with a rough swipe of the cloth.

"He wanted me to tell a war story. I said I don't have any good war stories. I said *he* was the storyteller, then the shit hit the fan."

"Oh," is all she says.

"Oh what? The left side of my face is on fire, for Christ's sake."

"The stories." She turns to the basin to rinse the cloth and soap it again. She feels incredibly sad. "He never said so, not outright, not sober, but he thinks that you know his war stories are all bull."

David is quiet and Nancy waits. Out the window, on the water, a fisherman and his stern man are in loud distant conversation over the noise of their radio.

"Garryowen," David says.

"What? I don't understand. Hold still."

"Garryowen. He told me he was with the Seventh Cav part of the First Cav. He had to be with the Seventh to have been at the Ia Drang. I said Garryowen, and he didn't know what it meant. Garryowen is the battle cry of the Seventh Cav, Custer's cavalry. There's music too. They say Garryowen every time they salute."

"He was with the First Cavalry Division, but he wasn't in a battle, not any battle," sighs Nancy "I'm going to change this water."

"Can I have some to drink?" David asks.

While she is gone, he thinks that he understands, that Simon is just another bullshit artist, and every time he was believed he revved up the stories a little more until he got in so deep that he was embarrassed by his own bullshit. David wants to ask her why Simon would call him a sensitive soldier with such bitterness.

When Nancy returns, she covers his face with a warm, wet cloth and asks him to open and close his mouth slowly while she feels his jaw.

"You jaw is okay and your teeth are fine, only a split lip. You might have a concussion; you should have one but your pupil isn't dilated."

With another cloth she cleans his hand, lifting it up to his chest from his stomach and belt to do so.

"You don't wear a shirt when you're out on the water, do you?"

From beneath the cloth he says quietly, slowly. "No Ia Drang. No smell of Johnson's baby powder from the dead brother. No door gunner and pregnant woman. No det cord."

"I don't know for sure, but I would guess none of it. I think they are stories he heard from others and embellished." She lifts the cloth, rinses it, and washes his cheek, a little gentler this time.

"But the details," he says. "They varied a little, but they're so real, so true, so convincing. The stories must be based on some experience. Ow! Jesus Christ."

"He's always been a good liar, a good storyteller. In high school he could make Friday night driving around with a six-pack sound like a wild and scary adventure when he told it on Monday morning. The war stories, those of battles, at least, can't be true. I don't know why he tells them," she says, lying to herself now.

"Why can't they be true?" David is surprised a little by how large and rough the hand is that holds his own while she washes it.

"If I tell you, will you promise never to tell another soul, never to use it against him? Never to tell him about this conversation?"

David says yes, of course, and waits until Melvin Hanson's boat with its big Cummins diesel roars past the cliffs beneath the cabin on his way south to haul, then promises that he will keep what she says to himself.

"He was a foot soldier. On his second or third day in Vietnam his platoon was ordered into enemy territory. He said while they were getting ready—saddling up—he fainted. He dropped right down; and not just that, but when they revived him he was paralyzed, really paralyzed, with fear."

"I've seen that," David says. "I have sure as hell felt it. But so?"

"So he didn't go with them. When it happened a second time, they moved him to the motor pool to wash jeeps and drive officers around. The other guys in his platoon never spoke to him again; he never got that combat infantry badge he so wanted."

"His stories were so real," David says as though to himself. "The one about being buried under the dead, the NVA bayoneting bodies on top of him, hiding his wedding ring so they wouldn't chop off his finger to take it, made me weak in the knees every time he told it."

"That's all he wants, I think." Nancy is not looking at David. "I think all he wants is to have us feel the fear he felt, and so to perhaps understand him, perhaps forgive him."

David, who can imagine what humiliation Simon must have suffered and still does, can't think of what to say. He wants to retreat into a deep, dreamless sleep, a healing sleep, a safe and quiet sleep. Nancy looks away, and he closes his eye.

"Simon may be a phony and a liar about what he did in Vietnam," she says, "but you'd be hard pressed to find anybody who hates himself for it as much as he does."

"For being afraid or for telling stories?"

"For both," Nancy says. "I'm not going to sew you up. Both that cheek cut and your ear could take two stitches, but I'm putting butterfly bandages on them, which means you're going to have to lie damn still for a couple of days. Will you?"

"I'll do my best."

ELEVEN

It didn't surprise me that that Simon lit into somebody. What surprised me was the amount of damage he did to the guy he lit into.
                                               –Fuddy McFarland

When the wind comes to Barter Island from the southeast, it arrives suddenly, rushing in from the open Atlantic, and it is dank and cold. It brings rain in sprays, trailers of fog so laden with moisture that they can be seen to tear apart among the trees, and it brings the wet salt chill of the North Atlantic. Few lobstermen will fish in a southeast wind as it baffles back and forth from southeast to east so quickly, so arbitrarily, that a man has a hard job coming around on the buoys with his gaff. When the wind is easterly, those few families who live on the seaward side of the island live in the face of the weather, with the cold gray sea before them and the green spine of the mountain ridge behind them, isolating them from the town and those who live in the comfortable lee of the mountain.

While the wind and fog and horizontal rain lasted during those three days, Gus visited the store to sit by the stove, and he visited the cove a couple of times a day to check on the *Betty B.*, which danced on a mooring chain that he has been meaning to replace. He visited David, too, though he quickly found that his stern man was being well nursed and attended to by Maggie and Nancy Cooper. David, Gus thinks, might have a face like a meatloaf and a headache of some proportion, but he got the better end of the stick. Simon, who whipped him, and who, according to Junior, is in exile in South Portland, will be allowed to return to the island only when his face has healed.

In the deep hours of Thursday night the wind backs to the south, and Myrtle Chafin wakes up sniffing the air in the bedroom. She sits up in the darkness and pokes Junior, who responds by heaving his huge midriff over onto his side, his back to the aggravation. This time Myrtle elbows him sharply in the middle of his spine.

He grunts and says,"What?"

"Smell," she says.

"Smell what?" He sniffs loudly to comply; her breath reminds him of embalming fluid.

"That," she says. "The wind's shifted. They're burning something. They're back."

Her breath notwithstanding, Junior does smell it: sweetish and acrid too. Something is burning, or has burned. It is not the smell of burnt wood, or vegetation, but the odor of rags smoldering, or of scorched metal and plastic mixed with the sweet-rotten stink of burning raw wool.

"Phew—Jesus," he says.

"They're back," she says. "And you've got to go up there as soon as it's light."

"I've got to haul my traps as soon as it's light. They've been setting three days."

"Well then, you can go up there now and be on the water at sunrise. You're the constable; you've got to apprehend those . . . those people."

"Now? In the dark? Good God. Look, it's not yet four o'clock. Apprehend? No. Question, you mean. The only place I'm going right now is back to sleep." He wants to tell her that she can go apprehend them, but he does not.

"How can you sleep when there's a fire in the woods and the wind southerly," she asks. "Are you crazy?"

"Whatever is burning isn't forest, as if you can't tell. The woods is soaked from three days of blowing rain and fog. For the sake of Christ, let me sleep."

Myrtle will not let him sleep when she cannot, not for anyone's sake, not when there is fire in the woods to windward of her house and the sickening, copulating criminals have returned and are lurking up there on the mountainside just as defiant of all human decency as they were before they robbed poor Christine McGregor. Now downstairs, she presses the pump handle to the right to make it squeak; she clamps down the lid on the empty teakettle, clamps it again when the kettle is full, and rattles and clatters yesterday's dishes as she puts them away, adding to the kitchen cacophony a nervous, very obviously fake, dry cough. To be absolutely sure, she turns on the CB radio and raises the volume until the static sounds like a raging sleet storm on a tin roof.

Junior lasts a half hour under his pillow before he mutters his way past her to have a pee in the dooryard. The hazy light in the east tells him that the sky has cleared; the wind is light and southerly. Outside, he can smell whatever it is that's burned, but just barely. Inside, he turns down the volume on the CB and sits down in his long johns to stir sugar into his tea while she slams and clangs about, making oatmeal and packing his dinner pail, carrying on only half listened to about how she said this would happen . . . What did anyone expect? . . . What was that McGregor thinking? . . . He ought to take the revolver with him, you can never tell . . . probably abandoned her and her baby on the mainland . . . and on and on until Junior lifts his last spoonful of cold oatmeal and soggy raisins.

Dressed, dinner pail and boots in hand, he leaves her still talking and steps out into the dooryard as the Willys pulls into the drive. Gus, too, is up and about an hour early; he sits in the Willys and waits for Junior to come to him, out of range of the kitchen door.

"They must of come back," Gus says. He reaches out and squashes a mosquito on Junior's forehead.

"Thanks," Junior says. "We smelt it too. Probably they're back and burning trash because it's wet now. I guess I got to go down there and ask him some questions."

"I thought you would. I'll go with you if you want. Bring your gear, and I'll drop you at your wharf on the way back. Or do you want to stop and see if that Simon wants to go too?"

"He's not *that* Simon; he's Simon. No. We won't be long; he can wait down there for me."

"They must be innocent if they came back," Gus says.

"Maybe. Probably, I'd guess. But maybe not, either. Maybe they stashed the money somewhere and are back to say they never."

Junior puts his boots and dinner pail in the back and settles in the front seat to watch with Gus as Myrtle, in a robe and dirty pink slippers, her hair tied up in an old linen towel, approaches them carrying the constable's revolver in her right hand as though walking to a gunfight.

"She's a sight when she's armed," Gus whispers.

"A caution."

✳✳✳

On the road, Junior tightens his left gallous strap and lights a cigarette, scratching the match alive with his thumbnail.

"Light me one, would you?" Gus is poking along in second gear. Ahead in the haze that is already beginning to burn off in the early sunlight above the road, he sees the McGregor truck coming toward them. Junior sees it too.

"First I lose a day of fishing because I am running around on the mainland looking for those goddamn freaks–they like being called freaks, I'm told." Junior picks a bit of tobacco from the tip of his tongue and flicks it out the window. "Then it's blowing easterly and a thick of fog. *Then* I lose a fair day when I could have hauled in a light rain, but Christ no, my mad-dog stern man has been in a brawl with Curly and has to be carried to Blue Hill to have his cracked nose X-rayed. We set there three hours to be told it's okay. And now, now these goddamn people are back and burning trash, and I got to go talk to them."

He finds the revolver, which has slipped down into his lap to hide under the shelf of his belly, and puts it in the glove compartment.

"I heard Simon go by around nine, racing down the east side," Gus says. "I thought he might be going to see David and shake hands, but he passed by not a half hour later going back. Up and down the road as always, probably with a snoot full."

"I guess," Junior says. "Look at McGregor wave; he wants you to stop, dear."

It is Eliot alone in the McGregor pickup. He is wearing a clean flannel shirt; his hair is wet and combed straight back. His thin lips are pressed shut, hidden between mustache and beard as though they are reluctant to let him speak.

"Hello Gus, Junior," he says. "I wonder, Junior, if you've heard anything about Willow and the women. From the mainland."

Junior leans ahead to talk across Gus. "No, I haven't. Nothing. Sorry."

Gus gives Junior a quizzical look, which Junior ignores.

"I'm going off on the morning boat," Eliot offers. "I'll see if I can learn anything. I have to go to a bank to see about a mortgage loan."

"Well, good luck to you," says Junior, and the Willys and truck drive on.

"Why didn't you tell him they're here?"

"Because he would of wanted to go with us, dear. If they're here, I want to talk to them alone, just us."

Gus steps off the road and across the drainage ditch to take the lead on the sodden path up to the tepee. He stops at a wet, lichen-covered boulder and cocks his head.

"Listen," he says.

Junior cocks his head too, breathing heavily through a wide-open mouth to hear better.

"I don't hear anything."

"Right," Gus says. "No barking. They heard us when we were this close last time, remember? Where's your revolver?"

"Down in the glove compartment."

Gus shakes his head. "Perhaps they took the animals with them. I should of worn my boots. My feet are soaking wet, socks too."

When Gus looks up from his shoes and the soggy path, he finds himself on the edge of the clearing before the reeking ruins of what was once the tepee, kitchen shed, and storage tent. Junior stands next to him, his hands in his pockets. Neither makes a sound until Junior gasps and points at the mutt and puppy who lie on their sides grinning in the mud and shit: they are still tied and their throats have been cut. The goat is gone.

"Oh, my dear God," Gus says quietly.

"Who would?" Junior turns around, his back to the clearing. "I'm going."

"No. Not yet. Let's look. There's stuff still smoking in the tepee."

Neither man speaks. Gus finds a stick; Junior does the same, and together they turn over the charred, smoking debris that is half covered by burnt pieces of sailcloth. The tepee poles are charred but still in place; the canvas at the top of the poles is intact, though singed. Junior shifts away from the smoke, keeping his back to the animals. He uncovers pieces of blankets, charred paperbacks, a wooden bowl, a shirtsleeve, a pair of leather sandals whose straps have been burnt away. He lifts the wretched remains of a sheep-skin vest.

"Here's what stank so," he says. "He must of soaked everything with kero or gas."

"Who?"

"Who? The guy who did this, that's who. You damn fool."

"I know that," Junior says sharply. "I meant who could he be, killing those animals. I thought maybe Simon; he said he would burn them out, and he drove by last night. But he wouldn't massacre tied-up puppies. Not ever."

"Willow," Gus offers.

"I guess so. I guess he came back for some stuff and then burned it down."

"And killed his dogs?"

"Christ, I don't know." Junior shrugs; he is at a complete loss.

"The goat's collar and chain are still here," Gus says. "He must of turned it loose. We ought to look for it."

"We need to douse that smoldering place first. Here's a bucket."

When they have soaked and stirred the mass inside the tepee and are satisfied that the pile is extinguished, Gus lights a cigarette.

"What was the goat's name?"

"Randolph," says Junior.

"No, it started with a G."

"It's Randolph," Junior is certain. "Nancy told it to me, and it's Randolph. How could Randolph start with a 'G' anyway–Christ."

"We need to find him," Gus says. "We'll look and call for him."

"How *do* you call a goat, dear?"

"I don't know. I don't know as you do call a goat," Gus says. "You go north and I'll go south."

A raucous gang of squabbling crows somewhere nearby in the woods reminds Gus that they will have to come back soon with shovels to bury the dogs. He turns to Junior to say so, but Junior has gone out of sight in a thicket of spruce, and Gus can hear his receding voice calling, "Here, goat. Here, Randolph."

With their winter visit in mind, Gus keeps an eye on the ground ahead lest he encounter a fresh coil of hippie shit. He finds that he is walking toward the noisy crows, thinking that it must have been Simon in a drunken fit of hatred, or, as they guessed, Willow come back and now gone again. He could easily have come and gone unnoticed had someone brought him down by boat, landed him, then took him and the animal off in some uninhabited cove.

Gus tends to his left, drawn toward the nearly riotous noise of crows that seems to be coming from a patch of penetrating sunlight beyond some young red maples. He gathers a handful of fair-sized stones.

It is a small natural clearing, a deep green floor of bayberry shrubs and blueberries surrounded by maples and scrub pine. In the center of the clearing is a crude platform, a large table made of limbs lashed onto horizontal spruce poles, the surface about six feet off the ground. In the center of the platform two crows dance on top of a bundle of sailcloth, black beak to black beak, their wings spread like hell divers; they are fighting over what looks like a large bloodworm that they have pulled from the bundle, until one lifts off with the worm in his beak to the delight of several spectator crows who croak obscenities from the trees. Gus hurls a stone at the crow still perched on the bundle, and two at those in the trees, dispersing them all, finally, with a hurled stick and a shout.

If he felt uneasy and a little nervous when they found the fire and the murdered dogs, Gus is now nearly smothered with a shapeless dread by the scene before him. The structure, he thinks, is about three days old, if the wilting of the garland of purple vetch on its borders is any indication. On each of its corners is a soggy spray of feathers gulls', hawks', and yes, crows'—tied to the platform with pink ribbon. The bundle in the center is perhaps the size of a thanksgiving turkey, and is secured to the platform with pink ribbons. He stands on tiptoe on a low boulder and looks over onto the platform. The bundle, he sees, rests in a bed of Saint-John's-wort, white yarrow, and daisies; it is decorated with a yellow sunrise and a rainbow, whose colors have run. In its very center, the crows have pecked through the shroud, tearing open a bloody hole, the smell and sight of which weakens Gus's knees, threatens his stomach, and sets his hands shaking. With a final push of resolve, he leans out onto the platform and feels first the top of the bundle, the head, then the bottom, the legs, before he falls back, shuddering. He lifts his eyes to the sunlight in the maples above on the mountain's slope and begins to bawl at the top of his lungs for Junior, his voice wavering and cracking in dismay and anger like the cry of a good boy being whipped unjustly for the first time.

Junior's answer comes from uphill among the spruce. When Gus hears Junior, he sits down on the rock and manages to light a cigarette on the second match. They call back and forth in the forest, Junior approaching, guided by the sound of Gus's voice. When Junior pushes his way cursing through the thicket, he stops to catch his breath.

"They got a clearing up there." He points up into the woods and wipes his forehead on his sleeve. "It's a big garden, with little mounds, and all the plants have been pulled up . . . What the hell's wrong with you, dear? You look like . . . "

Junior stares at the platform.

"What's this?" He stands on tiptoe. "The crows have been at it. Ugh."

"It's a baby."

"It can't be a baby." Junior's tone is disdainful; he hates it when Gus makes fun of him. "A baby off in the woods wrapped up on a, an altar? What is it, for Christ's sake?"

"It's a human baby; I felt of it. It's some kind of Indian or pygmy burial platform."

"What are you talking about?"

"I saw it in *National Geographic*. These natives, they put their dead on platforms instead of in the ground so the soul can get to heaven easier, or something like that."

"Help us, God," says Junior.

"I know it."

✳✳✳

The Barter Island Post Office is in Miss Lizzie Rich's parlor. The room is partitioned into Miss Lizzie's little office and a small sitting room by a wall into which a bank of mailboxes has been built. A Dutch door, the bottom half of which serves as a counter, is the only access to the little office. The mail-boat captain carries the day's letters and parcels from the morning boat in a padlocked canvas bag, property of the federal government. Miss Lizzie shuts and latches both halves of her door so she can sort the mail undisturbed. When she is done, she opens the top half of the door to attend to those who have received package cards in their boxes or want to buy stamps or money orders.

In July and August especially, the island natives go early to collect their mail, often sitting and chatting and watching the windows of their boxes for letters or magazines to appear while Miss Lizzie sorts the mail in silence behind her door, ears alert for gossip from the other side. They come early in the peak season to avoid the crush of summer people who do not check their mail until later in the morning. It is not that the natives dislike summer people, though some of the young new ones do on principle, but that the islanders have much to do and don't want to be delayed by summer rusticators who have nothing to do and would love to while away an hour talking about island arcana.

At 8:15 on this early August morning, Fuddy and Skippy and Skippy's little appendage Cecil sit on Miss Lizzie's front steps, Fuddy off to one side to allow clear passage to the door. Fuddy and Skippy, who are prodigious whittlers, are each at work on a piece of clear pine with a razor-sharp jackknife; Cecil is reading *Tintin In Tibet* and unconsciously blowing and popping pink bubbles of gum. Inside, Maggie and Betty sit facing the front window in two of the three chairs, talking quietly, almost mournfully.

Over Fuddy's head, they see Nancy walking down the hill from her house. Her hair is woven in a loose French twist; she is wearing blue jeans and a blue cotton shirt; the straps of her backpack draw her shirt tight over her breasts, and, as she comes closer, it is apparent to the women watching inside and the men on the stoop that she is not wearing a bra and does not need to.

"She's lost weight only recently," Betty remarks. "Look how narrow she is in the waist and hips. The girl is not built for birthing."

"No, she's not," Maggie says. "You once had a beautiful bosom like that, Betty."

"Didn't I though?" Betty laughs. "And I would've gone without a bra if I could have. They put Band-Aids over their nipples when they wear flannel shirts to protect them from chafing."

"Thank you," Maggie says.

Through the screen door they see and hear Nancy greet the whittlers and admire Fuddy's sculpture. Inside, she bids the women a cheerful good morning that seems forced to Maggie and sits down, setting her backpack on the floor beside her.

"Nancy, tell us how your husband is faring," Maggie says. "Is he quite healed? We were relieved to hear that his nose is not broken."

"Very nearly healed," Nancy says. "He still has two black eyes, well-deserved black eyes."

"And I am glad that he and David are on speaking terms again," says Betty, who is also glad to see that Nancy is uncomfortable with the topic.

"Are they indeed?" Maggie asks.

"Yes, Junior and Gus made them shake hands when they sent them up to bury the poor dogs."

The women fall silent, and behind the mailboxes Miss Lizzie stands stock-still. Nancy hesitates; she knows what they are waiting for her to say, or thinks she does.

"It sounds awful, I know, but I was relieved to hear that the dogs had been killed and how it was done," Nancy begins. "I knew then that Simon couldn't have done that burning; he could never kill a dog, kill a puppy with a knife." Nancy's voice rises. "He's done lots of bad things, but never anything like that, never anything evil."

Nancy does not say that Simon claims that he wishes he had burned them out, that he had "wrapped det cord around that fucking tepee and blown it all to commie hell."

"No, no," Maggie consoles. "Certainly not Simon. Who but the cruel lunatic who put that infant out for the birds to feed upon could have done such a thing to two dogs? Betty has just now been telling me the gruesome details. It seems that reality has indeed far outrun Myrtle's most horrible apprehensions. They took the poor thing up to the Jones brothers?"

"Yes," Betty says.

A terrified howl from the front stoop pierces the quiet parlor. It is Skippy's cry, and the women turn aside in time to see Cecil chasing his friend with something pinched between his thumb and forefinger.

"Spider," Betty says. "Skippy's scared to death of them."

"He'd eat one alive to please that boy," Maggie says.

"Who are the Jones brothers?" Nancy asks.

"The undertakers in Stonington." Betty is watching Cecil and Skippy running in delighted circles on the lawn. "Junior called the state troopers in Ellsworth. There's going to be a coroner's inquest, an autopsy to make sure there was no foul play."

"Surely no one could be so depraved as to..."

"If they were on some drug like the one they gave Skippy, they could have done anything. Remember what Charles Manson's beastly girls did to that movie star and her unborn baby?"

Maggie does remember; she shuts her eyes, thinking bitterly that this is not the dawning of the Age of Aquarius, but rather of the Age of Molech.

"It's Gus, Betty," she says. "It's Gus I'm most worried about."

"I am too, and for good reason." Anger strains Betty's voice.

"Why...?" Nancy tries.

"Because God has been cruel to him," Betty says. Her cheeks are flushed, her hands, fingers entwined in her lap, grasp one another. "Seeing David mauled-I'm sorry, Nancy–awakened images of the suffering he thinks that John went through before he died."

Maggie turns aside as if to see if a letter has slipped into her mailbox; Miss Lizzie is still again, listening.

"And now this." Betty lifts up her eyes to the ceiling. "This to remind him of his own baby girl, dead before she was born, killed with her mother in a highway crash. Last night he could barely speak. I had to grill him mercilessly to find out what happened, what they found. When he got to the part where Junior put the little bundle in a bassinet to take aboard, he choked and his eyes lost focus like they did when he heard that John had been killed. Now he has withdrawn again. He won't eat, not even a baked potato. He took a drink and went to bed. When I came to bed, he pretended he was sleeping, knowing that I knew he wasn't."

Betty looks down at her hands.

What you neglected to mention, Maggie thinks when Betty falls silent, is that Gus swore to me, twice, and probably to you too, that he did not know why the boys had fought, but David swears that he told Gus it was something to do with telling war stories, reminding Gus of what he alone believes: that it was his own war stories, exaggerated but told humbly to emphasize his own gallantry, that inspired John to join the marines, to go to Vietnam as an infantryman, to get himself killed.

After a moment's wait to be sure that Betty has finished, Miss Lizzie opens the top half of her door and says to Betty:

"Will you tell Fuddy his Sears catalog is here? He'll be some happy."

Nancy rises, her hand outstretched. "Here, Miss Lizzie. I'll give it to him."

"Oh, I can't do that, dear. It's the U.S. mail, you know."

"Oh Lizzie," Betty says. She turns to the door.

"Fuddy, your wish book's here."

✳✳✳

In the first early light beneath an overcast sky the sea is flat calm, the color of burnished metal reflecting the thin light that filters through the high clouds. Gus has not turned on the CB radio and drives the *Betty B.* in silence, sipping his tea, wending his way at half speed among the bearded ledges that are left so exposed by the departing tide. David sits on the washboard, his hands wrapped around a thermos cup of coffee watching the other lobster boats, all from the Stonington fleet, farther out to sea, thinking that those men would like to be fishing closer to shore off the east side of Barter Island early in shedding season.

David stands up for a better view and watches as three tiny cormorants scurry across the surface to climb onto their mother's back and ride away from the offending *Betty B.*, afraid to look back. He taps Gus on the shoulder and points to the retreating mother and her three passengers. Gus looks, sees, nods in acknowledgment, and turns back to the windshield. On another day Gus would have been delighted by the sight and would have offered a fond comment, but this morning he is quiet, withdrawn, distracted by some distant woe.

Gus's dark mood threatens to envelop David, as well. In a letter from a friend at Fort Bragg—one for some reason long delayed in coming—he learned yesterday that his worst fears for his Khmer friends have come true and that the soldiers and families from both the outpost and the village of Ba Xaoi have fled the Vietnamese, crossing the border to seek refuge in the mountains and villages in Cambodia. He does not want to imagine Neang, Chau Sinh, and Socheat, dirty, half-starved, and hunted in some makeshift mountain camp, or huddled beneath a tarp in a swamp of sewage on some side street in Phnom Penh with hundreds of other refugees, all strangers, all victims of corrupt police and soldiers.

Earlier, alone in his damaged kitchen, holding a cold washcloth on his bruised face, David resolved to be busy today, to keep his mind on the boat, to pay special attention to the needs of his captain, to find solace in the familiar tedium of gaffing, hauling, emptying, baiting, and launching two hundred sixty lobster traps. He had spent a fitful night, waking and half sleeping, plagued by the odor of burning in his nostrils and the sight, both remembered from Ba Xaoi and from hearing what Gus found on the platform, of a tiny child's hand—a perfect miniature human hand—its raised fingers curled in a final grasp in the backseat of his jeep, lighted by a red-filtered flashlight and a burning house beyond. Now, as he and Gus ride in companionable silence approaching their southernmost string just off the Eastern Ear of the island, he sees, then hears, Junior and Simon off the port bow; Junior's CB is turned up to hear some distant captain's whining complaints, and Junior and Simon are talking, nearly shouting, to one another above the noise, Junior laughing uproariously. Junior and Simon step back from *Myrmaid's* house to wave, and David does the same; Gus reaches an arm out in brief recognition, and cuts back on the throttle to come around on the first buoy, gaff at the ready. David pulls up his boot tops, ties his apron behind his back, spears a bait bag stuffed with herring, and stands at the washboard, ready for the first trap to break the surface. Gus hauls it out and slides it back to David, then brings up the second of the pair on this buoy. There are two lobsters in David's trap; both go the measure, and both, he discovers when he lifts them out, are soft-shelled shedders, the first of the season and harbingers of many, many more to come.

"Well," David says. "Here we go, Cappy. Shedders!" He holds aloft the climbing, snapping creatures.

Gus smiles slightly, pegs the claws of the one he is holding, and drops it into the barrel.

When they have hauled all twenty traps in the first string-and ten in the second, set in the wide Turnip Yard–they find that they are getting at least a pound a trap. On another day, this would have brought forth the happy, laughing claim from Gus that they were "dogging 'em" and a proposal for a drink or two when they got up to the lee of the Battery. Today it elicits only a quiet nod of satisfaction to what might as well be, David thinks sadly, an empty deck, empty forever without John.

An hour or so before noon, Gus takes the *Betty B.* out of gear and lets her drift on the smooth, windless surface while they sit to eat their lunch. Gus has not uttered an unnecessary word all morning and says little while he eats except to comment that the season for storms is almost upon them, telling David for the twentieth time how the hurricane of '36 wrecked so many boats and wiped out so much gear that some fishing families went hungry that winter and had to move off-island to find work. He recounts how, in '39, a storm out at sea sent in a rogue wave that nearly capsized his grandfather Amos's big Novi boat.

As the tide turns in the early afternoon and the southwest wind returns with it, they pass Eaton Cove as they run north between strings. In the meadow by the McGregor house, David sees Christine and Nancy standing together in conversation, and behind them in the doorway, a figure that can only be Eliot. Christine and Nancy look around when they hear *Betty B.* in the channel and wave to her. David returns the wave; Christine turns aside to Eliot, who pays none of them any mind. Nancy waves again, to David, a high-hand-ed, slow, pendulum wave that David matches, remembering her soft, persist-ent touch on his face and hands, his forearm brushing against her soft breast.

"You better be careful," says Gus, who is watching them watch one another. "He almost killed you last time, and isn't anybody blaming him."

"It wasn't about her," David insists.

"If it wasn't, I'm a horse's ass." Gus pulls back on the throttle and takes up the gaff, looking back at the McGregors.

"Buried under the Eaton's headstone, for Christ's sake. Everything they had: thousands in hundred-dollar bills. For a guy who hates banks and paying interest for normal reasons and high-toned ones too, taking out a mortgage must of been a bitter damn pill."

David slides the trap aft on the washboard. "He hasn't said a kind word to her since."

Gus shakes his head slowly to say that nothing makes any sense anymore. Nothing. Or what was it Maggie said? The center is no longer holding.

Running in toward the cove from the last string along the York Ledges, David looks up to the cleared height and the cabin and thinks that up there he is as safe from the outside world as anyone can be, but even there not entirely safe from the offenses of the present and the haunts of the past.

This time David does not notice the blue-and-yellow buoys strung a hun-dred feet from the shore along the cliff beneath the cabin, but Gus does, and turns toward them, saying simply, almost to himself, "Well then."

"I've never seen those colors," David says. "Not even up in the bay. It's not Milo Weed."

"It's his uncle, Roger. It must be that they're going to push harder this time. Roger is not a man to back down. They want to see if I am. These are Grandfather's waters."

Gus gaffs a blue-and-yellow buoy, clamps the line in the pot hauler, and brings up enough line to allow him to tie off the warning knot–two half hitches over the spindle—then drops it back in, turning *Betty B.* toward the next buoy.

"Why don't we go up to Stonington and tell Roger to take his fucking traps out of your waters?"

David watches Gus tie the knot, thinking it curious, but when the buoy is back in the water, he sees that the knot on the spindle makes the buoy swim backwards, bucking the tide and wind.

"We don't do it that way," Gus says. "Besides, he has the legal right to set out here."

"Jesus, then what's to stop him from appealing to the warden? Why didn't Milo?"

"Because that's not the way we do things." Gus's voice is weary with impatience. He drops the next buoy and line overboard. "The wardens are from away. Our customs are a higher authority than the law."

"What will he do if you cut him off?"

"Cut me off, probably."

"Then what?"

"Well, a trap war, I guess. There hasn't been one down here in years."

"And what's that mean, a trap war?" David asks.

"Hell to pay." Gus takes up another buoy. "We're being invaded on land, and now we're being invaded on the water, too. Christ." With the gaff he takes a couple of swings at a gull that is considering landing on the transom and dirtying it. The gull gives up and veers off to look for another perch.

"Let me tie these next ones," David says. "Then it will be both of us doing it."

Gus looks at David curiously, nods with a slight smile, then watches with approval as David ties the warning knot, drops the buoy over, and watches it turn against the tide, a freak among the other buoys in sight, whose spindles ride the current or wind. As they finish tying off Roger's lines, David thinks that next year he will have his own traps and will be fishing these waters with Gus, perhaps to inherit them when Gus is done, as John would have. He hopes that it will not come to cutting off or to violence; when you hold the high ground and they dare to come at you from all sides, there's nowhere else to go.

TWELVE

Frailty, thy name is not Christine McGregor.
—Christine McGregor

Sunday night
August 23, 1971

Ruth Dear,

Have I told you that I so love the early fall? No doubt I have five dozen times. But more so now with the advent of heating with wood down here, as the air, when the wind is just right, is redolent with the sweet smell of burning birch, of pungent spruce. I am thinking of getting a woodstove myself (Gus and Betty have—they are so "with it") and saying good-bye forever to the stifling petroleum stench of kerosene.

You asked about the hippies, and I neglected to answer you in my last letter—yet another lapse, ever so common nowadays. No, there has been no news of them from any quarter. We do know that the poor infant was indeed stillborn—never drew a breath—and if that tribe is somehow ever found, they will be interrogated about the theft and may be charged with improper burial and failure to report a death.

(I should make carbon copies of my letters to you to preclude repetition, but that would mean writing with pencil, or, God forbid, ballpoint pen.)

I had David and Leah for supper last night (ha-ha! you say), and I learned from them, via Nancy, that the cheerless

Eliot McGregor blames Christine for the loss of their (her) money. He avers that she must have told the thieves where it was hidden, and he hectors her day and night, bullying her with quiet disapproval of everything she takes pride in, from book-keeping to weeding. She has taken on evening jobs cleaning cottages for summer people after working like a dray horse on the "farm" from dawn till dark. And she confides only in Nancy; she has selected her own society and shut the door on the rest of us with a brave smile and a polite demeanor. I am reminded of the way poor Leah was treated years ago–I'm sure she is too–men can be so damn cruel when they are thwarted, especially greedy or uncertain men.

But for those who travail on the sea, these are salad days. Feast days. Gus and David are pulling up traps that are crowd-ed with lobsters, as are Junior and Simon, and a happier pair of pairs I haven't seen in a long while, not since the cove was teem-ing with boats and brothers and cousins; not since John was Gus's stern man, since Junior and Dunreath fished together. We women say secretly that we hope that David stays on the island and that Junior can calm the unruly Simon somehow, perhaps give him the confidence he so obviously lacks.

Leah left after the sherbet to work on the store's books. David stayed to help with the dishes and sit amiably in the par-lor with a glass of sherry. I find that I am of two minds about him: I want him to stay down here for Gus's sake and for the community which is aging too quickly, but I want him to go back to college, for his own sake and for his parents'. He says he cannot abide the "scene" on campuses these days and hates this cultural upheaval, this "revolution," this "movement," with all his heart. (He told me of the Chinese curse that says: "May you live in interesting times.") But when I bade him goodnight on the stoop, I felt quite sure that I had at least planted the seed of possibility for compromise: college during the academic months, lobstering with Gus in the summer months as he wishes (and for Gus's sake).

I am nearly finished with Cheever's *The Wapshot Chronicle* and find myself falling in love with the crotchety old sea dog Leander. Thanks for recommending it, dear one.

My love to all, as always.

Maggie

PS: They have found the goat. It seems that he appeared yester-day morning at the McGregors', gazing fondly at the cabbage through the garden fence. He's named for a wizard, I am told.

* * *

At her bathroom window, Nancy notices that the lights in the school-house are on, and she sees old Mrs. Carnidge the schoolteacher leaning over her desk in the corner. It is not yet dark, though it soon will be, and Nancy wonders for a moment why Mrs. C. is working tonight, when everyone else is preparing for the end-of-the-summer dance in the town hall, which will begin very soon. Then she remembers that this will be Labor Day weekend and that school will start on Tuesday, and with Mrs. C.'s crooked back in sight, Nancy's heart goes out to poor little Cecil, who so fears and loathes the old creature.

Beyond the little lighted schoolhouse and the dark alder swamp, Nancy catches sight of someone walking down Town Hill: a vague, slow-moving fig-ure in the near darkness, walking to town from the east side, its stride short-ened by the steep decline before the bend. The figure's swaying shoulders make her think that it is Christine, but she has never seen Christine walk with her hands in her pockets nor known her to wear a white shirt. In the light from Charlie Bowen's porch, she sees that whoever it is has short hair and decides that it is a summer person walking in to the dance from the Point Lookout road, a sailor, perhaps a young crew member from a yacht moored at the point come to town in clean shirt, chinos, and Top-Siders to find him-self a girl at the dance.

If Simon was here, she thinks, he'd have something cruel and crude to say about the guy when he walked past the house: he'd call him a rich fag-got, a candy-ass draft dodger, and, if he had had a few, he would say it loud enough to be heard almost perfectly by the boy passing. But Simon is not here; he has gone to South Portland to see the boys for the third weekend in a row, and that is fine with her. He goes home to raise hell with the boys Saturday night and well into Sunday morning; the boys, and, increasingly, she suspects, his blonde cousin Catherine. Nancy resents the money he wastes, but she is grateful for his quiet recovery Sunday and Monday and sometimes into midweek, when he is subdued (guilty?) and almost pleasant, working hard during the day, going to bed sober and smelling of soap.

But the walker's clothes are not chinos and Top-Siders; they are Carharts and work boots. Nancy hurries to push open the front screen door. It is not a boy from a yacht crew; it is Christine with her hair cut as short as any man's. It is Christine as cleaned up and shy and hesitant as Nancy has ever seen her. It is Christine come alone to go to the dance with her as Nancy has begged her to do for two weeks. It is Christine standing stock-still in the dooryard, her hands still in her pockets, her face tanned and turned full toward Nancy in the doorway, her gray-blue eyes wide in an anxious query.

"Oh, Christine, what have you done?" Nancy moves closer to her friend, noticing in the half-light that the back of her neck, bare now, is pink from the sun.

"You hate it, don't you?"

Nancy laughs and holds Christine's shoulders. "No I don't hate it; I love it." She can see that Christine does not believe her. "I do, I swear I do. Is it a statement of some kind?"

Christine pulls away. "A statement? What do you mean? No. It is simply practical and hygienic." Christine does not explain that the idea was originally to cut it as penance, but now that it is done, she also thinks that it is handsome.

"Did he do it?"

"Well, he cut it, but it was my idea. You don't like it."

"The more I look, the better I like it," Nancy says, and means it. "It was just a surprise." She caresses the back of her friend's head, now so soft and pink and vulnerable. "Your pretty face is even prettier."

"Eliot likes it. He says the island matrons will hate it."

A truck passes on the road, honks hello, and waves to Nancy and the stranger.

"Who cares what they think. I like it, too. You think they'll hate your haircut; they won't even notice it when they see this." Nancy does a pirouette, fists fixed on her hips, to show off her very short leather skirt, very long, very bare legs, and Christine laughs.

"Are we going to the dance, then?"

"You're damn right we are," says Nancy. "But first we're going to have a beer to get our personalities going. Come on in."

"Well, not a beer, no, but okay."

Nancy offers her arm; Christine takes it, and the friends step inside the house.

✳✳✳

For six years or so the Barter Islanders have referred to the houses, the town hall, and the store that sit on both sides of the road in town, on the western side, as the Lucky Mile. While the distance from the town landing to the schoolhouse at the foot of the Town Hill may not be quite a mile, those who live and work in the buildings along this stretch are indeed lucky because they alone of all the island enjoy electricity provided by the town's generator at the landing. Chief among those blessed with electric power is the large, square-shouldered town hall, built of boulders and hardwood beams at the turn of the century. Tonight the town hall blazes with light from every window, especially those that throw light from the hall itself onto the lawn and road where dozens mingle in laughing clusters while the orchestra warms up on the stage inside. Running shallow among the islands of adults is a current of chasing children; on the front steps and porch the teenagers, both native and summer people alike, are gathered in loose groups. Just inside the double doors, the ladies of the church are busy arranging two tables of refreshments; far across the lawn and road in the shadow of the alders, several fishermen are gathered around Fat Albert and Eben's open trunk to mix and down a quick one and have a smoke before the reverend goes inside and all others follow. Tonight the ladies have lined both sides of the entrance walk with little sand-ballasted bags in which burn gay candles to form a promenade.

When Nancy and Christine emerge from Nancy's house to walk the hundred yards to the town hall, it is full dark and most of the crowd has moved inside behind Reverend Hotchkiss. Nancy takes Christine's hand as they approach the lighted walk and the eyes of the teens on the porch and the few fishermen lingering in the shadows turn on Nancy and her unfamiliar companion. Inside, a voice that could only come from the giant that Jack met at the top of the beanstalk, or Reverend Hotchkiss, is lining up couples in preparation for calling of the "Lady of the Lake," the traditional first dance. Among those who are pretending not to watch Nancy and Christine approach, only Fuddy and Skippy, seated on Fat Albert's bed, recognize Christine and wave to her. The others, the teens especially, watch in wonder as Nancy, in short skirt, sandals, and peasant blouse, her own hair shoulder-length and unconstrained, approaches with this stranger, then their mouths drop open in undisguised awe when they realize that it is the calloused, hermetic Christine McGregor who walks with Nancy, looking more like a blue-eyed, freckled, vulnerable girl than the bereaved and abused wife of the iron-hearted ideologue of Eaton

Cove. As the silent teens part to let them through, Christine lets go of Nancy's hand and with a shy smile leads the way inside to face the astonished church ladies at the refreshment table.

Seated on one of the folding chairs along the far wall, Leah sees Nancy in the doorway beyond the dancers who are lined up awaiting the orchestra's opening. She recognizes Christine next to her and sees David, who is standing with the men in the near line, turn toward Nancy and raise a hand in greeting.

"Look there in the doorway," Leah says to Maggie.

"Heavens," says Maggie over the music. "I thought she was a boy. Now aren't the two of them a sight to remember?" She smiles, basking in the triumphant entry that the two have made.

On Leah's left, Myrtle overhears them and cranes her neck once, twice, to see past Betty who has just given Mabel a playful shove.

Myrtle is speechless, and she is immediately thrice glad that she has dressed the way she has–in a full, tiny-flowered skirt (three stiff petticoats) and a bright red blouse cut low, almost off her shoulders with little puffed sleeves-so that the younger women, who thought that their jeans and T-shirts and miniskirts and other racy get–ups were acceptable at a contra dance called by the reverend, can see how they *should* be dressed. A girl can have a good time, too, dressing up, even dressing up a little risky, but she can be decent about it.

Bernadine stands at center stage leading the three-piece orchestra with her accordion; at her side, mike in hand, the reverend begins to call the dance, and on the floor Leah and Maggie converse, their mouths nearly touching one another's ears to be heard. Myrtle, who is left out of the conversation next to her by necessity and left out of the dance by Junior, who lingers outside with Eben and the others, watches with displeasure as the lines progress, as Betty's full-skirted, red square-dance dress flies wide in do-si-dos and allemande lefts with Gus and her neighbors. With even more displeasure, she watches Nancy and Christine in the entryway chattering away cheerfully with anyone and everyone as if they were not the harlot and newly announced lesbian that they most obviously are.

The first dance done, nearly half of the dancers of "Lady of the Lake" find their way outside for fresh air and a little something to drink. Those who stay inside to form up for the "March and Circle" are joined by a dozen new dancers, including Myrtle and Junior, David and Nancy, and the beautiful

Lodge twins who are being watched by half the island teenage boys whose heads appear in a row outside the big window. Fuddy buttons up his flannel shirt to seal in his aroma and approaches Christine, who stands alone in the doorway. Fuddy holds his right hand flat against his tummy, the other behind his back, and bows deeply before her, asking for the pleasure of being her partner, which she grants happily.

As the orchestra returns to the stage, Myrtle says to Junior, "You didn't tell me your boy Simon was off-island again this weekend."

"Didn't think I needed to."

"How convenient," she says, with a nod toward David and Nancy ahead in the line. When she sees Fuddy and Christine take up places just behind David and Nancy, she turns to Mabel, just behind her.

"Today's the first of September, you know. It's the anniversary of when Hitler invaded Poland. He almost destroyed the world," she says. "He nearly did."

"Bow to your partner," the reverend commands, and Myrtle and Mabel obey.

An hour later, the reverend announces that tonight the last contra dance before "Good Night, Irene" will be "Duck for the Oyster, Dive for the Clam," and he looks around to find Skippy, who is in the entryway behind the refreshment table, and who perks up when he hears what's been said. "Duck for the Oyster, Dive for the Clam" is Skippy's favorite, with all the ducking under arches of arms and diving under clasped hands, with words like "Punch a hole in the old tin can / Turn the can inside out" that sing to his heart, and it is the only tune that he will dance to. Those around him, the delighted ladies at the punch bowl, gang up on him and usher him onto the floor, where Betty bows deeply before him, and he returns the bow, his hand hiding a misshapen and euphoric smile.

Only the liveliest and most experienced contra dancers dare to dance to the reverend's fast and furious "Duck for the Oyster, Dive for the Clam." Those who demur line the edges of the floor and windows to watch, clap, and laugh at collisions, stumbles, and to witness, finally, Skippy's wild ascent to the last do-si-do in which he lifts Betty clear off the floor and swings her around and around until she squeals for mercy, and his sixty-year-old heart nearly bursts with transcendent joy.

✳✳✳

"It's time for me to go home," Christine says to David and Nancy. "I'm all of a sudden so tired."

The three stand in the road in the light of the town hall windows, their shadows reaching across the road to the alders. Gus and Betty have just left, walking to the Willys parked past the alders, with Junior and Myrtle trailing astern headed to Junior's Ford.

"I shouldn't have tried to dance 'Duck for the Oyster,' " Nancy says. "I'm all sweaty." She holds her collar open. "Look, I'm steaming. You can't walk home, Christine; you'll catch cold, for sure. I'll take you."

"Let me give you a ride," says David. He lights a cigarette and says good-night to Gus as the Willys creeps slowly through the thinning crowd in the road. Most of the adults have left for home, the contra dance done, but the teens and other younger ones are setting up a record player in the hall for the second half of the evening, the rock-and-roll and locoweed half, that will go on until nearly dawn.

"Oh no," Christine says. She pinches the front of her shirt and shakes it in and out to cool herself down. "You want to stay for the rowdy part, both of you do."

Inside the hall, Mick Jagger is howling from twin speakers about painting things black. Nancy is watching two summer teenage couples passing a joint around in an ancient Chevy parked on the lawn.

"I don't really want to stay," David says. "I'm tired, too. Let me take you."

"Let's go, Christine," Nancy says quietly. "I don't know, but tonight I just feel, well, too old to stay for the party."

Nancy holds the door of David's truck for Christine, who slides across the camouflage seat cover to make room for her friend. Next to David, Christine strokes the seat.

"What is this," she asks as Nancy climbs in. "It's so soft."

"It's a poncho liner," Nancy says. "We have one too. They issued them in Vietnam; kind of a quilt liner for a poncho, for warmth."

David opens his little side window and tilts it to give Christine a breeze. Nancy does the same on her side.

"It's a seat cover now," David says. "The seat's coming apart; I need to pin the liner on permanent."

"Simon would never use his for a seat cover," Nancy says. "He treats it like a holy relic, rolled up smartly and tied inside his poncho on the closet shelf."

"Is it silk?" Christine asks.

"Probably synthetic," David allows. "Maybe Simon had a heavenly experience in his; maybe he . . ."

David catches the look that Nancy throws across the cab at him and desists. When he passes her house he says that he will bring her back after they drop off Christine; Nancy doesn't reply.

There is neither breeze tonight nor any visible stars, but when they gain the top of Town Hill, they can just see the moon in its third quarter through high thin clouds, and Nancy can feel a sharp promise of autumn in the air as she leans her head against the open window frame to catch the soft current, letting it dry the damp tendrils of her hair. David is driving slowly, not more than ten miles an hour in second gear, and Christine is nodding, slipping in and out of dream.

When he turns into the McGregors' long drive, Christine insists that he let her out at the road, saying that she would like to walk in. She thanks David for the ride, and outside the cab, she thanks Nancy for the evening.

"Don't thank me." Nancy laughs, then hugs Christine; she holds her cheek against hers for a moment and kisses her good-night.

David and Nancy watch Christine walk along in the right hand rut in the drive, then disappear from the headlights as she rounds the wooded corner.

"Do you want to go back to the dance, or do you want to go home?"

"Neither," Nancy says. "No. I don't know."

"Let's go around the island. I'll take you home the long way, and you can decide while we drive."

As they pass Gus and Betty's, they see a lamp move past the kitchen window. Nancy crosses her legs and leans an arm out of the cab.

"Are you and Christine...?" David begins.

Nancy glares at him, angry, surprised. "Are we what?"

"You know. I mean her haircut, and holding hands, and that kiss just now."

"Oh goddamn you," she says. "Let me out. Stop right the hell here and let me out."

"Don't be pissed. I was just curious. It wouldn't make any difference to me; I'd–"

"It wouldn't be any of your goddamn business, either. You're just as bad as he is. You're all the same. Let me out. I want to be alone. I want to walk."

"Don't, Nancy. Don't make me. Please. I'm sorry. Believe me, I am sorry."

"You can think what you want of me, I don't care, but you leave her alone. Jesus Christ, all because of a friggin' haircut."

"You have to admit it is a pretty manly haircut."

"Maybe she's feeling manly; maybe she needs to right now. That doesn't mean that..." She stops, waves her hand at him to dismiss him and the subject and turns toward the window as though she is deeply interested in the boulders that form the sharp turn called the Needle's Eye.

Very little, less than a quarter, of the only road on Barter Island is paved; the remainder of the fourteen miles is one-lane unimproved dirt, which often means boggy stretches whose ruts are filled in with rotting logs, steep hills strewn with loose stones the size of potatoes, and almost everywhere, deep ditches on both sides that make it impossible to pull over for an oncoming vehicle to pass. Though there are very few places along the road where the sea is in sight because of the high rocky cliffs of the shoreline, there are stretches that pass through hauntingly beautiful cedar bogs, some that pass steep granite cliffs covered with moss and lichen rising on the inland side, others that cross over deep streambeds alive with tumbling water, several spots where Long Pond can be seen, and some places where fields of hay-scented fern and ancient birch trees spread for acres. Even in daylight, some of the long passages through dense spruce forest are dark and menacing.

As they pass the fern-blanketed hillside above Long Pond, Nancy is thinking about Christine, then talking about her, as though concluding her thoughts aloud.

"It's just that she is not afraid. That's what I admire most about her, I think. And that she is always eager to learn. Learn everything."

David does not answer. He is thinking that he would like to lie down in the soft ferns with her, that if he allows himself to look at her long bare legs one more time, he will certainly make a drooling fool of himself somehow.

"I want to be more like her," Nancy says to her open window.

"You certainly aren't afraid," David says. "Nobody could call you timid."

"Maybe, but I could be more curious, more adventurous intellectually. She borrowed my nurse's textbooks. She wants me to continue my education and get my RN. I didn't think I wanted to, but now I do. Because of her."

"Would you have to go back to Portland? You would, wouldn't you?"

"Yes, and I'd like to take her with me, get her away from that abusive bastard."

"You really think Eliot abuses her? Beats her?"

"No, not physically, but mentally, which can be worse." David starts to light a cigarette. "Please don't," she says. "The night air smells so sweet. Thank you. She tells me everything, and I tell her everything, too, but there is something about him that she's holding back, even from me."

"About the hippies," he offers.

"Yes. I think he is the one who burned them out and killed the dogs. He hates useless things, especially animals, ones that took up her precious time to feed. And he tore up the marijuana plants. She must have told him about them; who else knew about them? She's protecting him, I'm sure of it, but still he treats her like shit."

At the tiny public beach at the foot of Long Pond, David turns his truck so that its headlights skim the misty surface of the pond and arouse the gulls that have been floating on the water and sitting on the exposed rocks. The pond is a mile long, very deep, and barely two hundred yards wide, a glacial slash running north to south. When the gulls return to the water and their perches, David shuts off the headlights and the truck.

"Maggie wants me to go back to college and finish," David says. "Let's sit on the tailgate so I can smoke."

He lets himself out and Nancy follows to settle upwind and at arm's length from him, saying that she is not surprised.

"She thinks I should compromise: spend the winter months in school, the summers fishing with Gus."

Nancy nods, watching his face.

"I don't want to compromise, though. I want to make a commitment. I don't want to be summer people. I don't want to go back to live among arrogant, simpleminded intellectual snobs who judge me in ignorance and hate me for things I never did. I want to fish with Gus, live here year-round, and maybe someday inherit his waters."

"Like John would have done," she says quietly.

"Like John would have done," he says.

Nancy does not say that it is only the prospect of spending another winter on the island with David here and Simon in Portland that causes her to hesitate about going back to school.

"I'm going for a swim," David says. "Come on."

Nancy hesitates, though she has expected this since he turned in at the beach. "I'll go first, but you have to turn your back until I say so."

"Okay," he says. "Watch out for the eels, though. Pete Gully dove into a ball of them, hundreds of them all tangled up."

"So I've heard," she says.

David does not watch her undress in the thin moonlight, but he cheats and watches her as she walks out into the water, watches her small round bottom as she gets deeper and deeper and finally calls to him when she is submerged.

While he is undressing, David does not see where Nancy swims to; when he gets out into the pond where she called him from, he cannot see her. Treading water, he calls her once, softly, but she does not answer. The water is surprisingly cold. He swims with his head out of the water toward the rocks and calls again, impatient this time.

He hears the truck door slam shut, but he cannot see that far in the dark. As he swims toward shore, he thinks briefly that she may have taken his clothes and is about to drive away as a joke.

When he comes out of the water, shivering and walking gingerly on the sharp stones, he cannot see her anywhere. He calls her name, but to no avail, then turns toward his clothes in the sand, hugging himself for warmth.

"Here," she says from the picnic table under dark shade of a maple. "David."

He can only see a vague form as he approaches; then he can see that she is naked and wrapped in his poncho liner, leaning against the edge of the picnic table. When he is close enough to see her face clearly, she spreads open the poncho liner for him. Neither speaks as she enfolds him with her arms and the soft quilt, then wraps her legs around his hips and draws him into her.

THIRTEEN

**I'm sorry the hippie kids left. And I don't believe they robbed anybody.
They were a spark of fun on this dreary old island.**
—Bernadine Bowen

On the inhabited islands farther out to sea than Barter Island, notably Matinicus and Monhegan, where the deeper ocean is much colder much later into the year, the islanders are wont to refer to August as "Fogust." On Barter Island and other islands in Penobscot Bay, June and July are the foggy months; August and the early fall are typically clear, breezy, cool, and sunny, perfect weather for sailing and fishing alike. But on September 3, 1971, the inhabitants of Barter Island woke up to fog, a cold offshore breeze, and a steady pelting rain that lasted well into the day with no sign of letup even past midafternoon. In spite of the weather, the waters off the eastern shore of the island and those farther out past York Island and the dark ledges called The Horsemen are crowded with lobster boats hauling traps, taking whole strings aboard to move into better water, and lying to one another over the CB radio about how many lobsters are coming up in their traps—"not getting anything over here" is the word of the day.

Simon wears a worn yellow sou'wester that keeps the cold rain from dripping down the back of his neck, but as he has been working most of the afternoon without a slicker, he is soaked through and through from his chin to his boot tops. He works mindlessly on the stern of *Myrmaid*, bending and lifting, picking and baiting; the exercise keeps him warm and has by now finally cleaned out the poison left in his blood from the hideous excesses of a very jolly, incestuous weekend in Portland with his friends and cousin Catherine. He is looking forward to finishing this, the last of Junior's string inside the York Ledges, and to a hot shower and dry clothes. He looks up once or twice at David's cabin, high in the clearing on the cliff, and thinks that he envies David the solitude, the freedom, of living alone like that and that some night this week he will take a jug over for a visit, now that the air between them has cleared, or whatever the expression Nancy used was.

On their way home south along the shore, Simon stands up against the exhaust pipe under the house drying his wrinkled hands. Junior is steering with one hand and looking back over his stern, squinting at something in the distance. When they pass the cliffs and the cove opens on their starboard, Junior sees that Gus has just taken up his mooring buoy and David has the bucket and broom out to begin washing down the *Betty B.* Simon is disappointed when Junior turns into the cove and cuts back on the throttle, obviously bound for a visit with Gus, but he consoles himself with the hope that there might be a drink involved, the lobsters being so plentiful again today.

Junior halloos the *Betty B.*, and Gus replies, stepping back out onto his deck to wait as Junior swings in alongside in a slow smooth arc. Both stern men are ready with gaffs, but it is Simon who pulls the boats together as they exchange muttered greetings. Simon tells David, who is wearing his wool watch cap, that he looks like a drowned rat. Gus notices his stern man for the first time today, sees water dripping from his soaked cap onto his ears, and for the first time in a week notices the livid slash on his left lobe, which causes him to involuntarily stroke his own earlobe for a pensive moment. He notices, too, that Maggie is on her perch up on the cliff in front of her house, out for air, a blanket over her head against the wet. He waves to her, and she waves back.

"I see old Roger took your warning when you tied him off, and he moved his traps off," Junior says.

"You seen wrong," Gus says. "He didn't take my warning. I cut him off. Just now we did."

"Did you, by God?" Both Gus, who is wiping his glasses on his shirt, and David, who is wringing out his soggy cap, grow in stature for the captain and crew of *Myrmaid*.

"You sound surprised to hear it," says Gus, as though he himself is not surprised that he did it.

"Christ, those were new buoys," Junior says.

"How many did you cut?" Simon asks.

"Ten, the whole string. They had new toggles, too; new traps, I'd guess. David cut half of them; he insisted."

Junior whistles. He looks out from the cove as though expecting to see Roger Weed steaming toward them for revenge.

Simon reaches across his washboard to cleat a line on the *Betty B.* and doing so knocks his broom overboard; he holds the boats apart to lean down and retrieve it.

Junior laughs and calls Simon some clumsy. Simon shakes out the broom, tells Junior to go to hell, then laughs with him.

"Well, I guess this calls for a little drink, don't it, dear?" Junior nods to Simon, who goes below for the jug. Gus looks to see if Maggie is still there, but she is gone. He has never taken a drink in her presence and never will; don't ask him why. He and David hold out their cups while Simon pours and Junior adds coke to the rum.

"He's got another string up in the Burnt Island thorofare; we ought to cut that too," Simon drains the contents of his cup and shudders appreciatively.

"No," says Gus. He does not like Simon's eagerness for trouble. "Those aren't my waters, only close. They aren't anybody's. There's going to be enough trouble as it is."

"There's going to be hell to pay," says Junior.

"He comes back at us, he's going to regret the hell out of it. Me and David, we know about revenge, about payback, don't we, man?"

David agrees quietly. Apprehensive, he avoids Simon's eye and busies himself with his broom.

"I didn't have any choice." Gus looks into his cup.

"No," Junior agrees. "You did the right thing. With any luck he'll just stay away."

"Here's hoping." Gus raises his cup, and Junior does the same.

Junior unties his apron, hangs it up, and rolls down his boot tops; he looks at Simon, who understands that he should start cleaning up now. Simon complies, saying to no one and everyone: "If he wants a trap war, he'll get one, by Jesus," in a voice of excited anticipation.

"There's nothing good to come out of a trap war." Simon's eagerness reminds Gus of John's before he left for Vietnam, and he stops his memory right there. "Everybody loses is what happens."

The same as in any war of any kind, you simpleminded sonofabitch. You'd think you would of learned that by now. You'd think you would of found the sense to be scared once in a while by now.

The two captains stand talking quietly while they finish their drinks and their stern men sluice the decks, scrubbing them down with heavy brushes and brooms. Junior tells Simon to watch he doesn't lose the broom again, and Simon tells him to go to hell again.

"Let's get in out of this Christly wet," Junior says. He starts his engine and unfastens the line to the *Betty B.*, allowing the *Myrmaid* to drift off slowly.

Simon pulls up the center deck plank, inserts the neck of the bilge pump, and begins to pump the stinking slime into a bucket. The pump belches up bilge water that is gray, swimming with chunks of rancid herring guts, and shiny with fish oil. When the bucket is half full, Simon lifts it and casually empties it into Junior's right boot.

"Oh! Goddamn!" Junior cries. His eyes are wide in disbelief and a hint of anger as he spins around to face his stern man.

"Oh, Jesus, Captain, I *am* sorry. God, how *clumsy* of me." Simon makes a punching motion with his right fist; his face is squinched up in a mockery of self-reproach.

Gus is laughing so hard that he is bent over, hands on knees, coughing, nearly choking. Junior dumps the horrible soup out of his boot into the water and rinses the boot overboard, then his lower right leg, swearing and promising monstrous revenge. On the deck of the *Betty B.* David waits until he gets Simon's attention, then renders him a perfect present arms with his broom; Simon beams and replies with a smart hand salute.

✳✳✳

Nancy sits by the open front window of Maggie's parlor, paging slowly through last month's *National Geographic*. Maggie has just ordered her out of the kitchen where she tried to help with the sandwiches, or at least to set the

table. With the tide coming on to full, the breeze has picked up, lifting a
curled orange maple leaf up onto the screen next to her chair, where it rocks
uncertainly. Inside, the thin curtain, too, is lifted and rises to drop again onto
Nancy's shoulder. She watches as Maggie takes a cupped handful of chopped
fresh chives to the little table and sprinkles them into the bowls of vichys-
soise that sit on opposite sides of a vase of thistle and aster. Nancy thinks that
today, even more than in the past, Maggie is looking straight into her soul;
that she can see her and David on the picnic table at the pond, see her
increasing aversion to Simon, her fear and doubt, but she does not care at all;
she even feels glad that Maggie can see.

From the kitchen Maggie says that she hopes Nancy likes chicken salad
because she has made too much of it. Before Nancy can reply, a tearing sound
rips past the window on the road and ends in a skidding clatter beside the
front door. Maggie comes out to see what it is, and Nancy steps toward the
front door.

Cecil shuffles up onto the stoop and lets himself in through the screen
door. He is breathing heavily; his hair is wet with perspiration and pushed
back from his forehead by his bike ride down the cove road.

Maggie stands in the kitchen entry, a plate of salad in each hand.

"Cecil Chafin," she says. "It is Tuesday, is it not?"

"I don't know." Cecil looks confused, a little resentful.

"It is Tuesday," Maggie says. "Why aren't you in school?"

"Oh," he says. "Skippy's sick, Aunt Maggie. I came to get Nancy; Myrtle
said she was here."

"Sick?" Nancy asks. "Sick how?"

"Fever and something about the cut on his leg. He won't let me in his
room. I went to see him at lunchtime."

Maggie tells him to sit down, but he does not. "What cut?" she asks.

"On his leg," Cecil points to his thigh. "He fell on something a couple
of days ago, and it cut him pretty bad. He washed it out with rum, but it still
hurts him."

"Lord," says Maggie.

Cecil nods his head in agreement just as a grown-up would. "Yesterday,
he couldn't walk on it anymore and took to his bed. He's burning up with a
fever and not making sense, and there's a smell in his room like there's a
squirrel dead under the floorboards."

"My God," Nancy says. "Was it metal that cut him?"

"I don't know."

Nancy looks around for anything she might have brought with her. Maggie takes the salads back into the kitchen.

"Why didn't you tell Nancy last night?" she asks over her shoulder.

"He told me not to. He said if I did fetch her he wouldn't let her into his room and he would take back the last arrowhead he give me. Now he won't let *me* in."

"I'll need to go back to get my kit first, Maggie," Nancy says.

"He won't let you in, Nancy. But he'll open the door for you, Aunt Maggie. He will."

"I should hope so," Maggie says. She carries the bowls of soup back to the kitchen and returns with a sweater.

"He's afraid you'll give him a shot, Nancy. He's afraid you'll make him take his pants off to see the cut and give him a shot in his bare butt."

"Well, I might have to do both; he'll just have to deal with it."

"You don't understand. Skippy loves you." Cecil wipes perspiration from his forehead, and Maggie hands him a glass of iced tea from the little table.

"Well, that's nice," Nancy says, smiling and nodding her head. "That makes him the first man who said he loved me and didn't want me to take his pants off."

"Oh Nancy," Maggie laughs. "You are wonderful." She pauses, then asks if Nancy has antibiotics.

"Oh yes," Nancy says. "We'll need to stop by the school to tell Mrs. Carnidge we have Cecil. You don't mind driving, Maggie?"

"Of course not." Maggie is herding Cecil out the door. "And where is Fuddy in all this?" she asks him.

"He went upcountry to see Harvey and go hunting. In Perkins Twerp."

"It's not deer season yet," Nancy says on the way to Maggie's car. Her loose hair blows across her face and she tucks it back behind her ear.

"It don't matter," says Cecil, echoing Fuddy's attitude. "Skippy's scared that Fuddy went to look for Autumn. Fuddy was all the time saying he wished she hadn't left and making a face like a codfish when he said it. Skippy's scared he's going to go off with her and leave him."

"He needn't worry about that," Maggie observes.

"That's what David said." Cecil looks at Nancy.

The road into Squeaker Cove is one lane, two deep ruts. Between the ruts rises a grassy hump that is wiped black with grease from the underbelly of Fat Albert, driven in and out of the cove all summer. Cecil sits deep in the backseat of Maggie's old Pontiac, watching ahead between Maggie and Nancy in the front seat.

"Watch you don't bottom out up ahead there, Aunt Maggie," he warns.

"Thank you, Cecil." Maggie slows to a cautious crawl. She looks at the pale boy in her rearview mirror and smiles. "You did the right thing coming to get Nancy," she says. "You may have saved Skippy's life, you know."

"We won't tell him you told us," Nancy says. "You can wait in the car."

"He knows," Cecil says sadly. "He can hear us."

"Oh pooh," Nancy says. "That superhearing stuff is a bunch of bull and you know it. Isn't it, Maggie?"

Maggie smiles. "There are more things in heaven and earth, Horatio. . . ."

"If he can't hear us now, he'll hear me in the car or in the kitchen, breathing. You watch."

Fuddy's and Skippy's kitchen table is piled high with dirty Depression glass dishes and a couple of crusted galvanized pots. A vise is clamped onto one end, padded with newspaper lest it mar the cherry surface; in its jaws is a crimped copper tube. In the center of the table, a hammer with a new hand-carved handle soaks its head in a coffee can full of water. A jar of peanut butter, scraped clean, holds a pewter spoon, and two empty cans of blueberry pie filling sit near the edge, their lids pushed back and licked clean. Nancy puts her finger over her lips, motions for Cecil to sit down and wait, then leads the way up the narrow stairs.

The upstairs hall is dark; the only light is from a salt-encrusted window at the far end. Nancy tries the closed door, then knocks soundly.

"Skippy," she says through the door. "It's me, Nancy. I want to see you and make sure you're okay. Let me in, please."

The women wait for an answer. When none comes, Maggie steps up and raps the door with authoritative knuckles. "Open this door, Skippy Groth. Open it now."

Nancy and Maggie watch one another's eyes as they listen to Skippy make his slow way to the door and unlock it. When he steps back from the door, his strength fails him and he slumps to a sitting position on the floor, his legs splayed. He is dressed in a union suit, gray with age and soil, and when Nancy enters the room, he hides his mouth with his hand and looks at the floor. As they lift him, moaning softly, to his feet, Nancy is afraid that she is going to faint from the stench of his bloated wound. They lay him on his side, and Maggie hurries downstairs to heat water, patting away her tears with the sleeve of the sweater tied around her neck.

✳✳✳

"He's sound asleep now and will be for quite a while, you can be sure of that." Nancy stands at the kitchen sink toweling her hands dry.

Maggie runs a hand through Cecil's hair. "If you'd like to go sit with him, you may. He's going to be fine, thanks to you, and to Nancy."

"We'll tell your mom you're here if you want to stay for a while," Nancy says. "I'll be back in a few hours to change the dressing and watch that fever. I'll bet you five bucks that you'll get another arrowhead when he wakes up and finds he's not in pain anymore. I'll bring you back a sandwich or something."

"I'm proud of you," Maggie says.

Cecil, who is still afraid, smiles shyly. He rises, takes an apple from the peck basket in the stove corner, and starts up the stairs.

On the way home, Maggie are Nancy are silent until they pass the drive into the McGregors'.

"Have you seen Christine lately?" Maggie asks. "I haven't in more than a week."

"I saw her yesterday. We picked pole beans." Nancy looks at Maggie, hoping for a further question.

"Is he still browbeating her?" Maggie's eyes are on the road.

"You knew it. I thought you would."

"You told us at the P.O. that he was treating her cruelly," Maggie says, remembering: *I measure every Grief I meet with narrow, probing, Eyes.*

"That, and you see more than most people."

"I've been watching longer. Besides, Christine's despair is quite evident."

"I don't think she would mind if I told you that she stood up to him the other day. Surprised him. But still she's afraid of him; I think it's because of what he did to those dogs, though she swears she doesn't believe that he killed them or that he's the one that burned them out."

"Good for her. She needs to stand up to him at every step. But she is deeply troubled, and I don't think it's just him."

"Me neither," Nancy turns to the open window. "It's not just the robbery, not just Eliot, but something else. I don't know. I wish I could be of help to her."

"You've been help enough today for several people. We might have lost that foolish Skippy. Imagine Cecil if we had. Oh, my, look at Pete Gully's raspberries. I'll have to bring a pail when I drive you back."

"You don't have to bring me back; I was going to ride my bike."

"And how would Cecil get home? He'll have schoolwork to make up if I know Biddy Carnidge. I'll drive you; I want to come too."

✳✳✳

Simon is sitting on an upturned trap on Junior's wharf, leaning forward onto his knees; he is exasperated.

"Jesus Christ, Junior," he says again.

"Well, I don't know. We're late getting started." Junior stands at the wharf ladder, his arms crossed over his begrimed sweatshirt, his eyes on the dark horizon to the southeast. "It's nearly nine," he adds. "And the weatherman gave—"

"Christ, you said that. You said he said it's headed for the Grand Banks. Listen, for God's sake, hear that? That's the *Betty B.* going by. Hear her? Even Gus is out and he's Captain Cautious. You're acting like a short-timer, for God's sake."

"Now what are you talking about?"

"A short-timer's somebody who has only a short time left in country, in Vietnam, and he's real careful not to take any chances. Closer he gets to going home, the less risk he'll take."

Junior might be listening, but if he is it is without much interest. His mind is on a line squall that nearly dumped him and Dunreath years ago, and the one that nearly drowned Amos, him in a Novi boat.

"When you get below ten days to go, you're a single-digit midget." Simon pushes back his hood. "Then you're so short you can play handball on the curb. When you get down to three days, or two, you're so short it takes a half hour to walk around a dime and you don't even leave the bunker. That's what you remind me of standing here."

Both men hear the distant low hum of a Cummins diesel engine.

"There," Junior says. "Hear that? That's Harvey Bridges coming in already."

"He always comes in early; he goes out before light. Jesus, as if you didn't know that."

"Usually not till ten or so."

"I give up." Simon stands and makes a blowing noise of exaggerated disgust. "I'm going home."

"Oh, all right, Christ, we'll go." Junior picks up his dinner pail. "Short-timer my ass," he says.

The stern of the *Myrmaid* carries a pyramid of ten traps taken up the day before to move to different waters today. The bottom row of four over-hangs the gunwales a tad on both sides, but the stack is well lashed and rides securely, as a pyramid of ten stacked by Junior always does. Yesterday, Junior planned to set this string north of the Turnip Yard in the kelp and in the rocks by the Sheep Ledges, and he also planned to take up at least one bal-last stone from each trap he has out, especially those that he set first and that have soaked the longest. But as he watches Simon let loose the mooring and noses her out of the cove into the low swells, Junior thinks that if it stays this rough he will most likely just bring this string in again and put it out when it calms down some, to hell with Simon's griping. He hikes his belt up over his belly, but it slides back under the ledge of his gut as he fishes for a Pall Mall and lights a match with a strike on the exhaust pipe.

The sea is a brownish gray today, and the wind is southeasterly. Simon has never seen the water this color before, nor has he seen it worked up like this: not choppy, but with little lapping wavelets and farther out past the ledges, some fair-sized swells breaking against both The Horsemen and the Spirit Ledges. He is glad to be out on the water–he had almost given up hope that Junior would set out–and he is hoping that the sea will pick up even more for an exciting ride on the wide-open water that just might wash last night out of his head.

Junior motions to Simon to take the wheel and walks back on the uneasy deck to check the lashing on the pyramid. The *Myrmaid* isn't as tippy as, say, the *Betty B.*, but she is tippy enough to make him nervous in these kind of waters. Gus, he sees, is coming north out of the Turnip Yard, and *Betty B.*, Junior has to admit, is riding just fine. Still, he doesn't like being out in this weather and plans to haul only the strings closest to shore, at least for now. When he takes the wheel back from Simon, for the first time this morning he notices the bags under his stern man's eyes.

Simon is wet to the waist as they finish hauling the second string; when he squints he can feel the salt crust on his cheeks. He sits on the washboard while they travel to the next string and is wringing out his mittens to have a smoke, when Junior asks him to check the lashing on the traps again.

"Jesus, you just did," Simon says.

The *Myrmaid* is slapped by a wave and a smooth, wet ballast stone the size of a squash slides off the top of the pile of stones onto the stern deck.

"There," says Junior. "What's bothering you today? You're dragging ass and looking like you're not here. You hungover?"

"I didn't sleep for shit. The nightmares." Simon steps over the pile of stones to tug on the lashing and finds it secure. He licks salt from his lips and lights his cigarette.

"Same one?"

"I guess. Sweating, couldn't hardly breathe, making noises in my chest, Nancy said. Noises that aren't my voice, like always. There was the smell of burning skin and shit, human shit. I only remember bumping and thumping noises and guys grunting. Somebody crying, always that. Somebody crying for his mom till they make him stop. No running away this time."

"What is it she says you say? Did you say it this time again?"

"Chet Roy," says Simon. "Remember? Chet Atkins and Roy Acuff's names is how she remembered it. And do re mi, or something like that."

"Maybe you're speaking Vietnamese. That's Myrtle's idea, at least. You ought to ask David about those words. He learned to speak it, didn't he?"

"That's what Nancy says, but it isn't Vietnamese. I never learned one word in that filthy fucking gook language. Where are you going?"

"I'm turning into the string by the Battery. I don't like this sea, and it's getting worse. Feel that wind?"

"It's not so rough that we can't finish hauling down here; it's just some swells," Simon says. "Look, Gus is still out there."

"Gus doesn't have a mountain of wet traps on his transom and a pile of stones canting him to starboard like I do. Not to mention a stern man who isn't paying any attention."

"I got up and drank a cup of coffee and never got back to sleep," says Simon.

And mixed a little something in with it, thinks Junior.

"You wouldn't be afraid of the water so bad if you could swim," Simon claims. He flicks half of his cigarette overboard.

"What the hell does swimming have to do with anything?" Junior hated this conversation the first time they had it.

"You know. If anything happened to the boat or you fell overboard, you could swim to shore this close, even out farther."

"Christ. You'd die of hypothermia in that water if ever you tried to swim ashore. That, or you'd be smashed and crushed between the hull and the rocks. Swim, hell. That water's so cold, David nearly sawed through his finger and didn't feel it. You saw that."

Junior signals for Simon to push the pair of traps on the washboard overboard and he is watching them sink behind the *Myrmaid* while a solitary, monstrous swell rolls toward his port bow. It comes on alone as if several swells have grouped and are seeking the shore in a single swollen mass that strains to keep from cresting before it strikes the shore. Simon turns to see it; he tries to shout "Rogue wave!" but he can only point. The *Myrmaid* rises broadside as if to meet it, drifting up the wall of moving water until her deck is almost vertical. The stack of traps goes first, tumbling off the transom, then Simon slides down the deck, fumbling furiously for something to grab, and goes over backwards into the water followed by an avalanche of ballast stones. Junior manages to hold on for another second, gap-mouthed with fear, before he, too, loses his grip and falls into the trough below; he strikes the surface and sinks, his body limp with surrender. He nearly lets out his breath and sinks with the familiar gear that drifts past him, but he sees Simon five yards away in the murky plankton and thinks that Simon can see him as they dance in the shifting gray brown light; he thinks that Simon is reaching toward him, stretched out for rescue. Climbing toward him, Simon is struck by a sinking trap; he pushes it aside only to meet the remainder of the ballast stones that tumble down on him, a slow rain of boulders, bumping his back and head. He flails at them, trying to climb at the same time, but one after another strike him in the face. He rolls over once, releases a cloud of bubbles, and begins to sink with the stones, following them down in a slow fall.

Junior does not look down. He thrashes and crawls up for the dark hull above, breaks the surface, catches hold of the washboard, and gasps through a rounded mouth, his legs tucked up beneath him. He thinks he must have taken the *Myrmaid* out of gear, but he can't remember. Before he can get his breath back, the cold and shock come over him at once and he has to rest his chin on the washboard to gather strength. With a terrible effort he hauls himself up over the gunwale and slides onto the deck where he lies wet and sucking for air with his eyes shut.

When he manages to push himself onto his feet, he sees that the *Myrmaid* has hardly drifted at all and the ocean's surface is almost calm, as if the giant wave rolled it flat as it passed over in its run for shore. He stands and squints, trying to see without his glasses. Only one buoy has come up, and Junior thinks that the distant shape must be his bait barrel.

"Simon!" He hollers, leaning over the washboard. His voice is strained and angry, demanding a reply. "Simon Cooper!" he shouts at the quiet surface.

Junior sets the boat in gear and starts out in a slow, helpless circle around the little gathering of debris that did not sink. After two luckless turns around the flotsam, he switches the CB on and fumbles for a channel with voices.

The *Betty B.* is alongside in minutes.

"Didn't you see it?" Gus asks. "You didn't see it?" David is standing on the bow scanning the surface for some sign; he does not believe this, not at all.

Junior says nothing. Gus calls David down to take the wheel and steps over onto the *Myrmaid*'s wet, stripped deck with a blanket. As the boats part, Gus makes a circling motion to direct David, who turns her out at half throttle, answering eager voices on the CB as he steers and watches the water.

Neither captain says anything while Junior puts on a dry shirt and accepts a cup from Gus. Junior plants himself in the middle of the deck, head hidden under the blanket, a stricken watcher, while Gus slips the *Myrmaid* into gear and turns out slowly to accompany the *Betty B.* in silence.

Within a half hour three other boats have joined them. When they come alongside they do not hail Junior or ask questions; they sail by him with their faces set to match his. The stern men ride high on the bows of the boats, legs spread for balance, bowline in one hand and gaffs ready in the other. Though they knew before they came they would find nothing and could say nothing, they continue in their slow circling ritual for several hours, then peel off one at a time, sliding by the *Myrmaid* and shaking their heads "No" once before they depart.

At home, Junior finds, as he hoped he would, a note balanced against the sugar bowl that says Myrtle has gone to sit with Nancy. You don't call for "Help! Man overboard!" on the CB without everyone within a hundred miles of coastal water hearing about it in a few minutes, word spreading outward in shocked waves. Junior puts on dry trousers, pours himself three fingers of rum, and carries it with bread and some cheese into the back room. He does not light a lamp that might be seen from the road but sits on the couch, food and glass balanced on his taut round belly, and shuts his eyes.

It will be more than twenty-four hours before Simon comes to the surface, if he comes up at all. They will look for him to wash up on shore during the day, carried in by the tide. What most don't know is that the tide, when it's going, strikes the point of land south of where Simon went down; it curls and turns so that it will carry him into the Turnip Yard. They'll want to bring him in and give him to Nancy so she can bury him. But they didn't see Charles when he was brought up in a scallop drag, his eyes chewed out, his cheeks eaten, and crabs clinging to his head and hands. The Coast Guard will get in on it. No, it is up to Junior to do it. He'll have to find Simon before he washes ashore and make sure that neither Nancy nor anybody else will have to see him and maybe remember him that way. It will want luck to have him come to the surface at the right time in the right place rather than stay down and come ashore that much later and that much worse to look at. They had to burn the crabs to make them let loose from Charles's neck.

✳✳✳

If there is anything at all that Nancy could say she doesn't like about the house the town has provided for her as nurse is that the picture window dominating the front room faces due west, so that every minute from 3:00 P.M. until sundown is glaring light, which in summer makes the front room unbearably hot. But she has not let herself close the curtains, shutting out the road and the passing islanders, as that might make people think she doesn't want to appear available, that she is shirking her nurse's duty, or that she has something to hide. But this afternoon she does not care. The curtains have been shut since Myrtle and Christine arrived in the early afternoon, and they remain shut now in the gray, drizzly dusk. It has been over three hours since Myrtle arrived with the news; in that time Nancy has gone from disbelief to a stunned silence. She sits at the kitchen table before a mug of cold tea; she has shed the blanket that Christine draped over her shoulders an hour ago, arranging it on the back of her chair. It is Myrtle's job to sit with Nancy, to meet visitors at the door and send them politely away in hushed tones, accepting from the women offerings of fresh bread, a pie, supper in a covered basket. Christine, as silent as her friend, sits in the oaken rocker by the stove, rocking and rocking, a silent sentinel. Trucks and cars passing the house slow to a quiet, respectful glide as they pass. In the store, Leah turns her back on two shoppers in the aisle and cries quietly in her apron for Nancy and for her Gus.

When the Willys pulls into the drive and parks behind Simon's Galaxie, Myrtle recognizes the sound of its engine and hurries to the side screen door. She meets them outside, out of earshot of the kitchen. Inside the rose-colored rims of her glasses, her eyes are red and swollen. She is still in her house dress, and the set of her jaw, which Gus has seen before, says that she is in no mood for any kind of compromise.

"We've just come to pay our respects and see is there anything we can do," he says, his arms limp at his sides. "Betty says to tell you she'll be here in an hour or so."

Myrtle says nothing, merely nods. She does not look at David until he speaks.

"I want to go in and see her, Myrtle," David says. He is wearing only a T-shirt in the light evening drizzle; his forearms, she notices, are covered with goose bumps.

"Well, you can't. She doesn't want to see anybody. She said so."

"Well, I'm going to go in anyway," David says quietly. "Only for a minute."

"The hell you are." Myrtle's knees flex slightly beneath her skirts as though she is preparing to pounce if need be. "You're not, David Harper." *You of all people at this time, for God's sake, and for her sake and for the sake of all of us who knew that boy.*

Gus puts a hand on David's bicep. "You heard her. Not now."

Gus asks Myrtle if she will tell Nancy that the two of them stopped by and paid their respects and if they can do anything to please let them know.

"Of course I will." She looks over at Bernadine and Kimberly, who are approaching, each carrying a covered dish.

"Oh," Gus says as he turns to go. "Where's Junior anyway?"

"He's to home." Myrtle is watching Bernadine and Kimberly.

"No he isn't. It's dark already over there. There aren't any lights. I stopped and hollered inside, past the kitchen."

"If I know him at all, and I guess I do, he's lying in bed in the dark; lying there blaming himself, running himself down to perdition, which is why I will be glad for Betty to relieve me here."

Fat Albert, in full grumble, gains the slight hill in second gear. At the house, Fuddy drops it into neutral, and he and Skippy bow their heads slightly in the doorless cab as they pass.

"That's not lasagna is it?" Myrtle asks Bernadine. "Mabel already brought a lasagna."

"It's my cream-of-mushroom chicken breasts," says Bernadine.

✳✳✳

The tide is coming when Junior goes down to the wharf in the early dark. He has a heavy flashlight, a gaff, and a thermos of soup. From the wharf he loads several of the flattest ballast stones into the bow of the skiff and slowly, not to get ahead of the tide, rows out of the cove, facing the bow, the better to see. There is a light chop on the water and the wind is southerly; when he turns and sits down to row against it, he meets little resistance, and staying close to shore, he rows to the Turnip Yard, glancing now and then over his shoulder for the first glimmer of the moon. Using the two looming shapes of The Horsemen as guides, he turns into deeper water and slows to watch the surface. The moon finally comes up, its light diffused over the water, but it is little help because it is still low on the horizon and the slanting silver creates deceptive pockets of darkness beneath every wave.

When Junior feels sure that the tide is beginning to turn, he rows into the Turnip Yard to cross against the wind toward open sea. At the southern end he stops rowing and lets the wind carry him back. He kneels on the seat and stretches over the stern, straining to see something that he does not dare to imagine, certain only that he will know it if he sees it. But what if he bumps it in the dark? The low, whitecapped waves, the only sign of life all around, slap at his stern, soaking him with a cold spray that stiffens his fingers on the oars.

Before he has made three passes over the Turnip Yard, the moon is high and he feels as though he has been out on the water all night. If he misses Simon this time, he will miss him altogether, and he begins to hope in spite of himself that he will miss him and not have to see him, his face all swollen in the awful gray light, his eyes emptied by what they have already seen. If he had to say, he would allow that the looking for Simon has been worse than watching him drown; at least underwater, it happened and was done. Here it is all waiting and the growing fear of what he has come to find.

On the next pass Junior fans the surface timidly with his light. He hasn't drifted a hundred yards when his beam passes over a dark, rounded shape bobbing among the waves. He must have passed the body twice in the darkness. He kneels and watches, colder now and surprised at his own reluctance to move, as Simon's head drifts away from him. He brings the skiff around and circles the shape, shouting at it: "Simon! Simon Cooper!" until he can no longer delay and backs in toward it.

Simon is floating standing up, as if still climbing, or else walking to shore on legs the length of shadows. Junior comes in behind him and ties one end of the line to the stern, looping the other end and letting it sink down over Simon's shoulders. He averts his eyes lest Simon turn and show him his face. When he has secured the body, he sits down to row out to open water. Once he slips and looks against his will: he sees Simon's shoulders break the surface and his ears bend back when Junior pulls on the oars before he sinks again.

"Almost," he says to encourage. "We're almost there."

He has towed things before—a skiff with two men in it—but never anything this heavy, never anything that strained against him like this.

He stops when he is in the way of the outgoing current. From here, once Junior frees him, Simon will be carried out beyond the bay and well into open sea before the tide turns and starts to come again. By then he'll be wedged on the bottom or taken so far out that it will be New Hampshire before he washes up on shore. With his teeth clamped shut, Junior reaches over his friend with the gaff and carefully lifts the line free of his shoulders. At first he thinks to drop the rocks down the back of Simon's shirt so he won't have to turn his face around, but that might roll him belly up, eyes to the moon, so Junior reaches gingerly around to his throat and slides the first ballast stone down into his undershirt. Simon's head tucks forward as if looking beneath him to see where he will settle.

Junior slips three of the biggest stones into his stern man's shirt all at once, and Simon hesitates, then sinks effortlessly like a weighted trap. Junior rows off a few yards to sit and watch in case the body comes back up. He stands up in the skiff, sculling to hold his place, and studies the surface of the water, mumbling at first, then talking almost aloud, angrily.

"It's all right for you now, Simon Cooper. You're not the one who has to go out alone tomorrow and every day after. I'm the one who has to start fishing alone all over again."

He rows for about a mile without looking around, then, when he gets close to land, he centers his stern on the tip of the second Horseman and starts back in toward home. Myrtle will be the only one he will tell, but even she won't understand. She'll fault him for not giving Nancy the chance to bury her husband and to pay her respects. She won't understand that Simon would have expected him to do it the way he did; like it was just more damn work, only this time far lonelier than it has ever been before. Like it was for Gus once, and probably will be again, the poor bastard.

FOURTEEN

**It was hard for Gus, but he did the right thing.
The brave thing. He's my Hector; he always has been.**
—Maggie Bowen

Maggie sits in the rocker by the front door, wrapped in a green shawl; a blank, sealed envelope is positioned in the center of her lap as though she has been studying it. Rain has been falling lightly but steadily all day, and the afternoon has grown quite cold for late September, but her front door is open so she can listen through the screen for the return of the *Betty B.* It has been unnaturally quiet on the water all day: the Barter Island boats are searching for Simon down off the southeastern tip of the island; the Stonington boats are not hauling their traps along the shore out of respect for Junior. Maggie rocks so slowly, so imperceptibly, that even when she goes adrift in a little sleep, the chair continues to move. An insolent and raucous trio of crows settles in the red oak in front of the house long enough to annoy her to wakefulness, then flies away as if satisfied.

Minutes later Maggie hears the familiar hum of the *Betty B.*'s engine as she approaches the cove from the south. She is out of sight, around the rocky outcropping and perhaps a half-mile away. Maggie closes her eyes to see Gus and David. Gus is stooped over the wheel, steering by instinct, his face pale and motionless. David stands up under the house with Gus, leaning ahead on the window shelf; the left arm of his damp flannel shirt steams from the heat of the exhaust pipe between them; he has a cigarette tucked behind his ear; his wet curls flare out from under the brim of his ball cap; and he is as still as his captain's face. "*Chips of Blank in Boyish Eyes,*" she thinks, recalling Emily Dickinson; they are coming home defeated, but they are coming home.

She rises to her feet, pats her beret onto her bundled hair, and slips into her rubber boots for the walk through the meadow to the wharf. She holds the envelope tucked under her arm to keep it dry. She knows that they have given up searching for Simon today, and for good, and that Junior will be following them into the cove soon enough. Nancy would want her to pass the note to David as discreetly as possible, and Maggie intends to get it into his hands before Junior and whoever is with him get to the wharf. At the water's edge, she passes beneath a slow-motion shower of brittle, yellow birch leaves—the first to fall—that are loosened by the steady patter of raindrops. As she steps onto the wharf, a pair of eiders, startled by the sudden noise of the *Betty B.* as she comes around the head of land, rises in unison and skims across the water for open sea.

Gus swings the *Betty B.* into the cove slowly, cutting her back to an idle, riding the slow heave of the tide. He looks up to see Maggie standing on the wharf, waiting for news, he supposes. When he has her eye, he shakes his head, no, twice, and she nods in reply. David stands ready with a gaff as they slip in to the wharf; he raises a hand in greeting to Maggie and smiles sadly. When Gus has shut down the boat and they have tied her off, Maggie tells them that she is sorry.

"It's a shame that Nancy and his family don't have someone to bury," she offers.

"Your memory is kinder than mine," Gus says. He pulls off his heavy flannel jacket and shakes it out. "Remember what Charles looked like when they brought him up? Those crabs? The sight of him drove Amelia mad."

"Amelia was already mad," Maggie says.

When Gus bends over his fuel tank with the measuring stick, Maggie leans forward to hand the envelope down to David, who takes it and thanks her quietly. Gus looks over his shoulder and sees the envelope.

"Why don't you go on up to the shack and see if you can get us a fire going in the stove?" he asks.

David tucks the envelope into his shirt and climbs up onto the wharf, whispering another thank-you to Maggie as he passes her.

Nancy didn't address it to David, Maggie thinks as she watches him walk up the wharf, lest someone see it and be finally convinced that there was, or is, something going on between them. Something more than just a little sneaker—some reason for an unbearable burden of guilt, for her, at least.

"Nancy is going off on the late boat, going home," she tells Gus. "Christine is going with her, bless her soul."

As he steps onto the wharf, they both turn to see the *Myrmaid* coming around the rocky head, and Maggie sees that it is Fuddy who has gone out with Junior today.

"You boys will want to be alone," she says. "I'll wait to give my condolences to Junior. He must be devastated."

"He blames himself for going out in heavy weather, even though there was plenty of boats out." Gus is watching the *Myrmaid* slide into the cove. A half hour before, in the southern end of the Turnip Yard, he told Junior that they were giving up the search and invited him and Fuddy to come for a drink. Junior said he would make one more sweep before he accepted that the boy is gone.

As Maggie passes the fish shack, she looks in the window in spite of herself; she sees David sitting on a stool reading the note, and though she wasn't told and hasn't read it, she is certain that she knows just what it says.

> Dear David,
>
> Christine and I are going off on the late boat to tell Simon's family and friends and my own family, too. I dread this, but Christine will keep me brave. I don't know when we'll be back.
>
> Please don't come to the boat tonight. I know you understand why I can't see you. Not now.
>
> I told Junior that Simon would like you to have his traps. He said he will see to it.
>
> Yours truly, Nancy.

✳✳✳

When Gus and Junior and Fuddy file into the fish shack, they drape their heavy jackets over the sawhorse in the doorway and find their way to a seat in silence. David has closed up the stove and sits on the stool next to it, rubbing his upper arms. Fuddy sits down on the stairs to the upper floor;

Junior settles on an upturned crate and crosses his legs; Gus carries his own stool to the window end of the workbench. David and Junior light cigarettes, pinching the match heads to be sure they are out before dropping them into the shavings and sawdust on the shack floor.

Junior is not saying that today on the water he decided that now he knows something of what Gus must have felt when he lost John. Nor is he saying that he feels far less than friendly toward David and that he wishes that he had told him months ago to lay off Nancy.

Fuddy is not saying that he had a feeling all day long, from the outset, that Junior knew he wasn't going to find any sign of Simon, either along the shore or out on the water. By noon he felt certain of it.

Gus does not say that he knows why Junior's eyes are hollow. Like Fuddy, he suspects that there is something more that Junior has not told them, and he does not expect to ever know what that may be. He draws a bottle of Bacardi from behind the paint cans and nods to David to scrounge some cups. David finds three cups and wipes out a small Mason jar for his own use; he does not say that right now he feels so crowded by collected grief and remorse that he cannot cry, though he would give anything to just bend down and weep.

Gus opens the window to let in some air and without a word raises his cup for Simon; the other three do the same.

"I suppose we should flatfoot this first one," Junior says. "He would of."

The others nod in agreement and knock back their drinks in unison.

As David goes from man to man with the jug to refill their cups, Junior says, "At least he won't have to suffer those hellish nightmares anymore. I think they nearly drove him to distraction. They scared him shitless. He acted like they didn't, but I could tell. Just the night before, he had the worst of them, the one about being buried under the dead. Chet Atkins and Roy Acuff."

David cocks his head.

Gus says, "What? He had nightmares about hillbilly singers?"

Fuddy feels right at home with this conversation.

Junior opens the stove door and throws his cigarette in; David's follows his.

"No, dear," Junior takes a drink. "That's how he remembered what it was that Nancy said he was yelling out; he yelled that and the other thing every time he had the dream. Chet Roy."

"Oh, my God," David says.

"That's what I thought," Junior says. "I've been meaning to ask you. It's Vietnamese, isn't it? What's it mean?"

"It means 'He's dead already.' " David lights another cigarette. Fuddy is nodding slowly in agreement with something.

Junior shakes his head. "He said he never learned a word of Vietnamese; said he hated that fucking gook language. It must be what he heard and he has forgotten in . . ."

"What was the other thing he said?" David asks.

"Do re mi," Gus says, uncertainly.

"Not *'do mer my'*?"

"Maybe. Jesus, I don't know. Why, what's that mean?"

" 'Mother-fucking Americans,' is what it means; it's what Vietnamese soldiers would be saying as they went through the dead, looting them, taking souvenirs, cutting off rings, and finishing off the wounded. The poor bastard."

"To have to keep living it, you mean?" Gus asks. "Yes, I guess that's over, for him at least. I'm tired. I'm going home. You want to stay and finish the jug, you're welcome to it, I'm just not in the mood." He sets his cup, half full, on the workbench.

"No, thanks." Junior says. "We'll be going too, hey Fuddy?" He and Fuddy finish their drinks and nod their way out.

At the foot of the meadow, Gus and David part without comment. David has kept his rubber boots on for the walk through the tall, wet meadow grass; at least his feet have stayed dry.

Tonight he will not tarry at the main house, nor will he bother to make himself dinner, just to have to clean it up. He takes the path up the hill to the cabin. In the clearing he sees that a band of thin sunlight lights the upper half of the roof—the sky is clearing in the west—and he thinks that there is at least an hour of daylight left. He gets a small fire going in the fireplace, hangs his wet clothes over the screen, and in a heavy sweater and dry pants, sits down on the front porch with a beer and a wedge of store cheese. Watching the water below and the rain retreating to the northeast, he thinks he sees something odd on the water, but he doesn't know what.

Perhaps Simon faked his nightmares to get Nancy's sympathy. But how would he have known *chet roi* and *do mer my*, both idioms? He could have learned them from a mama-san or looked them up in a dictionary, but neither seems likely. Perhaps Nancy was lying when she said that he had never been in a battle, that he fainted, and that he drove for the motor pool. But why would she lie? And why didn't he know what Garryowen signifies? Perhaps Simon lied to her, preferring her to think him a faint-hearted pussy rather than an abject fucking coward, but couldn't keep back the nightmares. Wouldn't she have guessed?

Does it matter, any of it? It does not. Simon is gone; his stories are not. Whether he was telling Nancy what was true or what he wished was true did not matter. In David's memory of him, Simon stands tall.

There *is* something wrong on the water. When the last of the sunlight from behind the mountain lifts and disappears, he squints out at the choppy surface and the thin blanket of buoys, then goes inside for the binoculars. All the buoys along the shore are trailing to the south with the going tide, except Gus's. His near string has been tied off; the buoys dip and kick, their flat ends slapping against the current. Running parallel to Gus's ten buoys are ten of Roger Weed's, riding lightly on the tide. David thinks that he should go see Gus but decides, no, nothing can be done at night. He will go get him earlier than usual in the morning.

Before it is full dark, David lights the lamp on the front table, builds up the fire, and wraps himself in a blanket in the rocker, his legs stretched out for warmth. Soon—in his mind—he is on the road into the mountains, pedaling furiously, swerving to avoid potholes, shirtless and drenched with sweat; his M79 is slung across his back, the metal sight digging into his shoulder with each bump. He is afraid if he does not hurry he won't find Neang and Chau Sinh and the others; there will be no trace of them. Nearly blinded by perspiration, he passes the two headless monks laid out along the road—one robe saffron, the other orange. Their heads, which had been cut off and perched on their chests the last time he was here, are gone, and so is the right foot of the one in saffron. He pedals past Sergeant Sirois, the team medic, who is walking back to the compound with a bucketful of human teeth. Sirois waves his hand and says they are all gone: the village is empty; their sleeping mats and pots, their chickens and ducks, their plows and hoes and little glass teacups are all gone. Nothing left but their little Buddha altars and the rice-filled Carnation milk cans with joss sticks burned down to nubs. You missed them, says Sirois. Gone. Fini fucking duke! Walked off the mountain and right into the meat grinder. Fucking wasted.

✳✳✳

While Junior sits alone, his elbows on the cleared supper table, his chin resting in his hands, his eyes closed; while Betty drapes a blanket over Gus, who is snoring in the big chair; and while David dreams in his rocker, Eliot picks up Christine at the town landing. Eliot takes her suitcase and a large cardboard box tied with binder's twine, and he hugs her warmly and kisses her, saying he is glad to have her home. The warmth surprises her: he was never a passionate man, even less loving since he passed forty; this is his warmest expression for her in years, and she thinks as they drive home that she likes it very much.

"Wait till you see the zucchini and the snow peas," Eliot says in a tone that is proud but not enthusiastic. "You've been gone almost a week; six full workdays."

"I know," Christine says. She rolls up her window against the sudden chill. "I came back as soon as I could leave her. I'll make it up to you. We'll catch up."

She looks at Eliot for confirmation, and she is rewarded with a slight smile when he turns toward her.

A wan smile, she thinks.

When they pass the store, Christine waves to Maggie, who is standing on the small side porch with Leah. Maggie has just come back to the island, too, having gone off for the day to see Dr. Boyer in Stonington and to visit the pharmacy.

Leah, too, waves to Christine.

"Did you sit with her on the boat?" she asks Maggie, holding the door for her.

"Well, of course I did."

"How is she? Christine?" They are alone in the store. Leah has turned off all the lights save the one at the counter to discourage late customers. They sit by the cold stove, and Leah polishes an apple on her skirt.

"She's tired." Maggie shuts her eyes. "One time she nearly fell asleep in midsentence. But her eyes are bright, and there's still that blush to her cheeks. She's glad to be home."

"And Nancy?" Leah offers the shiny apple—a Jonathan, Maggie's favorite. Maggie shakes her head to decline, and Leah bites into it.

"Exhausted. Too busy to grieve. She is staying with her mother, who is milking the loss of Simon for attention, grieving inconsolably for a man she despised in life."

Leah makes a *tsking* noise while she chews. Skippy comes in through the door and heads past them to the freezer for a late ice cream.

"She's not eating properly. Nor has Christine been, she who can only eat certain foods—foods rare as hen's teeth in South Portland supermarkets. They held a memorial service for Simon last night at his mother's church. One of his friends was so drunk, Christine said, that he lurched and fell down between the pews. Nancy left this morning."

"When will she come back?"

"I asked, of course," Maggie says. "Christine is not sure that she *will* come back. She thinks it likely that Nancy will send for their things sometime this fall and stay down there to start back to school."

"I hope so for her sake, though I will miss her here."

"So shall I." Maggie turns to look out the window into the thorofare, where the mail boat is steaming slowly through the shallow channel on its way home.

"I like Christine's short haircut," Leah says. "It's cute. Like a pixie. What did we used to call that cut, a pageboy?"

Maggie nods yes.

"She's a brave girl," Leah says.

On the far side of the island, Eliot downshifts on Bridge Hill to save wear on his brakes. He wants to tell Christine that he missed her while she was gone and that he worried about her, as he knew that she assumed a share of Nancy's burden of grief and still carries it. He has never seen her looking so worn.

"The island ladies certainly did their best to keep me well fed," he says instead.

"I'm not surprised," Christine says.

"Bernadine and Myrtle both brought meatless casseroles. Myrtle's noodles and creamed corn were covered with a layer of crushed potato chips." He looks at Christine's face for an expression of disgust but is disappointed. "Betty brought cookies, and Maggie brought pies from her and Leah."

"They meant well, I am sure." Christine does not look at him.

"I dumped it all into the cove at high tide," Eliot says.

"You didn't . . ."

"Tell them? Of course, I didn't tell them. Processed noodles, butter, refined sugar, canned vegetables . . . potato chips, for pity's sake."

Christine rides in silence, passing the Barters', where she sees Betty taking in the clothes in the side yard. Eliot has not asked one question about Nancy, not one word, as though he doesn't care about her, not a fig; but she tells herself that he does not, will not, discuss emotions of any kind.

"I thanked them all. I returned the plates and dishes and told them how much I enjoyed everything, every morsel. I was positively effusive," Eliot says with pride.

✳✳✳

It is still dark when David parks his truck in the road so as not to wake Betty and walks up Gus's drive to the house. Like the drive, the dooryard is paved with crushed clamshells dumped on the ground after every chowder eaten in the last seventy years and flattened by tires to keep down the mud. As he nears the house, someone–Gus, he assumes–lights a lamp in the kitchen and opens the door. A gray shape in the doorway, Gus in his union suit and woolen socks, pushes the screen open for David. Gus is holding his index finger over his lips and David nods that he understands as he enters the warm kitchen.

In a soft light and silence that satisfies both of them, David sits at the table while Gus quietly serves up tea and buttered toast thick with apple butter.

Gus does not ask why David has come to the house instead of meeting him at the wharf, nor why he has come so early. Gus thinks that something more than losing Simon may be amiss and that David does not want to face it quite yet. David has a look about him that Gus thinks is distant. At the sink, he pours boiling water over his dishes and the steam fogs up his glasses. He takes them off and, holding them away from the heat to clear them, squints at David, who is standing next to him drying a cup.

"Junior said Nancy told him that she wants you to have Simon's traps," Gus whispers. "There's forty-two."

"I know," David says. "She told me. In that note. I don't know that I can take them. It doesn't feel right; Junior should have them."

"She wants *you* to have them." Gus turns aside to pack his lunch. "I don't think you have any choice. Junior, he promised her he'd give them to you."

David says nothing. He sits back down and lights a cigarette at the table.

Gus looks at him. "So are you going to tell me why you came up here, and so early?"

"Roger tied off your string out below the cabin and put another one of his own right where he had the one we cut off."

"Tied me off in my own waters." Gus's voice is as lifeless and flat as a road-killed snake. "Well then," he says. "I don't have any choice but to cut him off again, do I? Why don't you wait here until I get dressed."

"I've got my truck," David says. "I'll meet you at the wharf. I forgot my boots."

"Maybe you shouldn't go with me this time," Gus says.

David acts as though he did not hear. He stands and lets himself out the kitchen door.

"When it rains . . ." he hears Gus saying as he leaves.

✳✳✳

David is tying his apron strings when the *Betty B.* slips out of the cove and turns to port, the northeast. By the light gray sheen above the horizon, David can tell that the sun will soon show its rising upper rim. It is cold on the water; there is a slight chop and the wind is northwesterly, carrying an autumn chill down from Canada. The *Betty B.* is the only boat in sight; if David can trust his senses at all, she is the only boat on the water east of Barter Island, other than a little gaff-rigged dory that seems to be inching southward out of the harbor on York Island, towing what appears to be a battered aluminum canoe. It will be another half hour before the sun is up high enough to let them see the surface to the eastward, toward the open sea, but any fisherman out that far would be no more than a speck, and the *Betty B.* would be impossible for them to see in the shadow of the island behind them.

Neither of them speaks as Gus starts at the northern end of Roger's string and cuts off the first trap. That done, he turns to port, gaffs the northernmost buoy in his own string, and unties the half hitches from the spindle, dropping the buoy back in. When he has cut loose the second of Roger's buoys, a loud crack over their heads makes David drop down onto the deck and Gus spin around to say "What the hell" before they hear the report of the rifle and see Roger's high prow steaming toward them from around the northern head.

"A fucking ambush," David cries.

Gus is still standing, staring in disbelief, when the second round slaps through the windshield three feet from his head. Gus pushes the throttle full forward to run for the cove; he is crunched down behind the wheel, barely able to see where he is going.

"He's turning out; he's flanking us. Goddamn!" David is shouting, though he doesn't know it. "Is this guy a good shot?"

"You're goddamn right he's a good shot," shouts Gus. "He's the best damn poacher on Deer Isle."

"Then he's not trying to hit us." David is on his knees, with only his head showing over the washboard. He can imagine a round striking his forehead as it blows the back of his skull onto the deck.

"Turn at him, Gus! Go at him!"

"What?" They are just passing beneath the cabin cliff, and Roger has steamed into the channel so that he is following on their port side.

David points out off the port bow. "Cut across there and bring us alongside him. I don't care how good he is, with so much motion he'll hit one of us shooting like that, or he'll hit the gas tank."

Never run from an ambush. Go right at it. Otherwise you're already dead. Chet roi.

David reaches toward the wheel, shouting "Please." Gus hesitates, then turns her to port. When Roger fires again—it is he who is shooting; his stern man is at the wheel, watching Roger as he steadies a heavy rifle against the side of the boat's house and fires again—David does not hear the crack of the passing round and assumes that they must have taken a hit in the hull.

As they approach Roger's boat, toward his starboard side, both Gus and Roger's stern man cut back on their throttles. David stands, holding onto the house for support. He watches Roger lower his rifle from his shoulder, chamber another round, and hold the barrel pointed at the *Betty B.* David is too shaky to light a cigarette, and he is afraid he is going to faint. Gus simply stares as the distance closes.

Roger, David sees as they draw closer, is a tall, wiry, pale man with a pointed nose and deep-set eyes. He holds the weapon at midchest level, his finger on the trigger; his eyes are on David and his ugly lips are engorged with rage.

When Gus brings her alongside, the two boats run slowly together for a long minute of silence: none of the four men is breathing.

"Give it up, Roger." David is surprised that his voice is not quaking. "Gus is going to give these waters over to me when he retires. You lose. You kill me to fish here and you'll be in Thomaston prison spending the rest of your life getting butt-fucked before breakfast by your cell mate. You let me live, and I'm not—we're not—going to let you fish here. Either way you lose."

Roger fires a round over David's head. Though David feels the hot rush in his groin, he holds onto the house and keeps himself upright.

"You can take the rest of your traps out, Roger," Gus says. "You know we can't let you in here; we do, and all of Deer Isle will take us over."

Roger says nothing. He ejects the brass from the old Enfield, lets the barrel drop, and turns to his stern man, swearing foully, before they steam away to the south.

Gus stares after them as David sits down on the washboard.

"Oh my God," Gus says. "Oh sweet Jesus." And he laughs, a building laugh of relief and delighted wonder.

David is afraid to laugh lest Roger hear him somehow and drop him like a bad habit. A buoy bobbing in the water alongside looks exactly like the lifeless head of Brother Stork bobbing between Reap's shoulders. David blinks it away, then smiles seraphically, beaming, and lights a cigarette with shaking hands.

"Jesus, mister, but that took guts," Gus says. "I know I couldn't of faced him down like that."

Now David does laugh. And he lifts his apron to show his captain the wide urine stain that has spread across the crotch of his trousers.

✳✳✳

Eliot does not wear or carry a watch—he doesn't need to; he knows from the position of the sun in the southern sky that it is two o'clock, and he knows that it is time for his hourly water break. He leans the bucksaw against the woodpile and sits on the splitting stump. Though he ate a hearty lunch not two hours ago, there is already a sharp pang in the pit of his stomach, which he welcomes with ascetic pleasure. Christine, he knows, is down in the little cove taking advantage of the low tide to collect sand and gravel to mix with cement when they are ready to pour the pond wall. He cannot see her but imagines with satisfaction that she is working slowly and deliberately, sifting each shovelful for the right consistency.

He can see the sailing dory that he noticed a few hours ago, and he can see that it is no longer tacking south down the channel, but has either put down an anchor or tied off on a buoy. When he first saw the boat this morning, he felt vaguely uneasy, so he fetched the binoculars to have a look. He saw that the dory was painted green and was towing a battered aluminum canoe. The man at the tiller wore his long white beard in two braids; his white hair fell over his shoulders, and he wore what looked like a leather Viking helmet without horns. The forward half of the dory was covered with a taut canopy and the man appeared to be talking to someone beneath it. On the boat's narrow stern three bronze letters of differing sizes and style read *Val.*

Since early morning the breeze has been erratic: sometimes slight, sometimes puffy. Eliot decides that the odd sailor is either waiting for a breeze or he is fishing, or both; when he squints to see him better, he realizes that the canoe the man was towing is gone. He walks out in the meadow toward the shore and finds that the canoe is sitting still at the mouth of the cove, a lone paddler poised in the stern seat. The paddler is a female, he thinks, dressed in a long-sleeved undershirt and gaudy vest; her hair, he sees, is cut like a man's, like Christine's.

When Christine sees the canoe, she stops shoveling and stands up straight. As she does, the woman in the canoe resumes paddling and enters the cove slowly. She waves to Christine with the paddle, and Christine responds hesitantly with a raised hand.

Neither Autumn nor Christine recognized one another at first, and for the same reason. Christine is wearing a ball cap and coveralls, and she moves like a man when she shovels. Autumn is entirely unexpected and looks even younger with her hair cut short. Christine crosses her arms over her chest as if to restrain the struggle between anger and fondness that rages within; she steps back from the waterline as the canoe comes in and Autumn steps out and pulls it ashore. Autumn is barefoot; the knees of her blue jeans are torn wide open. The two stand ten feet apart, both afraid. Finally Autumn says that she didn't recognize Christine because of her short hair.

"Nor I you," Christine says. "Why have you come back? And who is that?" She gestures toward the man in the dory.

"That's my friend Thor," Autumn says. "He lives in his dory and gave me a ride down from Deer Isle. I didn't dare come on the mail boat."

She steps back to the canoe and brings out a pouch that is decorated with pink-and-blue beads.

"Don't hate me, Christine," she begs. "I never thought that Willow . . . I mean, I just thought it was so cool that you kept your money buried in a grave, not collecting interest or being used by the capitalists. I never, ever, dreamed he would steal it. I didn't even know Willow had taken the money until we got to Bangor and he paid for a VW camper with hundred-dollar bills out of this."

She hands the beaded pouch to Christine, who takes it and thinks of a wampum belt, an offer of peace.

"I don't know when they did it, but it had to be both of them together. I hate Meadow Dawn even more than Willow because she knew that you gave me that three hundred to use for her if she had to go to a midwife. She'll do anything he tells her to do. Oh, Christine."

Autumn looks over Christine's shoulder and sees Eliot approaching across the meadow.

"Eliot's coming," says Autumn. "Please tell him to wait till I leave. Please, Christine."

Christine turns and holds up a hand to Eliot, shaking her head. He stops by the boulder and watches from the distance.

"Open it." Autumn nods toward the pouch.

Christine has guessed by the feel of the contents that it is their money, but she opens the beaded flap and looks anyway. She simply stares at the bills, then looks up at Autumn, mute with surprise.

"The camper was nine hundred," Autumn explains. "I kept the three hundred for Meadow Dawn, and it's in there. I would have come back sooner, but I was scared of Willow. I left and hitchhiked around in circles for a week, then I went to Bar Harbor and camped out in the park for a while. I did this there." She brushes her hand through her hair. "They said they were going west, and I hoped they would just go and not try to find me."

"Where will you go now?" Christine has found her tongue.

"I don't know. Will you forgive me, Christine?"

Christine closes the flap of the pouch and stands still, her head bowed slightly, as if she is lost in thought. She looks over her shoulder at Eliot, who has not moved but is watching intently, then turns back to Autumn.

"I'll forgive you if you'll forgive me."

Autumn shakes her head. "Oh, wow, that's crazy. What do you mean, anyway?"

"I burned down your tepee, and I killed your dogs," Christine says quietly. "I was so angry. I turned Gandalf loose, but now he's here and he's fine."

"You?" Christine whispers. "Holy shit, Christine. You killed them?"

"I hate myself for it, if that is any consolation. I have no excuse but anger, and that is not a valid one, I know."

"Willow said you would feed them, and we would go back for them. I should've known that was another one of his fucking lies."

"No one knows I did it, not until now," Christine says.

"And no one will ever know, not from me. I will never tell anyone, ever. I swear to you." Autumn puts her hand on her heart.

"And I promise you that everyone *will* know that you returned the money; everyone on this island, at least. And though you don't need to be forgiven, I forgive you. Will you me?"

"Of course. Oh, far out. Of course I will." She pauses. "And the people down here on the island will want to know that the baby got buried in Blue Hill and no charges were made against Willow and Meadow Dawn."

As he watches from the boulder, Eliot is prepared to sprint to Christine's aid should something go amiss. But he sees her embrace the stranger, and when the stranger turns toward the canoe, she looks up at him and waves, and he recognizes her. He pauses, then hurries down to the shore as Autumn paddles quickly out of the cove. When Eliot reaches Christine's side, she holds the pouch open so that he can see. He stands gap-mouthed for a long moment, then wraps his arms around her and the pouch.

✳✳✳

Gus and David are tired this afternoon, drained by fear and exaltation, by three instead of two drinks, and by hauling nearly three hundred traps. Gus shuts down the *Betty B.* and coasts her into the cove. He leans over his port side and gaffs the mooring buoy. Instead of handing it to David to take it forward and tie off the bow as he has done every day for a year and a half, Gus steps up onto the washboard and starts forward with it himself. The wind has breezed up considerably with the coming tide; it is westerly and has washed the sky clean of every last wisp of clouds. Gus pauses high up on the bow and looks around the cove at the evening light that is skipping across the tops of the turning maples. Maggie's oaks and house are already in the shadow of the mountain, and Gus thinks he sees her in the road next to her house, but he's not sure.

While David douses the deck and begins scrubbing it, Gus moves the lobsters, two by two, from the barrel into crates. Neither of them is talking—they talked all afternoon, and they are drained of that, too—but since they tied off, Gus has been avoiding David, with his head tucked low or his back turned as they work. When the second crate is full, he ties it shut, slides it overboard, and cleats its line. He heaves a bucket of seawater against the bulkhead and begins to scrub it down, though there is not a fleck of gurry on it.

"What's the matter, Captain?" David stands still with the broom.

"Nothing." Gus is bent over, scrubbing.

"Yeah there is."

Gus straightens and turns to David, then takes a breath and releases it with, "All right, yes. What's the matter has to do with what you said to Roger this morning, about these waters."

"Jesus, Gus, I'm sorry." David's cheeks redden. "I didn't mean to . . . I only said that for effect."

"It's not that, but it's about that. I want you to go to college. There, I've said it. I want you to work with your mind and not your back. Look at me: I'm forty-five years old and already my arches are collapsing and my back is giving in. I've got no social security to speak of, no health insurance, and a nest egg a sparrow wouldn't claim. You can still fish with me in the summers—God, I hope you will—but I'm not going to help you set yourself up for a lifetime of hauling lobster traps."

"How long have you been practicing that speech? A couple of weeks?" David resumes sweeping.

"All fricking afternoon," Gus says. "I mean it, you know."

"Did Betty and Maggie have something to do with this?"

"They feel the same way—Myrtle does, too—but it was me who made the decision to tell you."

"You're cutting me off."

"No, I'm not. I'm steering you in the right direction."

David says nothing as he rinses and stows the bilge pump, scrubs and hangs his apron on the nail next to Gus's.

"I guess I'm not surprised." David lights a cigarette. "I've been thinking about going back, maybe to a different school. I just hate to leave, Captain."

"I know it," Gus's voice is quiet, barely audible. "Why don't you bring the skiff alongside. I've got a headache; I want to lie down a little before supper. You think about it."

As David bends over the side to pull the skiff forward, Gus starts to put his hand on David's shoulder to reassure him, but he lets it fall, forlorn, to his side instead.

✳✳✳

At dusk Maggie sits wrapped in a gray wool blanket on the mossy seat at the edge of the cliff overlooking the cove. The tide is going and, though the *Betty B.* points to the west, there doesn't seem to be any breeze at all. She plucks a berry from the juniper at her feet and breaks it open with her thumbnail for the fragrance. The sun is behind the mountain and her back, and behind gray clouds as well, but it looks fairly clear over the sea, and she hopes that it will stay clear in the east past dark so she can see the light at Mount Desert Rock, eighteen miles out. Under the maples off to her left, a doe and her fawn, spotless now, graze in the meadow by the stone wall. The screen door to Ava's kitchen slams shut, and the doe snorts, her white tail snaps up, and she and her fawn bound over the wall into the shadowed woods.

Maggie thinks that David might be angry now, his feelings hurt, but when he thinks about it, he will realize how hard it was for Gus to discourage him. David will realize that Gus did the right thing, and that he did it for him. Gus, who almost had his son back, home from the war, or as near to it as he could ever hope. And we, too, she thinks, are suddenly without the kindness of Nancy, of a neighbor in the cove, of comfort for Christine. Once David goes back to college, he'll learn to endure being judged by the ignorant, maybe even learn to ignore them; he will gain strength and move on, to a profession, perhaps, to a family (with Nancy, perhaps), and they will be summer people, and the cove will be filled with kids once more.

Maggie draws the blanket over her knees and buries her hands in the folds in her lap.

She should see the light by now; it is certainly dark enough for it to be visible. She watches out two points north of the tip of York Island, counts to eighteen—one second for each mile away—and waits, but does not see it.

The light must be obscured by fog or distant clouds, she decides. So she shuts her eyes to watch it blink and blink toward her in its reassuring, eternal scanning watch over the surface of the dark sea all around.